Introduction

Spring practically tingles with the promise of new life, new beginnings, and, most especially, new love. This original quartet of contemporary, spring-themed novellas is no exception. You'll find the wonderful magic of new romance on every captivating page!

E-Love by Gloria Brandt introduces you to a painfully introverted computer geek, Gwen Paulson, who finds the flush of first love in an Internet chat room. But her hopes get surprisingly tangled when an old high school crush tries to spoil her growing cyber-space romance.

The Garden Plot by Rebecca Germany digs right into complication and intrigue when Debbie Julian inadvertently expands her new garden into the yard of her neighbor, a perfectionist landscaper. Can anything new bud from their old, thorny relationship?

Stormy Weather by Tracie Peterson puts you directly in the path of swirling trouble when Gina Bowden, a young widow, fights city council to regain funding for her son's Boy Scout troop. Something better than lightening hits when she teams up with the equally tenacious troop leader.

Bride to Be by Debra White Smith carries you over the threshold into Amy Matthews' bridal shop. Amy is thirty-five and reconciled to being single when God brings the man of her dreams through her door. She's instantly attracted. But Mr. Right is already engaged!

SPRING'S PROMISE

Gloria Brandt

Rebecca Germany

Tracie Peterson

Debra White Smith

ISBN 1-57748-501-7

Published by Barbour Publishing, Inc., P.O. Box 719, Uhrichsville, Ohio 44683 http://www.barbourbooks.com

Printed in the United States of America.

Spring's Promise

E-Love

Gloria Brandt

Dedication

For "taking me on" as a fledgling. . .
For offering more than just encouragement,
but a shoulder to lean on. . .in all times.
Thank you could never be enough.
This one's all for you, Sally!

One

The silvery screen faded into its normal zigzag pattern, a pleasant tone chiming from the tiny speakers.

"Good night to you, too." Gwen Paulson plucked her purse from the top drawer of her desk, her coat from her chair, and rounded the wall of her little cubicle.

"Gwen!" A voice carried across the nearly empty work area.

Tucking a strand of hair behind her ear, Gwen waited as Barb Wilkinson came trotting across the office floor.

"Glad I caught you before you left," her tall and slender coworker panted. "Just wanted to let you know, Bob said the crew starts tomorrow on the new offices. So. . .within a few weeks you should have a little more privacy."

Swallowing the self-consciousness she always felt in Barb's presence, Gwen smiled at the fashionably dressed, picture-perfect businesswoman before her and nodded. "That will be nice. Thanks for letting me know." She started to turn away.

"Wait a minute. I—we were wondering if you'd like to join us for dinner?"

She turned, eyebrows raised.

"Well, you know—our little group." A perfectly manicured finger traced an aerial circle around the surrounding cubicles. "After all, you've been here nearly a month already. We feel like we hardly know you." The neat blond brows formed a teasing arch. "We're beginning to wonder what sort of secret life you lead after hours."

Gwen laughed a little too loudly, a little too nervously. "Oh, you know. The usual. Hang gliding, trips to the Amazon, parties with dignitaries—all the while working on the great American novel."

A patronizing smile came back. "So? Will you come?"

Gwen yanked her cumbersome tote over her shoulder again. "I–I really don't think so." She fought the urge to cast her gaze to the floor, instead pushing up her glasses in nervous habit. "I. . .I kind of have plans for tonight."

Barb's blue eyes took on a shine again as she leaned against a desk behind her. "Really? What's his name?"

That same irritating fiery warmth flew across Gwen's face. She put her hand to her cheek as she smiled shyly. "Actually—well, his name is. . .Graham."

The woman's look mingled curiosity with more than a shade of doubt. Gwen felt her backbone tense slightly. It was true. She really had agreed to meet Graham later tonight. Barb didn't need to know that the date was via the computer screen. She hiked her chin and straightened her shoulders.

"Okay then. Maybe next time." Barb flicked a

parting smile over her shoulder as her stiletto heels clicked toward the elevator. Gwen wasn't sure if the quiet sigh escaping her own lips was one of relief. . .or disappointment.

The walk to her small car was uneventful. For a Monday, the office sure had cleared out in a hurry. As she opened the driver's side door, Gwen's eyes lifted to take in the glass-front building. *Reiser Business Systems* was prominently displayed on the etched marble monument centered in the perfectly kept landscape, now covered with the last traces of the late March snow.

With a wistful sigh, she slid into the seat. Was Barb right? Had it been a month already? Four weeks since she'd had to leave her self-made solitude? Easing out into the busyness of afternoon traffic, she couldn't help but muse over the turn of events—not only in the last month, but in the last decade of her life.

Since high school—she shuddered at the mere thought of the horrid experience—she'd promptly whisked herself away to a tech school, learned her present trade of computer programming/consulting, and applied for this job with RBS. How well she remembered her parents' initial reaction to the placement.

"It's over three hours away!" her mother had exclaimed.

Her father had only shaken his graying head in typical worry. *Who will watch out for my little girl?* was written all over his face.

Gwen had assured them that living on the outskirts of Hudson, Wisconsin, wasn't the worst she could do.

Besides, she'd be working as a freelancer out of her own little house.

With consenting but unconvinced nods, they'd let her go.

Besides, she added mentally, *it was better than staying in Carson for the rest of what would be a dreadful existence.*

But her comfortable, nearly eight years of solitude had come to an abrupt and unwelcome end a month ago. RBS had succinctly informed her that freelancers were no longer in their budget. So she had two options: come to work at their plush office building—or find a new job.

Well, it could be worse, she admitted. The office job was turning out a lot better than she'd thought it would. The other employees actually seemed friendly. And with her current salary, virtually no expenses, and a frugal mind-set nurtured by her parents, she had her little bungalow paid for. She was debt free. Completely dependent on nothing—no one. And more than aware that the fact caused an ache from deep inside.

And she did what she always had to get her through those yearning times—she'd prayed, every year a little longer, a little harder. Knowing that with the passing of time, the likelihood of her ever meeting someone and actually marrying was—

She promptly disrupted her thought process and gave herself a mental shake. *Get on with it, Gwen. Quit living in the past.*

With more than her usual rush, she headed toward

the house and flicked on the computer. Maybe there was an E-mail from Graham.

⁂

Gwen took another swig of her cappuccino as she waited for the website to come up, more than aware of the silly grin that was trying to cover her whole face. There had indeed been an E-mail from her special Internet friend. Along with explicit instructions to meet him in the private chat room he'd set up at seven o'clock. She'd already had to endure an endlessly long TV dinner while watching the news and reruns to wait for seven to come. She glanced at her watch for the hundredth time.

True to his word, Graham's chat room showed up on the screen. She typed in her name and password and was promptly greeted with a post stating, "*Where are you, Gwenivere?*"

Smiling at his alternative spelling to fit her name, she replied, "*Right here, Lancelot.*"

"*You're a whole minute late. I was beginning to worry about you.*"

"*Sorry.*"

"*How was work today?*"

"*Pretty good. Got the news they're starting on the offices tomorrow. Soon, no more cubicles.*"

"*Great! Well, you deserve it, you know. In fact, they should make you CEO of the place.*"

Gwen blushed and felt that smile creeping back across her face. She never failed to feel wonderful when she was talking to Graham. Too bad she hadn't known the guy in high school.

"I've got a surprise for you."

Gwen felt her heartbeat speed up. It seemed that no matter how often he said those words, no matter how small the surprise might be, she found herself almost shaking with anticipation.

"Don't leave me in suspense," she typed quickly.

*"*grin* Okay—two surprises actually. Look for the first one on my new webpage."*

She made a mental note to check out the long-ago bookmarked site as soon as their conversation ended.

"Next," he continued, *"I have something to ask you."*

She held her breath.

"I happen to be coming to St. Paul on a business trip in just a few weeks."

Gwen closed her eyes, almost afraid to keep reading the words on the screen. This couldn't be it, could it?

"And I was wondering if you might agree to meet me. Either in St. Paul—or I could come on over to Hudson."

There was an interminable pause as her heart hammered in her chest, her mind reeling.

"Whaddya think?"

Every inclination within Gwen screamed for her fingers to type out YES, YES, YES! But an odd feeling held her back. She'd been corresponding with Graham for a couple of months now. Nearly every night. Even shared several conversations on the phone. She felt so easy with him. So relaxed. So. . .accepted.

She eased the kinks out of her shaking fingers. *"Graham. . .can I think about it—just for awhile? You know, let me check my schedule and everything?"*

A big smiley emotion prefaced his reply. "*:) Sure, sure. Do whatever you need to do. You're worth waiting for. *smile*"*

Later that evening, as Gwen brushed through her hair before retiring, she studied herself in the bathroom mirror—and shuddered. Could this be the reason she was so hesitant to meet Graham?

Fingering her long, straight brown hair, she wondered why she'd kept it this way for so many years? The round glasses perched on her nose didn't help to display her green eyes any, either—her dad had always said those were one of her prettiest attributes.

With a sigh of resignation, she traipsed back to her bedroom, passing her office on the way. Stepping into it once more, she picked up the new photo she'd printed out from Graham's webpage. It was more close up than the last one he'd scanned for his personal site. And he was. . .gorgeous. Dark wavy hair, dark eyes—he almost had a Greek look about him with his classic features.

Taking the paper with her, she propped it on her dresser and sank into her warm comforter, staring at the appealing apparition.

He wants to meet me.

He wants to come here.

What do I do?

And for the first time in her whole life, Gwen went to sleep with an undefined, troubled spirit over the whole issue. For in the muddle of confusion, it never even dawned on her to pray.

Two

Gwen's distracting thoughts didn't dissipate overnight. By morning it seemed they'd only intensified. Her normal, scheduled, organized self appeared to have stayed in bed.

Somewhere, since just yesterday, she'd misplaced her Bible-in-a-year schedule. So, she flipped open to Proverbs for today, confident the missing paper would turn up later.

Warming her fingers against the piping-hot mug of cocoa, she delved into the passages she'd so often studied before: "Hope deferred makes the heart sick, but a longing fulfilled is a tree of life."

Gwen stopped. She reread the words. They'd never really stuck out at her before now. Could it be that the hope she felt every time she talked to Graham was God's way of fulfilling her heart? A smile eased across her face. It would be so like Him—to step in, when she least expected it, even after all these years. She allowed her mind to drift off on more than a few fanciful turns.

After all this time. . . Time!

She locked her gaze on the clock—and gasped.

She had exactly five minutes to get to work. . .in what normally took ten. Stuffing the last of the bagel into her mouth, she yanked on her coat as she sailed out the door.

Creeping in only a few minutes past eight, Gwen skittered onto the elevator, punched the usual button, and waited for the interminably long ascent to the sixth floor.

She leaned wearily against the polished chrome rail as the conveyance jarred to life. Then she frowned. Wait a—

A quick glance at the arrows.

She didn't even try to stifle the groan. This car was going. . .down! Most likely to the storage/basement area. Wonderful!

Well, not much she could do about it now. Might as well whip a brush through her windblown hair one more time. She began rifling through her tote.

Keys, lip gloss, wallet. . . Where on earth was that. . . ?

The cheerful ding of the elevator interrupted her mutterings. Propping her purse on the railing, she was vaguely aware of a group converging into the tiny space. . .with an awful lot of stuff.

With her fingers still fumbling in the jumbled contents of her bag, she glanced over at the tools, lumber, and miscellaneous other items surrounding the group of men.

Of course, the construction crew for the new offices.

She refocused on finding the errant brush, when the doors opened once again. With an inward sigh, she noted her watch. She was definitely late now.

Several of the men greeted the new passenger with typical male jocularity.

Gwen felt a light smile teasing her lips in spite of her harried morning. With a curious glimpse, she lifted her head to watch the interchange.

The look from those blue eyes hit her like a ton of bricks.

Trying to simultaneously start her heart beating again and stop the pathetic wheezing that was trying to help her draw breath, she felt her jaw go slack, along with her grip on her tote.

And her attention shifted to her feet as keys, computer diskettes, gum, photographs—and that stupid brush—went skidding across the floor in perfect pandemonium.

Shoving her glasses up her nose, she dropped to her knees and frantically began scooping up the errant items, unceremoniously dumping them in the limp bag. Anything—anything to keep her from having to look up again.

She drew in a shuddering breath as a pair of denimed knees knelt beside her and began helping collect the mess.

No words were spoken—thank goodness! She couldn't dare look up to verify if the person next to her was who she thought it was.

Right, Gwen, she railed inwardly. *Like you could ever forget that face.*

"Looks like that's everything," his low voice intoned, handing her the last stick of gum.

She felt her knees turn to jelly at the mere sound. His voice was lower than it had been in high school. *Stop it! Stop it! This cannot be happening!*

"Thank you," she muttered, realizing that unless she wanted to appear entirely rude, she'd *have* to look up. Steeling herself against her positively jumping stomach, she lifted her head and melted into the clear blue depths of his smiling eyes.

Alex Marshall. In the flesh. All six feet two of him. No doubt about it.

She tried not to wince as he returned her stare with that friendly grin she had never quite forgotten. It was only a matter of time. . .until he would remember everything, too.

The insistent ding of the doors interrupted her reverie. Glancing up at the numbers, she felt relief pour over her. Never had she been so glad to see that number six lit up before.

"This is it, guys," one of the other men announced.

With as much dignity as she could muster, Gwen hiked her tote over her shoulder and prepared to leave behind the construction crew. And found herself following *him* out of the elevator.

A new look at his tool-laden form made her close her eyes in sudden realization. *Dolt! Why did you think he was on the elevator?* she told herself.

Scurrying to the privacy of her cubicle, she slunk gratefully behind the small partition's confines, slowly, methodically putting away her purse, her coat.

He hadn't said anything. In fact, his face hadn't

even registered recognition!

A new conviction washed over her with gut-wrenching clarity. *He doesn't even remember me.*

Well, why should he? she argued with herself. *What were you to him?*

"Nothing," she whispered to the air around her. "Absolutely nothing. Other than a big joke." Decade-old tears began to sting behind her glasses. The fear and humiliation of him possibly recognizing her was nothing —not compared to the painful fact that he didn't even recall her at all.

"Morning, Gwen." Barb's cheerful voice floated over the top of the cubicle. "I see the crew's here."

Gwen finished stuffing her personal items in their places and managed a distracted nod as she flicked on her computer. At least she'd been successful in containing her tears.

"Well, well, well," her coworker's tone changed suddenly.

She looked up to find Barb's stare pointed in the distance. A glance over her shoulder showed the passel of men toting in armloads of lumber. She whipped her head around before she could pinpoint any of them in particular.

"Did you see that blond?" Barb whispered.

"Which one?" Gwen tried to ask nonchalantly as she typed in her password.

"Which one?" she echoed incredulously. "The one in the red flannel shirt. Looks like he's about ready to cozy up by some big ol' fireplace in a cabin somewhere.

Can't say I wouldn't mind joining him."

A solid lump was now lodged in Gwen's throat. *Let's see. . .what else could happen this morning to top all of this off?* Maybe if she gave herself a paper cut—

"We'll have to find out *his* name, won't we?"

Staring at the more-than-just-interested look in Barb's eyes, Gwen felt something within her start to rise to the occasion. And before she could even label it, she opened her mouth. "Alex."

Her friend's face finally swung toward hers. "What did you say?"

She cleared her throat. "Alex. His name is Alex."

Barb's tweezed brows frowned in doubt. "How do you know?"

Shrug. "I know—knew him. But his name *is* Alex Marshall."

"Really?" The light flicked on behind the crystal blue eyes.

Gwen tossed a dubious glance at the ceiling—the hunt was on. And she was more than aware that this time Barb's penchant for finding new blood hit a little too close to home.

❧

Trying to swallow around the last tasteless bite of her bologna sandwich, Gwen clacked furiously on the keys before her. Today she'd worked straight through lunch. Maybe she would tomorrow, too, and the next day. . .

She'd watched as Barb had sidled up to the construction crew, her usual coo in place. Her conversation had quickly narrowed on Alex. And in spite of the pain it caused just to watch the whole interaction, Gwen hadn't been able to help it.

With morbid fascination she'd kept her eyes glued on him—just as she'd done all those years ago in high school. No matter where. Whether he was on the playing field. . .frowning over his algebra text. . . accepting the Homecoming crown. . .with one of his many girlfriends. . .

Giving herself a mental shake, she crumpled up the empty brown bag and tossed it in the trash. Maybe if she got this project done early today, she could leave before—

"Hi."

Jumping at the sudden voice, she flicked her gaze up to the short wall's edge. Her heart stalled.

His muscular arms were leaning on the top, his eyes taking in whatever was on her screen. Then they slowly moved back to meet her face. "Did we find everything?"

Completely lost in his gaze, she shook her head. "Pardon me?"

"Your stuff," he said with a grin. "From your purse."

"Oh! Oh, yes. Thank you. It's all. . .fine."

He propped his chin on his forearms. "Good. So this hundred dollar bill isn't yours then?" His fingers displayed the folded-up currency.

"I–I—" Gwen frowned. "No, I don't—"

He eased into a light laugh. "Just kiddin'. It's fake." He turned the paper to show her that it truly didn't unfold, it was just a tiny square. "Here, though. You can keep it anyway." He handed it toward her.

She hesitated, then willing her fingers not to shake as much as her insides, she accepted the offered gift. "Thanks," she murmured, wondering why a dumb piece of paper could feel like such a treasure.

"You know," he said suddenly, his head tipped to the side. "You look kind of familiar to me. Have we met somewhere before?"

The dread rose up in her throat, nearly choking off whatever breath she had left. There was no hiding now, was there? "I—"

"Alex!" a masculine voice boomed from across the floor. "Lunch doesn't last all day, buddy."

Turning to her with an apologetic shrug, he grinned. "Guess it's back to work." He strode away from her cubicle, each step bringing a portion of her pulse rate back. Then he turned. "I'll remember," he said as he pointed at her. "I've got a thing about faces. If we've met before, I'll remember."

Gwen managed a weak smile as he whirled around. She turned to face her computer screen. "Oh, I pray you don't," she whispered.

Three

The one-dimensional face cards stared back at her haughtily. With a sigh, Gwen clicked to close the never-ending game of computer solitaire and shoved the mouse away from herself. What was her problem? Was this truly all her life consisted of? Just sitting in front of a dumb computer? She remembered when that was all she'd wanted. . . .

But now—something had happened. She didn't know if it was the disconcerting encounter she'd had today at work. . .or if she was finally just tired of living in cyberspace. Was it her turn to take her place in the world?

Well, at least she'd made it through the day—that fact was no small consolation. She'd fought every urge, every second, to glance over in Alex Marshall's direction—to watch his painfully appealing character shining from his smiling face, his boyish antics. . . She jumped up from the computer chair with a huff.

Why? Why did he have to come here? To her work? So far away from Carson—from where he was supposed to stay?

Now she sat in her too quiet house, waiting for the evening to pass by in nothingness. There wasn't even

Graham for a diversion. She'd come home to an E-mail from him saying that he wouldn't be on his computer tonight. Reading it had hurt—more than it usually did. Tonight she really felt like she needed to talk to him. He was the only one who really understood.

And in the back of her mind, his previous night's question ricocheted through her thoughts. She still hadn't decided about whether to meet him or not. Something, still undefinable, held her back.

Unaccustomed to the muddled state she found herself in, Gwen decided to have another quiet time this evening. If anything gave her some solace, it was meditating on the Word.

Rummaging through her tote for her small New Testament brought back all the horrid memories of this morning's elevator ride. She almost recoiled in an odd sense of fear; Alex Marshall had touched some of the objects in her purse.

Her fingers suddenly folded around a small slip of paper. Pulling out what she thought must be her missing Bible reading schedule, she inhaled quickly when she saw the corner of the fake hundred dollar bill. She pulled it slowly from the opening, studying it carefully—remembering the strength of his hands, his fingers when he'd handed it toward her own shaking grasp. A single tear rolled down her cheek, and the memories came back, entirely unbidden, completely unwanted. . . .

The last hour's bell buzzed noisily through the speaker on the wall. The mass exodus of pounding feet and laughing students prefaced Gwen's nervous breath. She efficiently gathered her books together and headed for the small round table at the front of the room, carefully wiping away the errant chalk dust from its surface.

Having just finished spreading out today's math assignment, she felt her heart trip over itself at the whistling that floated through the door. Never having quite accomplished the ability to look him in the eye, Gwen merely took her seat, fingers in a firm grip on the pencil, ready to get to work.

Fully aware that his usual cheerful "Hi" hadn't been uttered yet, she frowned at the missed step in their day's protocol.

His books slapped down on the table next to her, and he pulled out his chair, still quiet.

Out of the corner of her eye she saw it, a flick of his wrist, followed by a small envelope landing squarely on her notebook. Her name was scrawled across the front.

Confusion overtaking her normal nervousness, Gwen glanced up at him. That completely sassy grin was plastered across his face. He ran a hand through his thick blond hair.

"What is this?" she managed to croak out.

He leaned over and pointed to the writing. "Gwen," he read. "It's for you."

She merely kept staring at him.

He chuckled as he shifted in his chair. "You can open it."

Flushing with a burning warmth, she cleared her throat and flipped the envelope over, carefully tearing along the slit. Inside was a card—for April Fool's Day! She remembered trying to ignore the irritating letters emblazoned on her calendar that morning—the start of the week when all the girls in school were supposed to issue an invitation to the guy of their choice to accompany them to the Spring Fling dance. This day was no celebration for her—unless you counted a sole comical card from well-meaning parents on your bedspread cause for excitement.

With numb fingers, she studied the silly hand-drawn cartoon picture on the front. In the corner sat a young man with a "dunce" hat on, off to the side, a smiling young woman with an armful of books. Slowly opening it, she let her eyes follow the words:

Some call me slow
ain't never been too smart.
But I'm no fool when I say
you've a special place in my heart.
No fooling!

Under the verse, in his familiar scribble, was a big "Thanks!" followed by his signature.

It was thoughtful, touching. . .and it made her want to weep.

"Like it?" he asked.

She nodded quickly, frantically trying to bury the veil of tears already obscuring her vision. There was no way she could go through this tutoring session—not today—not now.

"Alex," she murmured, trying to keep her voice low to disguise its wavering. "I'm—I really. . .thank you. But—could we skip today's lesson? I can go over it with you next time and all—I. . .I just don't feel that well today." She began

shuffling papers together even before he could answer.

Just as she shoved her chair backward to stand, his large hand reached over and gingerly touched her arm. The shock that it sent through her system was nearly more than she could hide. All she could do was hold her breath.

"You okay, Gwen?"

A quick, jittery nod. She clamped her lips together. She wouldn't cry—she wouldn't. "Fine. Thanks again." Scooping up her books, she cradled them in her arms and shot out the door. The students milling around in the hallways were a blur. Not even stopping at her locker for her coat or anything else, she burst through the last set of double doors, immediately slapped by the cold of the early spring day. She trudged home, the tears nearly freezing on her cheeks as the sobs got lost somewhere between despair and self-pity. It was a card. It was from him. It had been given as a friend—that was the problem.

With the piteous cries shaking her defeated shoulders, she chastised herself with every tear. When would she ever stop thinking of Alex Marshall in any sort of romantic way and just get on with her life?

Dropping the folded bill as if it were ablaze, Gwen let it fall to the desktop and turned away from it, resolutely marching down the hall. Reaching her bedroom, she yanked open the rarely opened closet and began tossing aside box after labeled and alphabetized box. Where was it?

H. *High school.* She tore the cardboard cube from its position in the pile and stalked back to the living room. Unceremoniously ripping open the flaps, she was surprised to find it right on top—not looking a day older than the day she'd gotten it. Correction—than when her parents had gotten it for her.

With a sigh still rife with leftover embarrassment, she slipped open the stiff cover. It was the only annual she owned. And had her parents not gone to the school the day of yearbook signing to purchase it, she wouldn't have this one commemorating her senior year, either. To be honest, she hadn't wanted one. She didn't want anything to remind her of that place—that time.

But how could she refuse when they'd gone to such lengths for her? Buying the book and walking around the commons full of students, gently asking for signatures for their daughter's yearbook. The thought still brought tears to her eyes—ones of humiliation, and deep gratitude and love.

Opening to the page that she'd studied far more than she cared to admit as a teen, she found his smiling face. Alex Marshall. His long list of high school credentials stacked up like a veritable pedestal for his flattering photograph. And over the whole thing were his words, scrawled in black ink. *Gwen, good luck to you. Hate these yearbook signings. But I mean it when I say that I know you'll go far. Thanks for all your help. And your patience. Don't know if I'd even be in here if it wasn't for you. Just don't drill me on my square roots in ten years, okay? Alex.*

She couldn't fight the smile playing with her lips. He'd always been so nice. So appreciative. So—unavailable.

Surrounding his note were two or three other impersonal signatures under the myriad of other senior portraits. No more. No one else had bothered. She hadn't expected them to. She hadn't even expected this much.

She flipped to the back. The yellowed envelope fell from its dark hiding place. And with it, a whole other host of memories that she was more resolute in keeping squashed. Those she couldn't handle. Not now.

Hastily stuffing the old card back in, she slammed the book shut and tossed it in the box. With a heavy sigh, she sagged against the back of her small, pillow-strewn couch.

Why didn't life ever get easier? Why? Just when she thought she had a handle on who she was, all of this had to go and happen.

"Oh, Graham," she whispered to the irritating solitude. "I wish I could talk to you."

Her Bible caught her eye from across the room. She'd done it again. Gotten distracted. With a frown of renewed determination, she retrieved the desperately needed book. Sliding it off the desk, Alex's bill fluttered to the floor.

With a groan of exasperation, Gwen swiped it up from the carpet and prepared to toss it in the trash—when she noticed some words written on it. Curiously, she pulled it open—and nearly dropped the thing in shock.

Alex had given this to her, had told her to keep it.

Closing her eyes, she shook her head. "No way.

There is no way—" Prying her lids open, she peered at the startling words again.

So. . .you think this a treasure?
Think again.
"Store up for yourselves treasures in heaven,
where moth and rust do not destroy
and where thieves do not break in and steal.
For where your treasure is,
there your heart will be also."

This time the missive fluttered to the floor—and stayed there.

Four

I don't know. . ."

"Come on, Gwen." Trish Peterson leaned against the locker door, her blond hair cascading over the shoulders of her bright purple cheerleader's sweater. "He gave you a card, didn't he?"

From down the hall, the first bell rang. Gwen grabbed her text and notebook for the next hour's class and pushed against the metal door. Eyeing the tall, athletic girl next to her, she shrugged. "How did you know?"

"Oh." Trish waved it off with her hand. "People see things. How I know isn't important." She leaned in closer, her suffocating perfume filling up the space between them. "What is important is that you ask Alex. . .today. Before someone else does. The dance is only three days away."

A huge lump stuck in Gwen's throat. There was no way. She couldn't possibly—

The second bell resonated through the halls, and Gwen scrambled toward the classroom, Trish close behind.

"Don't blow your chance," the girl whispered as they skittered through the door.

Gwen tried to avoid the teacher's glare as she eased into her desk. All she needed on top of her confused emotions was a tardy slip. Throwing one last glance at the circle of cheerleaders rounding out the far section of the classroom, Gwen couldn't help but wonder why the captain of the squad, Miss Popularity, would care a whit about her all of a sudden.

But before a reason could come to mind, Trish caught her gaze and smiled broadly. "Today," the girl mouthed silently.

❧

Gwen bolted upright, clutching the sheets to her chest, her breath lost somewhere in the recurring dream—nightmare—past. Why did it always have to come back, always?

She glanced at the clock. Almost six. Close enough. She wasn't going to get any more sleep anyway. Tossing aside the covers, she padded toward the bathroom and set the hot water in the shower to high, waiting for the painfully slow water to emerge from the nozzle. As she picked out her outfit for the day, something she was still unaccustomed to doing after working out of her home for eight years, her eyes drifted toward the calendar. With an audible groan, she plucked a pillow from the bed and flung it at the irritating daily schedule. "Of course," she muttered. "April first. Happy April Fool's Day, Gwen." And she stalked toward the shower.

❧

Wincing as the power saw screeched in the background, Gwen rubbed her throbbing temples. With her back to the area under construction, she hadn't had the misfortune of meeting Alex Marshall's eyes yet today—to her great relief. And a little to her persistent disappointment.

Her stomach rumbled under the noise of the remodeling crew's poundings, a reminder that she'd also avoided the cafeteria so far. Anything to stay tucked in her little cubicle, awaiting the time to head for home. It was her greatest fear, now that she knew Alex didn't remember her, that the realization would hit him somehow. And she wasn't sure if she could deal with the pain of that memory on top of her apparent inablility to establish herself as any sort of memory to the man.

In the back of her mind, she kept rereading the words on that little dollar-bill tract. Was it even possible that Alex Marshall had somehow become a believer? The idea was nearly unthinkable. Although he'd not been one of the most aggressive "partiers" their little hometown had known, he'd certainly shared in his days and nights of revelry. . .or so she'd heard.

With a sigh, she reined in her wandering thoughts, trying to direct them toward something other than *him* and the recurring question as to why he had come—all the way up here to Hudson. After all, Carson was hundreds of miles away.

With a growl of disgust at her own frail musings, Gwen finally pushed back her chair and stood. She needed to get a breath of fresh air, Alex or no Alex. Without a second glance, she rounded her partition and headed straight for the elevators. She grimaced, remembering their earlier meeting. Maybe it would be safer to take the stairs.

The bell chimed as the arrow lit up, and the doors slid open. Caught right in front of the conveyance, she tossed a wary look inside. Empty. With a grin, she stepped in and punched the lobby's button.

She expelled a breath of relief at again having managed to avoid bumping into him. She started to chide herself for her paranoia; chances were better that she'd see him while actually working than while traipsing around the rest of RBS's expansive building.

After going through the short line in the cafeteria, Gwen even dared taking her lunch outside in the complex's courtyard. She wasn't sure if today's unusually mild weather was nature's way of playing an April Fool's Day trick, but she was going to enjoy it nonetheless. Just in case. One never knew in Wisconsin.

The mild sun shone down gently as she sat alone on the small bench. A few brave birds had already made the long flight back north. But she was still waiting to see that first robin—that much anticipated promise of spring. Before she knew it, her lunch was gone. With a satisfied sigh, she moved back toward the building.

Between the welcome solitary, meditative time and the beautiful day, Gwen had completely forgotten her earlier concerns. Without even thinking, she punched the buttons to the elevator and stepped inside.

"Hey!" a voice called from behind her.

She turned to see one of the workmen trotting across the long floor of the lobby, waving his arms frantically. "Wait!"

With a frown, she wondered if he could possibly be addressing her. The automatic doors slid shut. Most likely someone else. She hit the button for her floor and leaned casually against the rail, finding herself humming the tune "It Might As Well Be Spring."

The elevator vibrated, groaned, then lurched to a stop at the second floor. Waiting for the doors to open, she studied the number above the portal. The number two flickered and blinked out.

The doors did not open.

Feeling her breath beginning to quicken, Gwen jabbed several pads on the number board, then all of them—any of them.

Nothing.

"Hey!" she called out, banging on the shiny metal wall. "I think this thing is stuck!"

Trying to keep her frazzling wits together, she eyed the telephone reserved for emergency situations. Wrenching open the panel, she plucked it up and held it to her ear. "Hello? Hello?"

"Yes, ma'am," a low voice finally came through. "Just relax. We know you're in there."

A semi-relieved sigh.

"I don't suppose you know about where you are," the voice said.

"I think it stopped somewhere around the second floor." Gwen's breath caught in her throat; the overhead bulb was beginning to flicker as well. "No, please," she breathed. "Don't let the lights go. . .off."

Pitch black greeted her last word.

"Ma'am, are you still there?"

"Yes," she whispered. "What's wrong? What happened?"

"Don't worry. Someone is on the way to get you out. Just hold tight."

"Like I have any choice," she muttered.

The inky blackness seemed to close in on her, surrounding her in stifling oppressiveness. "Next time, Gwen," she railed aloud, "take the stairs."

Unsuccessful at replacing the receiver onto its proper brackets in the dark, she let the phone slip from her grasp, eased her back down the wall, and slid to the floor, trying to remain calm while she waited. Just a few minutes he'd said, right?

But in her fear, she prayed. "Dear, Lord. Why do I always get myself into these situations?" She shook her head in resignation. "You must get tired of bailing me out. But—" A lump rose in her throat. "Thank you for doing it anyway."

A sudden grating, scraping noise from overhead made her jump. Inching into the far corner, she winced, fully expecting the huge car to go hurtling to its demise . . .and herself along with it. She could just picture the shattered wreckage, her broken lifeless body. A new jolt of alarm shook her.

A straight beam of light permeated the enclosure, sending a circle of brightness to the floor in front of her feet. She strained to see against the glare, but to no avail.

"Gwen?" the low voice echoed in the chamber.

Her breath caught in her throat—cut off by a sob that rose highly unexpectedly. That voice. . .saying her name. How did—

"Gwen, are you okay?" The ray of light moved around the car.

She nodded. "Yes," she rasped. "I'm here."

The flashlight's glare found her and she lowered her face from the intrusive brightness, fearing it would only amplify her mortification.

A chuckle escaped the bodiless voice from above. "Stay right there," Alex ordered. "Company's about to drop in."

He landed with a thud a foot or two away from her. With one hand on the flashlight, he reached out the other toward her. "Come on," he said. "I'll help you out."

Her head jerked up. "Out? You mean, up there?"

"Yeah," he returned with maddening calm. "The elevator's power is being cut for a time while we're rewiring a portion of the new part of the building. I take it you didn't hear the announcement for everyone to use the stairs?"

Gwen shook her head miserably. "It must have come while I was outside."

Alex laughed. "Oh, well. At least you gave everyone some excitement for today. April Fool's and all that." His strong hand found hers and he effortlessly pulled her to her feet.

Gwen tried to ignore the supreme slamming of her heart.

"Okay, now," he said as he crouched down. "On my shoulders."

"What?" she gasped. "I can't—"

"You can think of a better way out of here?"

"I—"

"Get on," he ordered, good-naturedly. "I can lift

you, don't worry."

Swallowing the last shred of her self-dignity, Gwen cautiously placed a foot on his broad shoulder, then another. In the midst of her humiliation, she had the presence of mind to be grateful that today she had worn slacks.

Like a shot, Alex stood up, giving her no time to be afraid of falling. Her hands immediately gripped the edge of the small overhead door as he boosted her from below. Yanking herself through, she teetered on the top of the car.

"Okay," he called up to her. "I'm gonna throw you the light, okay?" He tossed it up to her, and she grabbed it. "Just shine it near the edge so I can see."

Doing as she was told, she heard a huff of exertion just before his fingers claimed the lip of the opening, the rest of him soon following.

Sitting completely amazed at his strength and agility, Gwen forgot for a moment where they were. . .who they were. "Thank you," she murmured. "I guess all those sports you were involved in came in handy for something, didn't they?"

Before the words had barely escaped her lips, she clamped a hand over her mouth. Her eyes followed suit. *Way to go, way to go, way to go! Oh, Gwen, you idiot.*

"I guess," he replied.

He didn't seem surprised at all by her comment. Gwen ventured to peer through one eye. His rugged face was smiling at her kindly.

"In case you're wondering," he said, "I did remember who you were. Right away."

She drew in a shaky breath and waited.

"I just didn't know if you'd want me to remember."

Gwen was torn between wanting to hug the man for rescuing her or shove him off the side of the elevator. Between wanting to cry in humiliation or scream in frustration. Incredibly, she started to laugh.

Alex's face registered first concern, then confusion before he finally joined her.

She couldn't help it. Everything, all of this, was just too absurd to take seriously anymore. Losing herself in a fit of giggles, she wiped the tears from her eyes. "Well, Alex Marshall. Happy April Fool's Day!"

Five

Are you all right?"

Gwen twisted the phone cord around her fingers and smiled as she curled up on the couch, hugging her chenille robe around her. "Yes. I'm fine. Actually, I've been kind of laughing over the whole elevator incident since it happened."

Graham's mellow voice chuckled. "Well, glad to hear you could laugh it off." He paused for a moment. "Wish it could have been I who came to your rescue though."

Gwen's heart caught midbeat and she felt her face burning with that now familiar warmth that came whenever Graham's words took on that low, secretive tone.

"I would have liked that, too," she murmured, half shocked at her boldness. Did she really just say that?

"Gwen," he said slowly. "Have you thought about my offer yet? To come and see you?"

Clenching her eyes shut, she took a deep, shaky breath. Had she thought about it? Oh, yeah! What else had been hurtling through her mind for the last several days? Well, other than Alex's surprising entrance at— "I have, Graham," she interrupted her own distracted musings. "I—can I let you know. . .tomorrow?" She grimaced at the sudden time constraint she'd placed on herself for a definite answer, but she also knew that Graham wasn't one to wait around for too long. He liked decisions to be made. Promptly.

He let out a painfully dramatic sigh. "Well. . .I guess so. Just don't keep me dangling too much longer."

With a laugh, Gwen glanced at the clock, amazed to find it nearly midnight. "Oh, brother," she groaned. "Graham, I have to go or I'll never make it out of bed tomorrow."

"I'd be more than willing to come and help with that," he stated suggestively.

She blinked, surprised at the words from the man who was normally so. . .mannerly. "Um," she faltered.

"Just kidding," he rattled off quickly.

She remained quiet, pensive. And several seconds of stillness hung between them.

"Gwen?" His voice questioned the silence. "You still there?"

"Yes."

"Only joking. Sorry if I offended you."

Shaking herself out of her brief discomfort, Gwen nodded. "Oh, I know," she assured him.

But the string of tension remained.

"Well, I'll bid you good night, lady fair." He now seemed just as eager as she was to end the conversation gone awry.

"Good night, Graham," she returned. "I'll talk to you tomorrow."

"I'll count the hours."

Replacing the phone in the cradle, she felt her smile fade as she contemplated the last few minutes. It was the first time Graham had ever said anything like that. With a frown, she tried to reason out why he'd said it. But the more she thought about it, the more she convinced herself she was being terribly paranoid, if not a little prudish. How many times had she heard Barb and some of the other women at work bantering with male employees, even when there was no romantic relationship involved. The talk had always made her uncomfortable, but perhaps it was just her sheltered upbringing. Maybe Graham's comment was more the world's norm than she realized. He had apologized after all. . .

And dismissing the subject, she headed down the hall to bed. As she flicked back her covers and then hung her robe on the nearby chair, her eyes fell to the yearbook that she'd brought in last night. In spite of her resolve to shove it aside, along with all other thoughts of Alex Marshall, she found herself powerless to control her feet as they took her to retrieve the annual.

Her fragile emotions of the night before now seemed a world away—after today's episode, at least. Now. . . now when she thought of Alex Marshall, the fear was gone.

Maybe that had been the whole problem. Perhaps all she'd needed was a jolt like this to wake her up from her recurring high school dreams and to get her on with living. Of course! Alex Marshall was just a man. Nothing to be feared. And she, Gwen Paulson, was a woman. A woman who was ready to get on with her life.

As her reflections reiterated themselves, she felt a growing confidence swell within her. It had been in God's plan all along—Alex's coming here, her getting startled out of her teenage mind-set regarding men and relationships. Her mouth rose in a shy smile. And now. . .Graham.

Yep. It was plain to see; the Lord was working everything out beautifully.

Then she decided right then and there—she would meet Graham. Definitely.

Taking one last look in her dresser mirror as she removed her glasses, Gwen grinned. But the first thing she had to do was talk to Barb. As soon as possible.

⁂

Crumpling up the last of her sandwich's cellophane, Barb tossed the garbage into Gwen's small wastebasket. She dabbed at her rosy red lips daintily with a napkin. And her artfully made-up eyes flared for a fraction. "Are you serious?"

"Quite." Gwen nodded and finished off her own carrot stick. "It's been too long already. I just. . ." She trailed off in embarrassment.

"What?" Barb prodded.

"Well. . .I've just never really done anything like this before. I'm not even sure where to begin."

A giggle escaped her coworker's lips as she leaned over conspiratorially. "Well, I'm free this Saturday. You wanna make a day of it? I'll show you the ropes."

"Really?" Gwen was amazed. "I didn't expect you to do all that—"

Barb waved her off. "I'd love to. But we'd have to start bright and early."

Gwen gave a chagrined shake of her head. "I can't believe you're willing to—just do this for me."

"Consider it a favor." Barb smiled, her perfect teeth gleaming.

"One I fully intend to try and repay," Gwen assured her.

Behind them, the sounds of people returning from lunch interrupted their temporary solitude. Gwen began cleaning off the counter in her cubicle, preparing to get back to work. But when her coworker didn't leave immediately, she glanced up.

Barb's attention was stuck elsewhere. Following her line of sight, Gwen found her gaze landing on none other than Alex Marshall. A fleeting twinge in her stomach prefaced a very odd feeling of. . .possessiveness.

"Actually," Barb broke the silence, "if you'd really like to try and return that favor. . ." She let the thought dangle, but her eyes never left Alex's brawny form.

A slightly sickening feeling rose up through Gwen's chest. "Oh. Well, I don't know," she managed to force past the tightness in her throat. "I mean, it's been. . . years and years since—"

"But you know him." Barb's pointed stare pierced Gwen's—what she wanted was all too clear. "I've seen him stop by your cubicle a couple of times. It couldn't hurt to just. . .put in a good word about me, right?"

Giving the woman a shaky smile, Gwen finally nodded. "Okay. I'll see what I can do."

"Good," she whispered as she bolted up from the chair next to Gwen. "Here's your chance."

"Huh?" Gwen swung around to find Alex striding toward her, a friendly smile covering his appealing face.

"Hey, Gwen," he greeted her as he leaned casually against one of the cubicle's walls. "I can't chat for long here, but I was wondering if you'd taken a look at that. . .uh, money I gave you the other day."

At first, Gwen's mind drew a complete blank. She was too caught up in just looking into those lucid blue eyes of his. . .that, and distracted by the fact that Barb was nearly yanking the sleeve of her blouse from behind her. "The. . .money?"

For the first time she could ever recall, Gwen thought she saw a trace of embarrassment wash over Alex Marshall's face. "Uh, yeah. The dollar bill—"

"Oh, oh," she interrupted. "Yes. Yes, I did look at it." She dared to search his eyes a little more deeply. "Very interesting. I quite agree." Then she gave him a smile. One that conveyed that she understood.

He nodded, looking a trifle relieved. "Great."

Another yank from the insistent Barb.

"Um, Alex. Have you met one of our accountants, Barb, officially?"

Barb stepped forward and coyly held out a slender hand.

He took it in a friendly manner. "I think. . .unofficially. On the first day here. Nice to meet you, Barb."

"And you," she cooed back.

"Barb!" a voice carried across the work area. "Your

phone is ringing over here."

A scowl of impatience flitted across her ivory brow for only a moment before she flashed another winning smile at Alex. "We'll have to get better acquainted sometime. Perhaps over lunch?"

Gwen desperately tamped down the urge to interfere in this little introduction that she'd agreed to mediate. Was Barb's help really worth all of this? But thoughts of Graham pushed aside all other discomfort and she stayed silent.

"Yeah," Alex answered. "We could probably do that."

"Wonderful." Barb fairly beamed. "See you later."

Watching her office mate walk away, Gwen was more than aware of the exaggerated sashay of the woman's hips, and more than aware that Alex had noticed, too.

Flopping into her desk chair, she clicked off the screen saver and began pulling up the files she'd been working on earlier.

"Sorry to interrupt your work," Alex said quietly, "but I was wondering if maybe. . .you could tell me where you go to church?"

Gwen stopped clacking on the keys and looked up at him with renewed admiration. He no longer looked embarrassed, but quite comfortable. Confident. Like he was confiding in a friend. She smiled warmly. "Of course. We'd love to have you visit. I think you'd really like it there."

Grabbing a piece of paper from her desk drawer, she wrote down the name, address, and service times, drawing a simple map explaining its location.

"Looks easy enough to find," he admitted as he pocketed the note. "Thanks. Guess I might see you Sunday."

"Great." Gwen watched him walk away, her heart much lighter than it had been in. . .she didn't know how long. She chalked it up to the simple, yet profound joy in discovering when someone had become a believer. That had to be it.

But as she settled back toward her computer, a new thought struck her—how long he might be visiting her church. . .and Hudson. If he was inquiring about churches, that didn't mean he intended to stay, did it?

Six

Gwen smiled, her cheeks already aching from the grin that had been plastered on her face for the last solid hour. Slowly pulling her hair down from the ponytail holder that had held the brown waves back, she clicked off her computer.

"Three weeks," she whispered into her home's stillness. "Twenty-one days." More confidently this time. She reined herself in from doing a little dance around the living room. Graham sounded just as excited about their upcoming meeting. In his usual charming manner, he'd more than once made her tingle and blush simultaneously as they'd chatted in their own private room over the Internet.

"Dinner at the finest restaurant," he'd promised her. "Somewhere in the Twin Cities. We'll leave Hudson behind for a night. Whaddya say?"

Fairly shivering in anticipation, Gwen had agreed. Leave Hudson behind—you bet. And on top of all that, she could leave a bunch of other things behind, too. Namely, age-old memories. . .including Alex Marshall.

But a pang of guilt surfaced just as quickly at the thought of Alex. She really had no reason to harbor any bitterness toward him. He'd never been an accomplice in all that had transpired back at Carson High. He'd been ignorant of the whole situation.

And now that he was a Christian. . .Gwen shook her head. No. If her only reason to "get away" from everything centered around fleeing Alex Marshall, she'd better find a new reason to meet Graham. Alex was no threat, not anymore.

As her mind worked through it all, bits and pieces of memories floated to the top of her consciousness. The crowded gymnasium, the roar of the students bantering on the bleachers, the band warming up for the pep rally. And herself, standing on the sidelines of the basketball court, awaiting her chance to catch Alex's eye.

Gwen threw one last questioning glance toward the section of the gym where the cheerleaders were stretching out and warming up for a few routines. Trish didn't even look up.

With a sigh of impatience mixed with fear, Gwen lifted her gaze back out to the middle of the court where the basketball team was tossing free throws and practice shots. Her nerves, which half an hour ago were nearly steel, had quickly melted to Jell-O. She was about to turn around and give up the ridiculous notion. But something made her stop. She couldn't define it. Perhaps it was just that deep-down feeling of needing to feel loved, needed, accepted. Whatever it was, she took a quaking breath, swallowed several times, and faced the commotion taking place on the gym floor.

At that moment, Alex caught sight of her and threw her a friendly wave. Willing her quivering lips to smile back,

Gwen lifted her hand slightly in return.

He seemed to sense her lingering attention, so with a cursory glance over his shoulder toward the coach, he jogged over to where she stood. His white teeth gleamed against his perfect complexion. "Hey, Gwen. How's it going?"

She managed a nod—nothing else. This wasn't going to be as easy as she'd hoped.

He tilted his blond head. "Do you need to see me about something?" His perfect face grimaced momentarily. "I didn't mess up my last math assignment that bad, did I?"

Gwen quickly shook her head. "No, your sheet was fine." Come on, girl. Spit it out. *"Actually, I was wondering—that is, I wanted to ask you if—"*

"Marshall!" a voice bellowed from across the cavernous interior of the gymnasium.

Feeling her stomach sink to her toes, Gwen watched in horror as Mr. Kelley, the basketball coach, sauntered over toward them. "What's going on over here? For Pete's sake, Alex. We've got the biggest game of the season tonight and you're over here pussyfootin' around with the ladies."

Gwen wasn't sure what she'd do first—die of embarrassment or throw up from sheer nervousness.

"I've been here all of a minute, Coach," Alex tried to explain.

"Yeah, well if it's important enough to take away time from warm-ups, then it must be important enough for everybody to hear."

Her eyes flared. This was not happening. . .this was not happening.

At the sudden shift of activity on the gym floor, most of

the assembly quieted, and their eyes turned toward the unlikely threesome on the court.

"Anything you need to say, missy?" Coach Kelley sneered, his bushy gray brows rising.

Gwen quickly shook her head. No way. This wasn't worth it. Not now.

"Go ahead," the pushy man urged her. "If it was worth taking the center away from his warm-ups, then spit it out."

Gwen felt her eyes beginning to burn under sheer humiliation. Her head wagged back and forth. "It was nothing. I–I'm sorry. I—"

"Hey, Alex!" a voice floated down from the bleachers. "Maybe she wants to ask you to the dance."

Audible chuckles followed the comment that made Gwen's knees turn to slush. And worse, Alex turned back toward her, his eyebrows raised a fraction.

"Is that it, Gwen?" he asked.

By now, the whole crowd watched in silence to see the outcome. Gwen wished the floor would just open and swallow her up. There was no way out of this. . .whether she asked him now or not. "I'm sorry," she croaked. "I shouldn't have interrupted your practice. I—" She turned to walk away, to try and escape.

She was met by Trish. "I think you left your notebook behind in accounting today," the cheerleader bubbled animatedly. Tossing the spiral-bound book toward Gwen, it plopped to the floor, landing squarely in front of them, exposing the page it had been opened to. . .the one emblazoned with scribblings and words across every available space. All too clearly they made themselves visible to Gwen and, she assumed, everyone else within visual distance. Including Coach Kelley. And Alex.

"What's it say?" one of the other cheerleaders questioned from the distance.

Trish gladly obliged, cocking her head and studying the handwriting. "Um, Mrs. Alex Marshall. Gwen Marshall. Alex and Gwen Marshall."

A few snickers ricocheted around the gym, and the majority of the basketball players went back to their dribbling and shooting.

And Gwen died.

Coach Kelley picked up the notebook and, rolling his eyes in impatience, tossed it toward Gwen's limp arms. "Come on, Marshall. Let's get back to work."

Whether Alex even looked at her or not, she'd never know. There was no way she would lift her eyes to find out. As if she'd be able to see through the veil of tears anyway. . . Her mortification was too great to even comprehend. Trish had done all of this on purpose. It had all been planned. That realization didn't come until later. After the weekend of the Spring Fling. After she'd heard that Trish, herself, had long before asked Alex to the annual spring dance.

❧

"That was a long time ago, Gwen," she reminded herself when the stubborn tears tried to resurface. "A long time ago, and many miles away."

Squaring her shoulders, she released a long breath, determined to not let that memory get the best of her. Not this time—not ever again.

For now, she had sleep to get. Barb would be here early. . . It would be a long day.

Barb's sporty little car whizzed into Gwen's driveway promptly at eight-thirty A.M. She honked the horn twice, just as Gwen was skittering out the door.

Piling into the car's low frame, she smiled at her coworker, who obviously wore as much makeup on her days off as she did at the office. "Good morning, Barb."

"Isn't it though?" she fairly tittered. Slamming the car into reverse, she peeled out into the street, heading directly toward the highway that would take them into St. Paul and Minneapolis. "Okay," Barb rattled off with the efficiency of a seasoned tour guide. "First things first." She reached out a hand and lifted a section of Gwen's long brown hair. "This goes. Right away."

The remainder of the day was a blur to Gwen. An exhausting blur, at that. The first stop, at a highly expensive hair salon, proved more than enough to break Gwen in for what the remainder of the day would entail. She watched in morbid fascination as the stylist snipped inch after inch of her long-neglected locks, their weight hurtling them to the floor in an abandoned pile.

Successfully dodging Barb's suggestions to "go red," Gwen opted merely for a few highlights to accent the chic new close-cropped style. Staring at herself in the mirror, she could hardly believe it was her. When did she ever have cheekbones before? And such a long neck?

After spending more for that one haircut than she had on all previous cuts combined, Barb dragged Gwen into an eyewear store, one of those one-hour places. She emerged with a new pair of "way stylish" glasses, according to Barb. And a pair of extended-wear contacts. They were even tinted the slightest shade of green to accent her own eye color. She hoped she'd get used to sticking the ridiculous little discs in her eyes.

From there, it was a flurry of makeup counters, dressing rooms, perfume samples, and shoe stores. And by the end of the day, she was absolutely shot. And she didn't even want to think about the dent this had put in her savings account.

"Well," Barb said with a satisfied smile as she surveyed the pile of bags, packages, and boxes in the backseat of her car. "I'd say we had a very successful day. Wouldn't you?"

Gwen could only nod. Was this success? She didn't know. She'd never done anything like this before. And would it really make that much, if any, difference?

At that moment, a group of young men passed by Barb's car on their way to the mall's entrance. Obviously entranced by the sporty vehicle, they sidled closer to it. Once they saw the occupants, several whistles broke the air, followed by chuckles and wide grins.

Gwen shifted her gaze to Barb and smiled faintly, assuming their attentions were directed at her friend. But Barb was jabbing her finger toward the group. Gwen swung back around to see, and there—directed straight toward her—was a particularly fetching smile on the face of one of the men.

Her lips curled in a shy smile as she self-consciously threw her gaze to the floor. Maybe it had been a good day after all.

Seven

Closing her eyes and losing herself in the chorus of the worship song, Gwen's heart fairly swelled. "Thank You, Father," she whispered. "Thank You for all You've done for me. . .all You continue to do for me." It had come back to her over the last week—with all of its events—that God was still in control. Always had been. And watching her life take that upward swing in the area of a "significant other," she could only marvel at His timing and profound wisdom. She simply hadn't been ready before now.

Slowly the music drifted off, leaving the pastor to close the service in prayer. Gwen echoed his amen and grabbed her purse from the padded pew.

"Gwen?" she heard a friendly female voice ask.

Turning around, she found Lori Bentson, one of the other young women in the adult Sunday school class, staring at her incredulously. "Good morning, Lori."

Her jaw only gaped further. "Is that really you?" She walked a circle around Gwen, taking in her hair, face, and new trim-fitting pantsuit. "I saw this gorgeous new woman in class this morning and wondered who on earth it was."

Dipping her head in embarrassment, Gwen found

herself warming under the compliment. "Thank you, Lori," she murmured.

"You're most welcome," her friend beamed. "So how's life? Seems like ages since we've talked."

"Oh, pretty good." Gwen didn't really feel like going into any deep details concerning the events of the past week. She just didn't feel she knew Lori well enough. Or anyone for that matter. Forming close, personal relationships had never been her strong suit. But now that she had exciting news to share, she realized how much she actually missed it.

"Hm," Lori commented as she looked over Gwen's shoulder. "You must be on everyone's list to talk to today. Here comes Pastor Hutchins."

Gwen glanced over her shoulder to find the man walking in her direction, deep in conversation with. . . Alex!

Tamping down her nervous stomach and trying not to release too audible a breath, she swallowed. She could do this. It was no different from every day at the office.

But taking a second glance at Alex, she decided she was wrong. If he did justice to a simple flannel shirt and jeans, he was absolutely born to wear dress pants, shirt, and a tie. He looked. . .incredible.

As the two men neared her, their voices slowed. "Well, here you are, Alex," Pastor Hutchins said as he stepped toward the women. "This is Lori Bentson," he indicated with a bow of his dark head. "And you said you already know Gwen."

All Gwen saw was Alex's eyes flare and his jaw nearly fall to the floor.

She hoped she kept her lips from tweaking into too much of an amused smile.

"Good morning, Gwen." Paul Hutchins pumped her hand in normal exuberance. "Glad to see you asked a friend to come today." He nodded toward Alex. "He had a hard time finding you." The minister chuckled kindly. "I shouldn't wonder why."

"Thank you, Pastor," she mumbled, never quite able to let her eyes leave Alex's surprised blue ones for too long.

"You all have a splendid afternoon." He turned toward Alex, extending a hand before striding away. "Nice to have met you, Alex. Hope to see you again soon."

Alex seemed to be having difficulty pulling his gaze off of Gwen. "I'm sure you will, Pastor. Thanks. I really enjoyed your message." He returned the warm handshake.

"Me, too," Lori spoke up. "Well, I've got company coming this afternoon and my apartment's a wreck. I'll see you next week, Gwen. Nice to have met you, Alex." She walked down the aisle, leaving Alex and Gwen alone in the midst of the semicrowded sanctuary.

Neither spoke for a time.

Some of the color began to return to Alex's normally healthy complexion. And he finally sputtered into a laugh. Gwen couldn't help but join him.

"Well," he sighed as the laughter finally died down. "I don't know about your plans, but I'd love to take you out to lunch. We can't let someone looking like a million bucks go completely unnoticed now, can we?"

Smiling at his compliment, Gwen shook her head. "I–I'd really like that, Alex. But I'm afraid I'm expecting a phone call this afternoon."

His face fell a fraction, along with his shoulders, but he maintained a cheery disposition. "All right then. Maybe next time."

Gwen shifted her purse to her other shoulder and started to side step around him.

"Can I at least walk you to your car?" he interrupted her steps.

Swiveling back around, she nodded with a grin. "Sure."

❧

The short hike to the parking lot was spent in silence. Alex wasn't sure if that was a good sign or not. But Gwen didn't seem to be minding the companionable quiet.

But he did know that he had to voice the intent he'd come to church with. The one that got waylaid when he'd looked at her. He had cared about Gwen as a friend in high school; as the years passed, he realized more and more how special their friendship had been. It was obvious to him that God had placed him in Hudson to renew their friendship. But there was something different in his feelings for her—something he hadn't felt for her before. Even now, he tossed a quick glance in her direction, restudying the transformation that had taken Gwen Paulson from a painfully shy computer programmer into. . .he didn't know what.

Something incredible, that was for sure.

She looked over and caught him staring. He felt his face redden for the first time in a long while.

She halted before her well-kept little two-door and placed her fingers on the handle. "Thank you, Alex. Guess I'll see you tomorrow."

"Yeah," he muttered, losing himself somewhere in the green depths of those huge eyes that had previously been hidden behind glasses. As she started to enter her car, he shook himself out of his reverie. "Uh, Gwen?"

She paused, just before taking her seat, her face questioning.

Clearing his throat, he shoved his hands into the pockets of his pants. "I just wanted to let you know. . .I was going to ask you at work tomorrow if you'd want to join me for lunch. Down in the cafeteria."

"Really?"

He nodded. "Yeah. But as long as we're here today, I thought I'd ask now."

Somewhere from within, he thought he detected a shadow of doubt in her features. Instinctively, he knew. Chalk it up to having three sisters. He jumped in before her doubts grew. "Gwen, you look fantastic today."

She blushed prettily.

"But," he smiled kindly, "I was going to ask you tomorrow. Really. Before. . .all of this."

A light came on behind those emerald eyes, and he felt himself relax a bit.

"Thank you, Alex." She smiled shyly. "I appreciate that very much. The offer. . .and all of this."

He grinned. "So, is it a date?"

He watched her face fall slightly. And he felt his chest sink at the same time.

"I'd really, really like that. But. . .I'm afraid, I just can't." She lifted her eyes in an apologetic stare.

Not wanting to press the issue, Alex simply shrugged. "Okay. Whatever." He couldn't quite place his finger on it, but it seemed as if she'd wanted to accept his offer—the battle of her thoughts was almost visible on her face.

Slowly closing the door behind her, he lifted a wave as she drove off. As he strode toward his pickup, Alex tried to think of something else to do with his afternoon. Anything at all. But with a wry grin, he realized that anything else would probably pale in comparison to his hope of getting to know the young woman he'd just watched transform.

Gwen's entrance at work the next day was nearly a carbon copy of her arrival at church the day before—save the more crude comments uttered by a select group of men at work who had nothing better to talk about.

She noted Barb's approving nod over the cubicle wall before she sat down and carefully smoothed out the pinstriped skirt of her new form-fitting business suit.

Today's getting ready had gone slightly smoother than yesterday's. She'd even attempted taking in and out her contact lenses. After the fifth time of jabbing herself in the eye, she'd gotten them in place. The makeup, so far, seemed to be the biggest challenge. The amount the cosmetician had put on Gwen at the counter was a bit much for her own tastes. She muted it somewhat, happier with the overall outcome.

Alex had met her eye as he exited from the elevator. The brilliant blue work shirt he wore seemed to make his eyes positively light up. Maybe she'd been wrong about the whole issue of his Sunday clothes; these certainly did suit him, too.

"Gwen," a hushed voice floated over the top of her partition.

She looked up to find Barb's expectant face. "Morning," she greeted her.

"Well?" Barb questioned, her eyes drifting toward the construction crew.

"Did you talk to him yet?"

Gwen chuckled. "Barb, I just got here."

A sigh of impatience. "Okay. I'll check back with you later."

Shaking her head, Gwen flicked on her computer. Guess there was no worry as to whether Barb would expect immediate paybacks for this weekend favor. With a sigh, she tried to figure out why it should bother her so much anyway. She had agreed to try and set the two of them up. And after all, she had Graham now.

A whistling song from across the floor caught her attention and she lifted her chin to peer over in the general direction. Alex was busily stacking a pile of two-by-fours. Gwen quickly recognized the melody as "What a Mighty God We Serve"—one of the songs they'd sung in church yesterday.

Gwen smiled and shifted her attention back toward her screen.

A new thought struck her. Would Alex even be interested in Barb—since she wasn't a believer? That part of the deal hadn't even occurred to Gwen. And she tried to squash the feeling inside that sincerely hoped he wouldn't be.

Eight

Gwen wiped the tears from her eyes, slowly patting the ache in her stomach from laughing so hard. What was it about Alex that had this giddy effect on her? She'd never laughed so hard in her whole life. At least, not until the last couple of weeks.

What did this make now? Six—seven times? Just in the last nine workdays? Gwen had lost count; it had been easy to do. In fact, never had her noon hours moved so swiftly before.

It had started out innocently enough. He'd merely taken a companionable seat near her with his own brown bag in hand. She tried not to read anything into the fact that he'd never packed a lunch before. Even though she'd refused that initial invitation, it seemed that this was still a suitable arrangement. Part of her still battled with guilt, half out of promise to Barb, the other half out of her growing relationship with Graham. Lately, though, their evening computer and phone conversations weren't nearly as frequent as they had been. She wondered about it, but then remembered that she would be meeting him soon. In fact, in just a little over a week. The thought thrilled her. . .and scared her just a little.

But even in the talks that she and Graham had, she'd found herself on more than one occasion beginning to mention some little incident with Alex and quickly changing the subject altogether. If Graham noticed her choppy conversation abilities, he didn't let on.

Alex wadded up the remains of his empty bag and tossed it in Gwen's trash can. "I'm glad to hear I wasn't way off base on that last Bible verse. A lot of this is still real new to me. I really appreciate the time you take setting me straight."

Gwen blushed and flipped closed the Bible they'd been studying. "My pleasure," she assured him. "Guess I never really lost that tutoring role, did I?"

She watched him try to grin, then hesitate before lifting his eyes to hers, suddenly more serious. After a moment, he shook his head. "I wish somebody would've explained all of this to me in high school."

Immediately feeling guilty, Gwen grimaced. "I guess I wasn't very good at witnessing back then. Or now. At least, I feel that way sometimes."

"No, no," he quickly assured her. "It wasn't your fault." He leaned back in his chair and ran his fingers through his thick blond hair. "I don't know. I probably just wasn't ready to hear it. I always knew you were. . . different. I might have called it 'religious' back then. But you spoke volumes more through just who you were than anything you might have said." He grew thoughtful. "Especially considering that episode you had to endure in front of everybody. If anyone has cause to hate people, I'd say you'd definitely be justified."

Gwen returned a quiet smile. Over these last couple of weeks, she and Alex had discussed a myriad of things as they ate their home-packed lunches together and conversed after church on Sundays—including all of what had happened in high school. It no longer caused her the supreme shame and humiliation. She finally felt she'd completely given it over to God. . .for good.

"No," she responded. "I don't hate anybody. I think I hated myself for a long time. . .but the Lord's pulled me out of that slump."

"Yeah," he nodded slowly. "I guess that's where Graham comes into the picture, too, eh?"

Feeling her cheeks flame scarlet, she tried to reason why the mention of the man's name should cause her such embarrassment. Or perhaps it was only because the word had come from Alex's lips. Part of her had thought that sharing her encounters with Graham would make her feel proud, a little less like that tongue-tied schoolgirl that came and went occasionally when talking with Alex. But sharing her growing relationship with her Internet friend had proved frustrating. . .if only in her own soul. Something niggled in the pit of her stomach regarding the whole issue, but she was just as quick to squelch any further thoughts along that line and quickly change the subject.

However, Alex wouldn't let her get away with it. For some reason unbeknownst to Gwen, Alex often got edgy and more than a little bossy when she brought up Graham's name. He'd said he'd read about people meeting someone on the computer—and he cautioned her about some very bad outcomes that had resulted.

She'd laughed off his warnings, assuring him that she knew what she was doing. And that Graham seemed to be completely on the up and up.

But here they were, back on that subject again.

Tossing her own garbage away, Gwen released a measured breath and faced her computer station. "Oh, Alex. I appreciate your concern." She gave him a level stare. "But you don't know Graham. He's. . .he's. . ."

Alex's clear blue eyes widened, waiting.

She let out a huff. "I don't know—I just think you're concerning yourself about nothing."

His look—a cross between hurt and anger—made Gwen retreat a fraction.

He opened his mouth to respond just as the ding of the elevator doors brought their discussion to a close. Alex promptly got to his feet, returning the chair he'd borrowed from a nearby table, and Gwen made herself busy shuffling papers and redirecting her mouse to the last file she'd opened, trying to bury the image of Alex's last look before he'd strode away. What was his problem anyway? They'd been having such nice chats over these last weeks, why did this one subject always have to come up and ruin everything? More often than not she ended up feeling muddled, confused. . .emotions she thought she was done battling with.

Out of the corner of her eye, she saw Barb exiting the elevator, her gaze leveled in Gwen's direction. *No, no, please. . .not her right now.*

Too late.

Biting her top lip, Gwen tried to look intensely busy as Barb's determined gait brought her over to Gwen's cubicle. The blond leaned over the partition, her eyes not wavering, yet saying nothing.

Swallowing a lump in her throat, Gwen looked up at her coworker and tried to smile. "Afternoon, Barb. Can I help you with something?"

The blue eyes narrowed. "I thought you could. But I didn't realize that you had designs on 'Mr. Carpenter' yourself."

Blowing out a breath, Gwen dropped her gaze to her keyboard. "It's not what you think," she tried to explain.

"Gwen," she continued in a forceful, hushed voice. "I'm not blind. I've seen you two. The lunches you share nearly every day. Don't tell me that you've been using all that time to sing my praises to Alex."

"Actually," she started to explain, then abruptly stopped. She couldn't tell Barb about her and Alex's Bible studies. It was against company policy. RBS had no problems with employees involved in such activities on their own time—like lunch. But any time taken away from work hours or used in pressing it on other coworkers who weren't interested. . . Well, Gwen could quickly lose her job.

"I'm sorry," she finally stammered. She had made a deal with Barb. And after all the woman had helped her do that weekend. . . "I'll speak with him right away. I promise."

The icy blue eyes looked doubtful.

"I will. I swear." Gwen held up her right hand solemnly.

Barb didn't totally lose her skeptical stare, but she nodded and turned to make her way back to her own workstation.

Releasing a long breath, Gwen closed her eyes. *Yet another mess you've gotten yourself into, girl. Nice job!*

"Gwen?" A whisper from behind made her jump.

Whirling around, she found Alex squatting within the small confines of her "office," hidden from everyone else's view. That same unsettled fluttering rose within her. And she was getting increasingly annoyed with it.

Perhaps she had been enjoying Alex's company a little too much. Maybe Barb was right. Maybe she was just being selfish.

"I have something to say to you—" they both blurted out at the same time.

Smiling, Alex nodded his head in deference to Gwen.

She took a deep breath. *Okay, here it goes.* "I just wanted to let you know that I think you should strike up some conversations with Barb. Maybe take her to lunch. I think you two would. . .really hit it off." There. She'd done it.

His face remained expressionless for a second, then he glanced at the floor.

"You really think so?" he asked when he met her eyes again.

That same old lump rose up, choking off almost all of her air. How was she supposed to answer that? She couldn't look into those cerulean eyes and. . .lie. Could she?

Not knowing how to respond, she didn't. She simply muttered, "Did you have something to say?"

"Yeah. But I'm not sure if it's that relevant anymore."

She frowned in confusion.

He slowly stood and looked in Barb's direction. "You really think we'd have that much in common?"

Gwen shrugged her shoulders, desperately trying to ignore the painful spasms in her heart. "Guess you won't know until you ask, right?"

With a slow nod, he began to head back toward his work.

"Alex," she interrupted him mid-stride.

He turned to face her, his face completely devoid of any of its usual exuberance.

"Did you have something you wanted to say?" she asked, trying to keep her voice to a minimum.

A pointed stare was all he returned. Then he shook his head and walked away.

Several days later, Alex pounded in the last nail from his carpenter's pouch, then ran a sleeve across his sweaty brow and glanced at the clock. Good! It was quitting time anyway.

He carefully packed up his tools and laid aside the heavier equipment that they would need Monday. Right now, all he knew was that he desperately needed this weekend.

Sunday would be Easter. His heart crimped at the

thought of what he'd like to be doing on the holiday. Thoughts of other people joining together with scores of relatives had crossed his mind more than once. But what did you do when your parents were divorced and half of your siblings weren't even speaking to each other?

No, going back to Carson didn't appeal to him. But sharing the day with *someone* did. *Tough luck, Alex.*

Almost involuntarily, his eyes swung in Gwen's direction. She was just grabbing her purse and closing up her desk drawers. He assumed that she had plans for Sunday. But maybe he shouldn't assume anything anymore. After their last discussion a few days ago, little if anything, aside from polite hellos, had been voiced between them. And all because of that stupid Internet "hero" she thought she'd found—

He squelched the rest of the thought. Deep down he knew the main reason for his defensiveness. The reason that had taken him so off guard when he'd finally admitted it to himself. The fact of the matter was that he had been, among other things, a blind, ignorant fool in high school. For all the time he'd spent with Gwen Paulson, even then, to not have seen her charming personality, her fun sense of humor, her incredible wit and intelligence, and the fact that she was a Christian. . . Whether he liked it or not, he'd fallen for Gwen—head over heels. And nothing ever had taken Alex Marshall by surprise like that before.

But even more, he knew there was just something about this guy she spoke of—this Graham. Even hearing his character filtered through Gwen's praises of him, Alex didn't like him. The thought of their upcoming meeting caused him no little alarm. But he was still trying to think of what, if anything, to do about his concerns.

If only he could talk to her again. Maybe even on Easter. Just to make her see what this guy might be. . . And to try and make her see what he, himself, had up until now been too afraid to admit in his own heart.

He sighed. A measure of comfort came to him. At least he had a reason to celebrate Easter this year—he finally understood God's gift of His Son. That was more than enough. The rest, he'd have to let God deal with.

Nine

Gwen passed the bowl of mashed potatoes back to her mother.

"Thank you, dear." Evelyn Paulson's round face beamed. "You've done me proud. This meal was excellent."

Gwen grinned. "See. . .I didn't sit in front of a computer *all* the time when I lived at home."

"No," her Dad chuckled. "Just most of the time. I'm surprised that you didn't figure out some sort of program to have the computer actually do the cooking."

"Oh, Daddy," she laughed. Standing from her place at the small, lace-covered dining table, she leaned over and gave her father's balding head a kiss, then began clearing the dishes.

Her mother jumped up. "Oh, let me help, dear. You did so much just having us up here today. Just like old times, right?"

Gwen smiled as the two of them paraded into the kitchen with their plates and utensils. For some irritating reason, her thoughts kept drifting to Alex. Maybe it was because of the expression he'd been wearing in church that morning—one of almost dejection. After having introduced her parents to him, she'd battled with asking him to join them for Easter dinner. She knew that most likely he had nowhere to go, no one to celebrate with. And there would be more than enough food.

But if Gwen's charity fell short, her mother's didn't. Mom had asked point-blank if he'd care to come and eat with them. Watching his reaction, she'd thought he'd really wanted to. But after gazing for an uncomfortable moment straight at Gwen, he'd graciously declined. She was surprised at the depth of her disappointment.

Going through the motions of placing the flatware in the sinkful of sudsy water, Gwen realized that her mother had been chattering at her and she'd completely missed most of what had been said. "I'm sorry, Mom," she began when she was able to get a word in. "What did you say?"

"That nice Alex fellow at your church. You mentioned that you went to high school together?"

"Yes, Mom. Alex Marshall. You couldn't forget him . . .he was the star of everything. I used to stay after school to help him out in math."

The older woman's mouth pursed in thought, still uncertain. "Hmm, was he on the Academic Decathlon with you?"

"No. Try the 'track and field' variety."

"Seems like a nice young man," her mother continued. She ambled on for several more minutes, Gwen settled for giving yes or no answers. She felt badly that she wasn't more sociable, her parents having driven all the way from Carson. But she couldn't seem to keep her thoughts together. She couldn't count how many times she'd wanted to share with them about Graham. After all, in only five days she'd be meeting the man in the Twin Cities. But something held her back. She knew their usual overconcern, and she really didn't want to burden them with extra worry that was unfounded. That, and she just didn't relish answering the onslaught of questions that would follow such an announcement. She'd had enough of that from Alex. Alex—

Shaking her head, Gwen dumped a dish a little too quickly into the steaming water and was promptly greeted by the shatter of china. With a groan, she pushed her hands in to retrieve the broken bowl—only to feel the edge slice sharply into her palm.

The gasp that exited her lips must have alerted her mother because before she knew what was happening, a dish towel was being wound around her hand and her mother was whisking both Gwen and her father toward the door and out to the car. "Come on, Russell. The girl's bleeding all over the place. Most likely will need stitches." Returning her attention to Gwen as they all piled into the front seat of the four-door, her mother clutched the towel tightly against the wound, clucking her concern all the way to the emergency room.

❧

"Where did you say you are?"

"Hudson. Wisconsin." Alex picked up the TV remote and flicked off the sound so he could better hear his long-distance friend's voice.

"Hudson. Huh." Jim Greer sounded somewhat surprised. "Thought if you were gonna leave Carson, that you'd get out of the state completely."

"Says you from sunny Florida," Alex laughed. "Look, Jim. The reason I called was to ask you a question. A computer question."

A surprised chuckle came through the line. "You? A computer question? Okay. . .the 'on' switch is right behind the—"

"Funny, Jim. I'm serious. I need some help here."

"Okay, I'll do my best. What's up?"

"Is it possible to find out the uh. . .the. . ." he sputtered off, frustrated in not being able to explain what he needed to know.

"So far so good, buddy," Jim laughed.

"Okay," Alex growled. "The Internet. People get on there and talk to each other, right?"

"Sure. Chat rooms."

"That's it! How can I get into one?"

"Well, there are a number of search engines you can use. You just type in what type of subject you might be interested in discussing and it will pull up a bunch of different sites with—"

"Whoa, whoa." Alex rolled his eyes and let out a breath. "You're over my head here. Search engine?"

Jim started again, slowly, as if explaining things to an extremely dense child. "A search engine finds the places that you'd like to visit. The type of people you'd like to converse with."

"No, no. I already know what—chat room I want to get into."

"You do? So what's the problem?"

Alex sighed with frustration. This was getting him absolutely nowhere. "Look, Jim. Here's the deal. There's this girl I met—"

"On the Net? Watch out, buddy. She probably looks like Attila the—"

"Jim, come on. Lemme finish here."

"Sorry. Go ahead."

"I know this girl. She's. . .a computer whiz. She goes into this chat room and talks to this guy pretty frequently. I want to know how to get into that room."

"Ah." Jim's tone suddenly conveyed understanding. "Some online competition, eh?"

"Never mind my reasons for now. Just tell me if it can be done. . .without her knowing it," he added.

"Hmm. Does she talk to him at home or at work?"

Alex thought for a moment. "I think usually at home but—oh, wait. No. Sometimes she talks with him during lunch. She mentioned that a couple of times."

"Okay then. Your best bet would be to get on her computer at work and pull down the favorite sites that she's bookmarked. Chances are that she'll have marked the page for easy log-on."

Alex's brain started to swirl. "Jim, you're doing it again."

"Alex, get a piece of paper. I'm gonna take you through this thing step by step."

With a sigh of relief and determination, he grabbed a pen and a sheet of paper. "Okay, I got 'em. Let her rip."

❧

Alex poked his head into the darkened, quiet office. Not a soul around yet. Good. The piece of paper clutched firmly in his hand, he strode over toward Gwen's cubicle and sat down at the tidy desk. Flicking on the computer, he momentarily panicked when he realized that he didn't know Gwen's password to get into the system. His tension released a fraction when the menu came up with the proper icons.

Clicking awkwardly on the picture for the Internet browser, he pulled it up without incident. Casting a glance at the stairwell door and the elevator, he quickly restudied the sheet in front of him. "Okay," he whispered. "Here goes nothin'. Favorites, favorites. . ." Down the list came, displayed neatly on the screen—the chat room right on top.

Clicking on the title, he watched as the address showed at the screen's base. He jotted it down, double-checking to see if he'd gotten all the characters right.

Off to the side, the ding of the elevator doors resonated through the empty area.

Cramming the paper into his shirt pocket, Alex punched off the computer and hit the floor.

The sound of heels clicking first across the tile and then moving to the carpet, pounded through the already roaring sound in his ears. *Lighten up, Alex. It's not like you're James Bond or anything. What could happen to you?*

"Comfortable?" The surprised feminine voice floated down from above him and he rolled over to find Barb staring down at him. He wasn't sure if he was relieved at that or not.

"Uh, just. . .checkin' Gwen's chair." He felt the sudden pressure leave his chest. "One of the casters wasn't working right the other day. Thought I'd look it over." He gave the seat a few last shoves across the floor before jumping to his feet with a satisfied nod. "Good enough."

Barb crossed her arms and studied him carefully. "You certainly seem to watch out for her."

"Oh, you know how it is. Old high school buddies and all that." He swallowed when her expression didn't even flinch. He cleared his throat in the deafening silence of the empty room.

"You know, Alex. Something bothers me here." Her gaze was unwavering. "I've invited you to lunch. . .how many times now?"

He looked up at the ceiling, trying to recall. "Three . . .four?"

"Right." She dipped her blond head in seriousness. "I'm getting rather tired of being shot down. If you'd rather not. . .ever, could you please tell me now?"

Gaining a measure of respect for her forthrightness, Alex gave her an understanding smile. "Barb, you seem like a great gal. And I'm sure that in time you'll find the guy who's right for you." He took a breath for courage. "But if you want to know the truth, I can't commit to seeing anyone who I know doesn't feel the same way about God as I do."

A flicker passed through her eyes.

He wasn't sure whether to shield himself from the onslaught or just take it like a man.

Amazingly, Barb slowly nodded her head. "I guess I can respect that. I've heard Gwen talk about something like that, too."

"Really?"

"Mm hm."

Suddenly, Alex was curious. "Barb, has she ever mentioned a 'Graham' to you?"

"A few times. Not a lot. She seems to like to keep that part of her life pretty private."

"Yeah, I figured that out, too." He lost himself in his thoughts momentarily, wondering why Gwen would go to such great pains to keep this guy so under wraps.

"Well, guess I'll start working. Maybe get done early today," Barb said.

He brought his gaze back around to Barb's and smiled. "Guess I'd better, too." He started to walk toward the area housing the tools, retrieving the crumpled paper from his pocket and carefully folding it before replacing it in his wallet.

"Alex?"

He swung around again.

"I just—" Barb looked unusually flustered. "Thanks," she finally murmured. "For being honest with me."

He gave her a kind smile. "You're welcome."

❧

Giving the librarian what he hoped was his most charming smile, Alex tried his appeal one more time. "I understand your dilemma, ma'am—it being nearly closing time and all. But this is rather urgent. Otherwise I wouldn't be asking such an obviously conscientious person as yourself to bend the rules. . .even just this little bit."

Shaking her salt-and-pepper dark hair, she finally broke into an amused grin. "Well," she drawled. "I guess I could sort some of the new books that came in."

Alex beamed.

"The computer is over here." She beckoned him with her hand, and he stepped around the checkout desk to follow her. "The rule is that everybody gets thirty minutes. No more." Her firm look stated that was one point she wasn't flexible on.

He gave her a salute. "Understood. Thank you."

She walked away, leaving him to stare at the blue screen and battle with his thoughts. Should he? Shouldn't he? Back and forth. But, figuring that the impetus had already gotten him this far. . . .

He pulled out that now familiar paper and typed in the address.

Ten

Eyeing the bandage on her hand disdainfully, Gwen sighed and gave up trying to figure out a way to clasp the new necklace. She'd have to forego the jewelry tonight. Who'd have thought that such a silly thing as a cut could turn into three days of missed work, leaving the remaining two days of the week less than productive on top of it all? She might as well have not even gone into the office.

If she'd skipped out of work this week it would have meant avoiding Alex as well. The odd strain that had crept between them seemed only to intensify with each day. And yesterday and today he'd been nearly unbearable. Every time he came near and she issued a polite greeting, it seemed to trigger his turn on the soapbox—berating Graham, a man he'd never even talked with. The mere memory still rankled her.

She'd managed to sneak out of the office a bit early, bypassing what she was sure would be his final parting shot toward Graham. No, whatever Alex Marshall's problem was, he'd have to deal with it on his own. Gwen glanced down at her watch. She had her own plans for the evening. And if she didn't want to be late, she'd better leave now.

Giving her reflection, clad in the new black evening dress, one last look, she nodded in satisfaction and whisked out the door.

❧

Alex pulled the borrowed car into the crowded parking lot. Judging by the make and year of most of the vehicles here, this restaurant didn't come cheap. He patted his pocket, making sure his wallet was in place. He'd definitely need that credit card tonight.

Having gained the eatery's name and location from Barb, he'd waited in the lot until Gwen's familiar vehicle drove in. He gave her what he hoped would be ample time to meet that guy and find a seat. He only wished he knew what this Graham looked like. More than once he'd caught himself staring at the string of patrons filing past his car, wondering if any of them might be the scum he was ready to punch out.

Straightening his tie, he ran a hand through his hair and stepped out of the car, pulling on his suit coat as he started toward the door.

As the imposing entrance neared, he started second-guessing his decision. His earlier musings of James Bond seemed more appropriate now. He'd never actually tailed anybody before. And that the anybody was Gwen made him feel a little more than sheepish.

Get a grip, Alex. Let's not lose it before the evening's even started. . .

In the classy atmosphere, it was hard not to stare. But function took over feeling, and he focused his thoughts on his directive—save Gwen. The first step would be avoiding the overly helpful maître d'.

Waiting until a large group commandeered the tuxedoed gentleman's attention, Alex unobtrusively slipped into the dining area, trying to blend in with the crowd, all the while looking for Gwen and her. . .date.

From across the section of dining room populated with intense foliage, he grinned as he spied Gwen's dark head. And wonder of wonders, the table on the opposite side of the plant-strewn partition was open! He made a beeline for it, avoiding moving into Gwen's direct line of vision.

Plunking himself into the plush booth, he leaned in his neighbors' direction, straining to hear all that was being said. Difficult. They seemed to be talking kind of low.

He leaned closer. Every so often, he'd hear Gwen's delightful little laugh. And it made him want to march around—no, through this wall and absolutely flatten Graham's face. If she only knew what this jerk was up—

"Good evening, sir." A sudden voice from his side made him bolt upright in the seat.

A smiling waiter handed him the menu. "Would you care for a drink?"

Rolling his eyes, Alex released a breath. Man, if he hadn't given up drinking— "No," he started, then clamped his jaw shut. Gwen was right over there. If she heard him. . .

Clearing his throat, he lowered his voice drastically. "No, thank you," he rumbled.

"Very good. I'll be back shortly to take your order."

The young man strode away with quiet efficiency.

Plopping the menu aside, Alex bent his head in the other direction again. His attention perked up. He could finally hear them. Settling close to the lattice-topped divider, he listened. . .and waited.

❧

"I am so sorry about your accident," Graham crooned. He tenderly picked up Gwen's bandaged hand and placed a reverent kiss against the back of it. Little jolts of electricity shot up her arm and she felt herself shivering. Apparently Graham noticed, too.

"Are you chilly?" he asked, concern in his deep brown eyes.

Not anymore, Gwen thought. She gazed at his classic features and realized that the photos she'd seen of him had not done justice to his "beauty" at all. He truly was beautiful. Not a hair out of place, not a wrinkle on his trim suit. Everything, perfect. Perfect.

"You know, Gwen," he murmured as he grasped both of her hands in his. "I don't think you realize how long I've been waiting for this moment. How long I've wanted to meet you. To see you." He lifted her fingers and brushed them across his lips. "To touch you."

Those same little shivers were skittering down Gwen's spine. Her head felt as if it were beginning to spin. A dizzying, warm feeling kept intensifying somewhere deep inside her.

She desperately wanted to respond, to say some profound, romantic words back to him. But none would come. All she could do was lose herself in the depth of his intense dark eyes, his full lips.

A brief moment of clarity fell on her and she shook her head, as if to slough off the surprising feelings. "Thank you, Graham," she whispered when she finally found her voice. "I've really been looking forward to this, too."

In a split second, her mind took off on a path of its own. And to Gwen's irritation, it was Alex's face she saw instead. And from the recesses of her brain came the words he'd thrown at her over the last week repeatedly, *"Are you sure this guy's even a Christian?"*

With an inward groan of exasperation, she met Graham's eyes, determined not to let such negative thoughts spoil her evening.

"You know," he continued, his brows knitting together in seriousness. "I know we've only 'met' each other just a mere half hour ago or so. And yet, I feel such an ease with you. Like I've known you forever."

"Well," she admitted. "We have spoken extensively. On the computer and on the phone. I guess that would have something to do with it."

He nodded with a smooth smile. "So, you feel it, too."

She shrugged, not sure of his meaning.

"This." He leaned closer, his face a breathless distance from hers. "Do you feel it?"

The warm fuzziness washed over her again. She nodded dumbly, aware that if Graham had chosen this moment to declare the world flat, she'd likely have agreed with him.

"I'm so glad," his low voice intoned. "Some people are

foolish enough to get caught up in the confines of 'knowing' someone. I think it goes beyond that, don't you?"

Gwen found herself semi-nodding again. She was starting to lose her place in the conversation. Maybe it was the ridiculous way her head kept spinning.

"I'm going to be somewhat bold here."

She drew in a breath and held it.

With his finger tracing a line up and down her bare arm, Graham leaned in again. "I feel like we need to leave here. We need to be. . .alone. I want to get to know the 'real Gwen.' The one who's not caught up in the day-to-day world around us."

Swallowing hard, she tried to keep her eyes on his. "I'm not sure what you mean," she admitted softly. "I feel. . .almost alone with you here. It's a very intimate place." She nodded at the surroundings, her appreciative gaze taking it all in.

"Not intimate enough," he insisted. "Please, Gwen." The look swimming in his eyes was almost pleading like a little boy begging for candy. Then it changed. To one much different—mature, passionate. Even predatory.

Feeling her lips part as her breath left in a quiet gasp, she simply stared. She had to find her voice. . .say something. "Graham," she whispered. "I—"

"Gwen!"

Startled, she whipped her head around to find none other than Alex Marshall, his face beaming down at her from above the leafy fronds. *What on earth—?*

"Fancy meeting you here." Alex laughed a bit loudly.

In utter confusion and consternation, she watched as Alex reached an arm through the greenery and pumped Graham's hand enthusiastically.

"You must be Graham. Nice to meet you. Gwen's told me a little bit about you. But I'm sure glad I'm finally able to meet you in person."

"Yes, same here," Graham acknowledged politely, as he stole his hand back and tucked it safely under the table.

To Gwen's horror, Alex didn't make a quiet exit. The man actually came around the lattice partition, grabbed a nearby chair, and pulled it to the edge of their table!

Ready to die of sheer embarrassment, Gwen locked her gaze onto the tabletop, too horrified to even meet Graham's eyes. Would he think that she'd planned this?

"I'm afraid I'm at a disadvantage," Graham spoke. "You know who I am, but I'm not acquainted with you."

"Oh! Alex. Alex Marshall."

Gwen lifted her lashes to find her old friend clapping her date on the shoulder with exuberance.

"I see." Graham retreated a fraction, and Gwen watched as he made a subtle motion for the bill to be brought. Yes, she was more than ready to leave now. Of all the nerve. She didn't know what Alex thought he was up to but—

"You know," Alex continued, in a way-too-loud voice, "I thought you'd remember me. But then, I guess since we've never actually met face-to-face, it would be hard."

Gwen frowned at him. What was he talking about? Graham's expression echoed her own.

"Hm. Maybe I could refresh your memory." Alex fairly grinned. "Let's see. . . Um, five-feet eight-inches tall. Red hair. Hazel eyes. Single. Currently working as an office temp. . ."

Her frown deepening at Alex's monologue, Gwen was about to tell him to leave when she noticed Graham's face. His usually tan features had paled.

"Linda, I believe, was the name I chose," Alex finished. He sat back in his chair, his face never leaving Graham's.

"What is going on here?" Gwen demanded as she watched Graham's eyes close slowly.

Neither of the men even looked at her.

"You gonna tell her?" Alex prompted. "Or should I?"

"Somebody say something," she nearly screamed.

Alex seemed only too glad to comply. "Well, it seems that your buddy here has a habit of meeting young women on the Internet. Lots of them."

Feeling the blood drain from her face, Gwen simply stared, waiting for the rest.

"I got to 'meet' him in a chat room last Monday. Of course, then I was Linda. But, he seemed interested enough, anyway." He tossed a look back toward the defeated individual next to him. "When were we gonna meet? Next week, was it?"

Fury boiled within her. Clenching her hands, she tried hard to control her voice. "You got on my computer. . .and pretended you were a. . .woman?"

"I used the library's terminal for that," he admitted. "And, yes. I pretended I was a woman." For a moment, he looked sorry, but then his blue eyes took on a steely quality as he looked back toward Graham. "And he," he indicated with a nod, "he pretended he was a. . . gentleman."

In the meantime, the waiter had deposited the bill on the table, a look of curiosity on his face. Gwen noted several other patrons seemed to be staring in their direction as well.

Swiping the bill from the table, Graham stood to his feet. Taking several deep breaths, he looked down at Gwen. "Sorry," he muttered. And taking huge strides, he left the dining area before she could even fully fathom all that had just happened to her.

Feeling rather shell-shocked, she continued to stare at the table. The empty plates, the half-drunk glasses. Gradually feeling the eyes of others bore into her from all sides. It had happened again. Ultimate humiliation. Intense embarrassment. And the common denominator suddenly was clear.

Raising her eyes to Alex's expectant face, she glared. "You," she whispered, seething. "You—you had no right. No right whatsoever to—"

"Gwen," he interrupted, his look desperate. "That guy was trying to get you into bed!"

"And you think that I—that I'm just too stupid to take care of myself? That I would have blindly followed him to. . .wherever."

His face fell, along with his shoulders. "I'm sorry, Gwen. I was just worried about you. I didn't think that you—" He sputtered to a stop, the reality obviously sinking in. "I'm sorry," he finally whispered.

"So am I," she whimpered as she jumped to her feet. Blindly running through the blurry maze of the restaurant, she slammed through the door and stumbled toward her car, sobs overtaking her. Just as they had a long time ago.

Eleven

Alex stared dejectedly at the shining ring of gold as he twisted it in his fingers. The small diamond solitaire caught the light with every turn, glistening brightly. Why he had done something as foolish as buying a ring on impulse, he'd never know. For that matter, why he thought Gwen would accept it after last week's tragedy—he must be dumber than he thought. She hadn't even shown up at work this whole week.

Shoving the jewel back into its velvet-lined box, he pushed it across his magazine-strewn coffee table.

Tomorrow would be his last day at RBS. His job was done. He knew the opportunity for jobs in the area remained. He also knew that his heart couldn't take staying here for any longer than necessary. No, he'd inquire about placement in a different city. What-ever God's reasons for bringing him to Hudson, they must've had to do with learning some humility—and perhaps more than a shred of understanding and empathy—to grasp what Gwen must have gone through all those years ago. Having one's heart completely laid on the line. And stomped on.

Blowing out a breath, he knew he needed to contact his landlord. Thankfully, he had a month-by-month lease. But first things first. Whipping out a sheet of blank paper, Alex began to draw.

⁂

With a sigh filled with more trepidation than she'd ever known, Gwen stepped into the elevator. *Elevator. . .* Even thinking of the conveyance brought ridiculous tears to her eyes. It had been just one month ago, when she'd first laid eyes on him after all these years. When she'd gotten stuck and he'd rescued her.

Swallowing painfully, she swiped at her eyes just as the doors opened. Without meeting too many people's gazes, she'd briskly strode toward her cubicle, only to find a note from her boss:

> *Gwen,*
>
> *The offices are ready to move into. You may start relocating your personal items today and a crew will be responsible for moving and hooking up your terminal this weekend. Hope you enjoy your new space.*
>
> *Jackie*

Even the thought of the privacy an office would afford—Gwen could find little pleasure in it. After all, whose hands had built that office?

But at least he wasn't here. Her initial reaction to that fact was strictly relief. How could she face those eyes of his? Especially when she knew that he'd been. . .right. All along. And she'd been too blind, or too stubborn, to see through Graham's obvious facade.

But part of her desperately wanted to cling to that anger. It was the only sure thing she felt right now. The rest of her unsettled emotions were just too confusing to deal with.

Anxious to get busy, she picked up a few miscellaneous pictures and pretties from her desk and started toward the wide hall, looking for the room with her name plaque.

"Hey, Gwen!" a voice called from the office's din. "Happy May Day!"

Smiling politely and throwing a wave over her shoulder, she trudged through the marked door and plopped her things on the wide oak desk. She crossed the carpeted floor and took in the view of the St. Croix River below her window. At least she'd be able to see outside now. It did seem to be a cozy place.

Returning to the heavy piece of furniture where her computer would sit, she ran a hand over the smooth finish—and stopped abruptly.

As if in some sort of relived dream, she stared at the envelope lying innocently on the desk. . .her name scrawled across it in a very familiar script. Next to it was a tiny basket of May flowers.

With shaking hands, she picked up the envelope and stared at it for a time. The furious half of her erupted. When she considered all that had transpired in the last week. . .

Wrong, Gwen, a voice inside of her argued. *For the last month? The last lifetime. Face it! You know you never quit loving Alex Marshall. And you are just a coward.*

Afraid of giving your heart to someone fully. . .because sometimes it means being hurt.

Breathing erratically, she finally tore open the edge of the envelope and yanked out the homemade card.

A simple cartoon covered the front. A young man carrying a variety of tools, oblivious to an anvil that was about to drop on his head, stared at a beautiful woman standing next to a computer screen.

Not being able to help the tiny smile that came to her lips, she flipped open the paper.

We may come from separate worlds
my tool's a hammer, yours, a mouse.
But I know I'd never make you regret it
if you could just forgive this louse.

Her spontaneous laughter turned into several minutes of tears. . .then mirth once again.

Plucking up the phone that had already been placed on her desk, she punched in her boss's extension.

"Jackie? I have a tremendous favor to ask of you."

Alex stuffed the last of the magazines in the magazine holder his sister had gotten him for Christmas. Standing in the middle of his now spotless living room, he sighed. "You've got it bad, Marshall. You're actually *cleaning* just to have something to do." He might have found it funny if he hadn't felt so pathetic.

He knew that Gwen should have seen his basket by now—if she'd even gone to work. "Nope," he murmured as he moved into the small kitchen. "If you were gonna hear from her, you would have by—"

The buzz of the doorbell interrupted any further words.

With a frown, he strode toward the door and yanked it open. He was met by a. . .box. With legs.

Standing back a bit, he tried to see around the huge cardboard obstruction. A tiny voice came from somewhere beyond it. "Are you gonna make me hold this all day?"

With a disbelieving smile, he reached over and grasped the surprisingly heavy load to find Gwen's sweet face staring up at him, pure sass shining from her green eyes.

"What is this?" he asked in amusement.

"Computer," she informed him and gradually helped him back it into the confines of his apartment. "You need to learn a few things about sending messages to people more privately," she said pertly. "Like E-mail."

Feeling his own face spread into a grin, he promptly shoved the box onto the couch and, whirling back around, grabbed her tightly, daring to lose himself in the emerald depths of her clear eyes. "No way," he murmured huskily. "No E-love for this guy. From now on it's only the real thing."

Leaning over slowly to savor the sweetness of the moment, he tenderly brushed his lips over hers. And again. From there, he wasn't sure how long they remained. . . each seeming to say "I'm sorry," "Hello," and "Forgive me" all at the same time.

Gwen felt her eyelids flutter open, amazed at the deafening pounding of her heart. Never had she felt so loved, cherished, treasured.

But an impishness inside wouldn't let go. Pursing her lips to ward off another grin, she leveled her gaze at him. "So, you're saying that you won't even consider learning to use the thing?"

Glancing at her sidelong, his blue eyes aspark with secrets, he shook his head. "I didn't say that. But. . ."

She watched as he leaned behind the computer box and came back toward her, in his hands, a small blue box. . .its size and shape immediately giving away its contents. She felt her throat begin to ache from sheer joy as the tears threatened to spill over.

"But. . ." he continued as he flipped it open, "you can't get one of these to go through a modem, can you?"

With a little giggle, all Gwen could do was give a silly shake of her head.

Alex's crystal blue eyes grew serious. "I know I'm no great Romeo, Gwen. And the Lord knows you deserve better than the likes of me. . . But I'm gonna ask, just the same."

Clearing his throat nervously, he knelt down on one knee and looked up at her earnestly. "Gwen Paulson, will you marry me?"

Clamping her lips together to fend off the now inevitable tears, she nodded adamantly. "I've never dreamed of marrying anyone else," she whispered. "Don't you know that by now?"

Rising to his feet, he gripped her in a firm embrace.

"I wish I would have known sooner," he said hoarsely.

"Thank the computer," she returned.

He pulled back, studied her, and then laughed. "You're right. For as much as I've hated those stupid machines, maybe there's a place for them after all."

She grinned, then her eyes widened as his face moved closer again, that intense longing evident once more.

"Just not right now," he said with a smile and reclaimed her lips once more.

GLORIA BRANDT

Gloria Brandt resides on a dairy farm in Wisconsin with her husband and four daughters, who keep her non-writing time occupied with home-schooling and life in general. She is active in her church, helping host a weekly Bible study and playing piano on the worship team. Writing has always been a very needed outlet, considering she started dabbling in poetry and short stories as a grade-schooler. For now, she contents herself with concentrating on inspirational fiction, poetry, and songs, on occasion. For her, the greatest reward in writing to God's glory is the pile of letters she receives from lives she's been able to touch in a very tangible way. "I always want to encourage people that no matter what their circumstances or background, there is hope."

The Garden Plot

Rebecca Germany

Dedicated

. . .to my wonderful family—
the families of
Germany, Betts, Acheson, and Royer—
a network of parents, grandparents,
siblings, aunts, uncles, cousins, and more
who have made my life complete.
Thank you for carrying
the torch of Christianity,
demonstrating the walk to me
and the generations to come.

❧

"Arise, my darling, my beautiful one,
and come with me.
See! The winter is past; the rains are over and gone.
Flowers appear on the earth;
the season of singing has come,
the cooing of doves is heard in our land.
The fig tree forms its early fruit;
the blossoming vines spread their fragrance.
Arise, come, my darling;
my beautiful one, come with me."

SONG OF SOLOMON 2:10–13

One

Few things have disturbed me more than watching my children and grandchildren move away from this town. It's good to have you home, Dandy."

Debra Julian giggled like a young girl. It had been years since she had heard her grandmother use that nickname for her oldest grandchild. Debbie, as a toddler with arms full of the flowering dandelion weed, had earned the nickname in this very backyard and on just such a warm spring day.

"Well, Gran, it is good to be home. I'm sorry I haven't been able to unpack and get organized much the last couple of weeks while I've been learning my job," Debbie said as she gently propelled the wicker porch swing for the two of them. "Walking the halls of Dover High School again sure makes me realize that I'm not a kid anymore. So many of the students are taller than me and only a few of my old teachers are still around after ten years, but the whole attitude is different. Each new class of teens is in such a hurry to grow up."

"Maybe your counseling will help them slow down. Have you been able to figure out the system?"

"The school secretaries have been very helpful, but it is obvious they still grieve the loss of Mr. Knight. He was a well-liked middle-aged man and no one was prepared for such a sudden death. He had requested two weeks leave for his surgery, so some things were in good order."

"Just goes to show that no one knows when the Good Lord will call them home," Grandma said with a soft, reverent tone.

"Why does it seem that his loss was my gain just when I needed to find new work and make the major decision about moving back and buying your home?"

"God's timing is perfect timing," Grandma almost sang. "He knows what each of us needs. Now, if your parents would only stay home for more than a week at a time they could enjoy having you back, too. But they—" Grandma suddenly stopped. She jumped to her skinny legs, waving her handkerchief at two dogs that were very interested in her flowering lilac bush. "Now scoot!" Soon the dogs ran into a neighboring yard. "Some of my best perennials have been ruined by those pesky strays," Grandma huffed as she settled back onto the swing.

"I'm surprised you never fenced in your yard, Gran. This corner lot is tempting for cross-through traffic."

"It's just not the neighborly thing to do," she crooned. "Besides, I don't want to cut off the little view I have. If I had a fence, I wouldn't be able to see Mr. Kelly's pink crab apples in bloom or Myrna Yoder's birdbath. . .and I may not have met my new neighbor."

"You could always use a see-through chain link or a low picket." Debbie sighed and rose to go inside. "Don't you think you ought to put your sweater on, Gran? The wind is picking up."

"Don't you want to know who he is?"

"Who?" Debbie paused with the back door open.

"Oh, never mind, dear." Grandma shook her gray head.

Debbie soon returned with a soft white sweater and helped Grandma slip her frail arms inside.

"Do you remember the Robillards?" Grandma asked.

"Of course. They lived in this neighborhood as long as you and Grandpa."

"I sure hated to see them pass on. . .and so close together," Grandma spoke softly as she picked at the balled wool on her sweater. "The house sold back in September."

"I've noticed the yard is looking very nice again." Debbie looked across the backyard. The Robillards' large Victorian home faced Sixth Street while Grandma's house—now hers, too—sat on the corner of Sixth facing Maple Street with her backyard bordering the south side of the Robillard lot. She remembered that the Robillards were always good neighbors and friends to her grandparents. Good neighbors could be hard to find. Debbie only hoped that the property had sold to a friendly family. *That house was made for a large, happy family,* Debbie mused.

"Debbie, girl, why don't we put in a garden this year?" Grandma asked, bringing Debbie back to their conversation.

"A garden, Gran?"

"I always had a garden until about four years ago. It got to the point that I hurt too much to bend down and tend my plants."

"A vegetable garden?"

"Why, yes. You'll have the whole summer free to work on it." Grandma paused. "Or, don't guidance counselors get summers off like teachers do?"

"Yes, Gran, I'll have a few weeks free, until August, when I will be helping the cheerleaders train."

"Who needs to train to know how to jump around and shout?" Grandma muttered.

Debbie just laughed and volunteered to fix them some lunch.

❧

The very next Saturday morning, the first in May, Grandma called from the bottom of the stairs and woke Debbie from her slumber, insisting that Debbie start breaking ground for the garden that day. After spending all but one evening of the past week helping her grandmother with various projects at home and at church, Debbie had anticipated Saturday as her catch-up day. She was beginning to understand one of the reasons why her parents enjoyed spending most of their retirement in Arizona. Grandma could be quite demanding, but Debbie loved being near family again, and she was happy to be in the position to buy Gran's Cape Cod style home. Gran needed to be relieved of the responsibility and have someone around part of the time to avoid going into a retirement home. And Debbie loved this old house, full of sweet memories. It would at least make a good starter home for her while she waited for the right man to come knocking on the door of her heart.

Debbie peaked out the dormer window to check the

weather. Many yards in this small Ohio town showed signs of new life in the landscaping as well as the people who had come out to enjoy the warm spring day that promised even sweeter days to come. She left her laundry in sorted stacks around her bedroom and school files strewn across her tiny desk and headed downstairs.

Debbie found Grandma in the living room, wrapped up in an afghan as she quilted.

"Gran, don't you feel like coming out and helping me plan the garden plot?" Debbie asked, suddenly concerned about her grandmother's health. Grandma had just hit seventy-nine without having had any major health complications, unlike her long-deceased husband, but her family worried that arthritis and age were wearing Grandma down.

"Oh, I better stay in out of the breeze today," Grandma spoke slowly. "I know you will do fine without my direction."

Debbie didn't know what to make of Grandma's mood. She didn't look ill, but Grandma usually didn't miss a chance to be near the action. Still, Debbie decided it would be best to start the work.

"Now, I don't need to tell you how to operate a rotary tiller, but the old one in the shed will need a bit of oil and could take a few cranks to get going," Gran instructed.

"That's all right, Gran."

"And. . .the garden is your project, but I would suggest that you go to the back of the lot, past the grape trellis, to start your digging. My other gardens were always right along the west side of the shed, and I'm afraid there wasn't sufficient morning light there."

"Fine, Gran." Debbie tried to head for the back door.

"Now, I like rows that are no longer than about twelve feet, and there should be plenty of room between each, especially when it comes to cucumbers. I just hate it when those vines twine through my other plants. But you build it how you like it."

Debbie smiled and nodded.

"About fertilizer. Did you buy the natural kind?" Grandma smiled sweetly. "You know. . .the kind from farms?"

Debbie prayed silently for patience. "No, Gran."

"Well. . .it is your choice, but natural is always the best."

After a trip to a nursery for bags of natural fertilizer and a couple of tools, Debbie was finally ready to step off her garden plot. She would make it twelve feet wide and twenty-four feet in length, starting the length at Grandma's grape arbor and working back toward a grove of evergreens near the neighbor's yard, where the Robillards had always lived until they passed away and the house had gone up for sale. Debbie knew a bunch of rabbits were just waiting among those pines to eat her plants as soon as they sprouted, but there was no other spot big enough for the garden—except along the shed.

Inside, the shed smelled like damp earth, the floor covered only by a thin layer of gravel. One whole wall was lined with shelves of flowerpots in every imaginable shape and size, while the opposite wall housed a collection of Ohio license plates that dated back to the late 1930s. Once, the building housed Debbie's grandparents' car before her grandfather had had a new garage built that connected to the house.

She pulled an old rug off the tiller and tugged the machine out into the yard. It took more than a couple cranks, and a lot of tinkering on Debbie's part, to get the old relic running, but eventually she directed the bouncing dirt digger to her garden spot.

It required every ounce of her strength to keep the tiller moving in a straight line, but by noon she had dug up the whole garden. It would need to be gone over again to work out the clumps, but she stopped for a much-deserved rest, her hands numb from the strain and vibrations.

Debbie slipped her dirty tennis shoes off on the porch and paused inside the kitchen door to watch as Grandma bustled around preparing tomato soup and sandwiches. She looked as happy and healthy as ever.

"Are you feeling better, Gran?" Debbie asked as the porch door slammed behind her.

Grandma jumped and gripped the counter. "Mercy, girl, you scared me. I was just getting ready to call you in. From what I can see from the window, you are making real progress out there."

Debbie washed up before joining Grandma at the old Formica table.

"Let's pray that God gives you a very successful afternoon," Grandma insisted. And before long, she was shooing Debbie back outside to her project.

Debbie went over half of the freshly turned garden

again with the tiller before she had to stop and rest. The sun was shining directly down, and she wiped away a stream of perspiration as she tucked her long chestnut curls behind her ears. It would have been a good day to wear a ponytail. Her hands and arms ached from the tiller's vibrations. She rolled her shoulders.

"Hey!"

Debbie spun around with a gasp, startled by the angry male voice.

"It's about time you turned off that antique and listened to me."

Debbie stared at a man of about thirty who wore old jeans and a polo shirt that were tailored to his athletic frame as if they had been a classic business suit.

"I came out here to clean leaves from my flower beds," he gestured widely with lean arms, "only to find you digging up my seed grass."

"I. . .uh," Debbie had a hard time finding her voice as her cheeks flushed hot with her embarrassment. "There is no clearly marked property line. Did I get into your yard?" was all she could think to say.

"I'd guess that at least half of your mess is in my yard," he grumbled. "Who gave you permission to dig here anyway?"

"My grandmother assured me that this was the best spot for our garden," Debbie said lamely, feeling like one of her scolded students. This handsome man stood at least a head taller than her and could have every right to be upset. Debbie detested her sudden lack of communication skills, and anger at herself and the situation began to rise. "Perhaps we should speak with her about the matter," she gritted through clenched teeth.

Without a word, the man followed Debbie across the backyard and up the porch steps, then waited as Debbie shed her dirt-caked shoes and went inside to find her grandma. She searched the whole house, upstairs and down, calling for Grandma. Debbie couldn't find her anywhere and had to assume she walked to visit a neighbor, as she was often known to do. Debbie dreaded facing the grim neighbor again, but she straightened her shoulders and returned to the back porch.

His back was to her as he leaned against a post. She had to admit that he was nice to look at but wondered how she would ever make a friend after such a poor start.

Two

A much relaxed face turned to greet Debbie. "You wouldn't be little Dandy that Maxie speaks so fondly of, would you?"

"Maxie?" Debbie's mouth dropped open in surprise. "My grandmother is Maxine Julian. I've never heard anyone call her Maxie."

The man chuckled, transforming his whole face into a wide grin, and though it didn't seem possible, he became even more handsome. "Mrs. Julian and I have become good friends since I moved in last September. You know, she makes the best apple crisp I have ever eaten. By the way, I'm Scott Robillard, the town's newest optometrist. I bought my grandparents' house. You may not remember, but I spent a few summers here."

Debbie looked closer at his masculine features and her face flamed. How could she not have recognized him? She was just fifteen and he was a "mature" seventeen-year-old who, along with a couple of his cousins, spent most of a summer with his grandparents. Debbie clearly recalled having spent her whole summer trying to gain his attention.

Oh, how foolishly she had behaved. It all came rushing back to her like it had been a month ago instead of thirteen years full of growth and change into adulthood.

Debbie was confused by this revelation and his sudden friendly change in attitude toward her. "Uh. . . Scott. . .my grandmother appears to have gone to a neighbor's." She pointed a thumb over her shoulder toward the open back door.

"Yes, feel free to call me Scott, if I may call you Debbie?" he said, seeming to ignore the issue at hand while his gaze roved her face.

She nodded and hurried on. "Would you like to call her later? I promise not to dig any more until we talk to her." She punctuated her sincerity with a timid smile.

"That won't be necessary. I am sure we can work something out. Let's take another look at the situation." He took off at an easy gait down the porch steps and across the bright green lawn.

Debbie followed slowly and watched as he walked along the boundary line, starting from the street inward. He was tall, though being five-nine Debbie didn't really have far to look up at him. He had a lean, athletic frame without the bulging muscles of a serious jock. She found him as appealing to look at as she had as a teen. He even had a boyish lock of rich chocolate brown hair that flopped across his broad brow. Debbie suppressed the urge to grin.

"That azalea bush by the sidewalk is really the only thing that marks the property line," he said as he marched across the middle of her tilled plot. "Our grandparents never worried about the details of property boundaries. It is no wonder that you got into my yard, but Maxie should have realized that there was not enough room for this size of garden here. It should have gone alongside the shed."

Debbie sighed and swallowed a sarcastic laugh. "She was quite specific about how the garden should be dug. I'm truly sorry for the mistake."

"I usually don't let anyone mess in my yard. It is kind of my stress-relieving hobby that I have taken to the level of obsession. But since you're Maxie's granddaughter. . ."

Debbie was back to feeling like a kid under the scrutiny of his dark brown eyes. She nervously smoothed her curls away from her rounded face. *He obviously still sees me as that silly teenage girl.*

"Ah, there's the old girl now," Scott whispered with a sparkle in the depth of his eyes.

❧

After iced tea, several cookies, and pleasant conversation about the weather, Maxine Julian still avoided discussing the issue of the garden.

"Dandy, did Scott tell you that he recently bought his grandparents' house?" Grandma asked. She patted Scott's large hand and shoved a paper napkin under his glass.

Debbie nodded as she chewed the cookie that seemed to stick in her throat. *Though* you *failed to mention that detail.* Debbie tried to resist the tug to feel irritated at her grandmother. It was really the easy comradery between Scott and Grandma that was gnawing at her sensibilities.

Scott leaned back in the kitchen chair. "It seemed to take forever for the estate to be settled after the back-to-back funerals. Everything had to be equally divided. . . but I'm glad I was able to buy the house and keep it in the family," Scott shared with them, then downed another cookie in large bites.

Gran nodded in agreement. "I told you that is what Dandy is doing for me. There won't be much to settle when I'm gone."

Debbie didn't like the direction of the conversation and her grandmother's matter-of-fact tone. Sure, these things were inevitable, but they didn't have to be discussed in casual conversation with a. . .non-family member.

Scott suddenly raised his head from contemplation of the cookie plate that was out of his reach. "Do you remember that neighborhood bonfire we had in these backyards? That's back when they allowed that sort of thing inside town."

"Oh, yes," Debbie recalled with renewed interest. "There must have been nearly a hundred people coming and going from that party."

"You were there?" Scott asked, and for the first time his gaze really met hers.

Debbie was confused and could feel her cheeks flushing. *Surely you remember the girl who followed you so closely that I can still repeat every move you made that summer.*

"Dandy was here most of the summer that you and the twins stayed," Gran declared and, reaching behind

Debbie, she deftly clasped Debbie's hair back into a ponytail. "You probably would remember her best in pigtails and braces."

Debbie gasped and pulled away from her grandmother's hands.

Scott chuckled. "Sorry, all I can remember of that summer was the stupid way I followed my cousins, Mike and Matt, all around. The twins had just finished their second year of college. They were here to help Grandpa with the closing of his store, and I begged my folks to come too because I idolized those guys at the time."

Debbie couldn't believe what she was hearing. How could he not remember her? Why, she had played a movie theme song over and over when she heard him say he liked it. She played it from her bedroom window when he was in the yard; she hummed it when they were in the same room. She was desperate to show him they had something in common. She even went as far as to join the neighborhood gang in a game of flag football. How could he not remember her—and her crush?

"It's funny," Scott said. "I've never been big on sports, but I played every imaginable game that summer just so I could keep up with those guys." Scott shook his dark head.

Debbie barely heard his words. She should still feel embarrassed, but now she was offended by his lack of ability to even recall her presence. Everyone knew she had been starry-eyed for Scott. Her grandfather had teased her mercilessly. Her best friend Penny had listened to hours of woes when Scott failed to give Debbie the attention she craved.

Of course, she had moved on from her adolescent behavior to more mature ways of looking at relationships—hadn't she? Certainly. Then why were the memories still so raw for her?

Grandma was speaking as she refilled Scott's glass of tea. The subject had obviously changed. "Now, Scott, I wasn't able to be out there this morning when Dandy started her digging, and I have left all the planning to her. She is a good, hard worker, but also very good with . . .why, she's a good homemaker." Grandma smiled and nodded in Debbie's direction.

Debbie's mouth dropped open. What was Grandma saying? She sounded like a sales pitch. *First, I'm the hormone-crazy teen, and now he'll know me as the desperate woman who has to rely on Gran's matchmaking.* Debbie picked up the plate that had just been passed. "Cookie anyone?"

Her offer was ignored as Scott continued to follow Grandma's conversation with no sign of emotion. Debbie's gaze glued to his left hand. She hated it when married men didn't wear wedding bands, but then, Scott was probably very much single. That was an unfortunate state for her jumbled emotions to deal with.

"I had no idea that Dandy would go into your yard." Grandma shrugged and petted Debbie's hand like she was a child. Debbie pulled her hands into her lap. "I can certainly pay for new grass seed."

"I don't blame anyone," Scott said, smiling at Debbie as she took a large bite from an oatmeal cookie.

"I'm sure I can get another good patch of grass started by summer, but I'm more interested in a compromise."

He couldn't help feeling like this wasn't all a simple mistake, but he was willing to play along with these apologetic females and reap some benefit. Leaving the garden on his property should allow for more opportunities to see Maxie's beautiful granddaughter, and even he could sacrifice some landscaping perfection for that prospect. He wasn't in the market for a wife, at the moment. He was just enjoying the beautiful scenery.

"What would you say if I offer my land in exchange for a share of the vegetables you grow?" Scott offered the ladies. "I wouldn't really have time for my own garden anyway."

Maxine appeared to sigh in relief, but Debbie looked to her grandmother nervously. "Gran, are you sure we will have enough to split with Mr. Robillard. . .uh, Scott? You know that you will want to give vegetables to Mom and Dad as well as Aunt Carol."

"Then we'll pack it full of plants," Maxine decided.

"But you like wide, neat rows, Gran," Debbie quietly reminded.

"If you think the garden should be a bit bigger, we can look at extending it," Scott quickly offered before thinking.

"Ah," Maxine laughed, "first you are ready to lynch us for ruining your new grass and now you propose a bigger garden. Kids. . ." she chuckled.

"Please," Debbie said and paused for breath, "forget I said anything. We'll make this plot work and have plenty to share with you. . .Mr. Robillard."

Scott noted the use of formality and the icy waves that Debbie emitted. Was he missing something? Had he overstepped the boundaries of her personal space? He had enjoyed the play of color in her cheeks when they first met, but he didn't understand why her sparkling blue eyes now appeared frosty and her blushed cheeks were now set like stone.

But it was settled, and Debbie went back to work on smoothing the clumps from the garden plot, while Scott finally got to work on his flowerbeds. But, though Scott worked on the opposite side of the house from her, all he could envision were large chestnut curls and round, pink cheeks flushed in embarrassment.

He had the distinct feeling that he should remember her, and he tried to play through his mind the summer of thirteen years ago. But it was useless. All he remembered was sweeping, dusting, and stocking his grandfather's hardware store. Then there were the football and basketball games every evening with Mike and Matt. The only girls he could remember were a group that hung around the park whenever his cousins went there to shoot hoops. His cousins were good-looking college freshmen who drew the girls like magnets. Scott, on the other hand, had still been a gangly teen at age seventeen and didn't give the girls much thought when he had so much to learn from his older cousins.

Scott dug his trowel deep into the soil. He wasn't sure how well he was going to like his new neighbor. She stirred strange, confusing emotions in him. In his profession, he should be used to dealing with all types of personalities of his patients. It could be a long spring . . .and summer. . .then fall. He was already thinking that he had better plan a garden on his own next year.

A loud clanking noise came from around the house. Scott tried to ignore it, piling debris higher in the old bushel basket. He knew the noise was coming from the garden, but he was afraid if he rushed to offer his assistance, his growing interest in Debbie would be obvious.

The tiller was shut off and the quiet returned to the peaceful neighborhood. Even the birds soon started twittering again. Scott found himself holding his breath as he waited for any sound that would tell him what Debbie was doing now. His hands moved in slow, fluid motion as he tried not to make a sound.

He couldn't wait any longer. He rose and brushed the knees of his jeans, annoyed with himself for his nagging curiosity. He would make a trip to the garage so that his path would give him a clear view of the adjoining backyards and the tilled plot.

Scott rounded the corner of his house and immediately stopped in his purpose-filled tracks. In the middle of the dark brown rectangle of soil sat Debbie. Her long hair was pulled into a loose ponytail and hung down her back. She sat cross-legged beside the tiller, her elbow on her knee and her head resting in her palm as she stared at the still machine.

Scott glanced up at Maxie's house and caught the movement of curtains at the kitchen window.

He knew he should move on to the garage and keep

to himself. Debbie seemed to be quite the independent type, and after all, this garden was her mess and problem. But his feet slowly propelled him to the edge of the turned earth.

"Uh. . ." He ran a hand across the back of his head. "Do you think you threw the chain?" he heard himself ask.

Debbie turned her large blue eyes upward, the sunshine illuminating her face. Scott dropped his gaze, trying not to stare, and shifted nervously.

"You wouldn't know of a repair shop for antique yard equipment, would you?" Debbie asked with little life in her voice.

"No." He slowly exhaled the word, and even though he knew he was treading in dangerous waters, he offered, "Maybe I could take a look at it." He stepped closer to the machine, and Debbie suddenly jumped to her feet and beat at the dirt clinging to her loose denim pants. She twisted to reach her backside and bent to brush her calves.

Scott turned his back to her actions and gulped for air, as he forced his heart rate back to normal. He poked at the chain cover, knowing he would need a screwdriver to loosen it. He deliberately looked the tiller over from top to bottom before turning back to Debbie.

She was gone. He was surprised to see her disappearing through the back door of her house. Scott turned back to the machine in dazed confusion. *So, fix the machine, Robillard. Isn't that what you came to do?*

Three

Debbie changed her clothes, then grabbing a file of work papers, she sat down in the window seat of her cozy bedroom. Two dormer windows gave her nice views of both the front and back yards. The window seat gave Debbie a clear, bird's-eye view of the garden plot. She watched as Scott returned from a trip to his garage and bent over the rusty tiller.

You ran from the scene, she scolded herself. *But to stay would have shown interest in the situation and to leave was a display of indifference. Wasn't it?*

Debbie had a feeling that, even though she considered herself an adult who happened to be in a job that placed her in authority over teens, she was allowing herself to be pulled back into adolescent games. She flipped open the file folder and took out the first sheet. She tried to study the print, but her gaze returned to the window. Scott made several trips to the garage as twenty minutes lapsed.

Watching him, she could picture Scott as a teenager bending over an old bike. That summer he stayed with his grandparents she had witnessed his kind acts to many people in the neighborhood. Though a busy kid, he always found time to lend a hand where needed.

Grandma called from the bottom of the stairs as Scott was placing the chain cover back in place. "Dandy, come and carry this glass of pop out to Scott for me, please. The day has sure warmed up and he has been working so hard."

Debbie rolled her eyes toward the slanting ceiling. To refuse would be very rude. She pulled herself up from her comfortable cushions, descended the stairs sluggishly, and took the cold glass of soda pop from her grandmother without a word. She had a feeling Grandma was reading her every action with great clarity.

Her leisurely pace brought her to the garden in what seemed to her to be record time. She held the glass out at a stiff arm's length. "Gran thought you could use a cool drink."

She let her gaze drift to the trees as he straightened and dusted his dirty hands.

"I'm very grateful." He took the glass and his fingers brushed hers.

She pulled her arm back. *Oh, would you stop reacting like a kid!* she screamed at the tingling sensation in her hand.

"Let's see if this thing will crank now," Scott said, and she noticed that he set the empty glass in the grass.

With two cranks the old tiller was noisily running again. The chain worked properly and the rotors were once again greedily searching for dirt to devour. Scott motioned her to take the handles. She nodded her thanks, stepped behind the machine, and followed it to the edge of the rectangle.

As she turned to chop a new row of dirt clogs, she saw a car entering Scott's drive and Scott making a beeline to his back door. It was getting to be late afternoon. Maybe he had a dinner date. The thought relieved and distressed her in the same wave of emotion. She pushed the tiller harder and deeper into the soil.

❧

It had been a long day, and after nearly an hour of working on the garden dirt, Debbie was on the last round at Scott's edge of the garden. Her pace was slow, but she pushed on. She brushed stray hairs back behind her ear and felt a splash of water.

Looking up Debbie's face was doused. Scott's sprinkling system had suddenly come on, and she was positioned between two sprinkler heads. Water ran down her forehead, cheeks, and chin. She no longer paid attention to the path of the tiller as she swiped at the rivulets of water tracing her lips. She huffed at the water and gave the tiller a disgusted shove.

All of a sudden the water was coming from every direction. Streams flowed over her shoes and sprayed the tiller from under the blades.

"Oh no," she screeched.

The tiller had gone out of the straight edge of the garden and cut deep into the sprinkler pipe. Debbie killed the motor of the offending dirt digger and scurried across the yard, dodging sprinkler heads that still spouted showers of water.

She searched alongside the back door for a shut-off valve. Finding none, she moved on to the side of the garage and even peeked inside the door. No luck. She looked back at the mess of water pooling in the soaked garden and running through the thin, new grass toward the stand of pines.

Debbie wanted to scream in frustration and cry in despair. She wrung out her drenched tee shirt and trudged to the back door. Her knock was not answered. Sure that Scott was home, she moved to the side of the house where French doors opened from the dining room. She could hear loud music blaring, and she knocked hard.

When Scott finally came to the windowed door his eyes widened. She must look frightfully bad.

"What happened to you? Is it raining?"

Debbie was fearful that she detected a smile around his handsome lips.

"I have a bit of a problem and could use a hand," she forced herself to admit. Two problems in one day were really going to look like a play for his attentions. She sighed and resigned herself to continue. "Do you think you can shut off your sprinkling system?"

Scott's brow creased in confusion. "Sure. I'll have to go down to the basement."

"When you are done, I have something I need to show you."

Debbie stepped away from the door and waited for Scott's return. She noticed that the music was lowered to a more moderate level.

When Scott returned he was not alone. At least six teenage bodies followed in his wake, eyes wide with curiosity. Debbie picked at her wet clothes and wanted to shrink away from embarrassment.

"So what do I need to see?" Scott asked, calm and controlled.

Debbie glanced at the heads behind his shoulders. "Uh. . .the garden. . .backyard. . ." was all she could manage to say with her tongue tied in a fool's knot.

"Give me a minute, guys. I'll be right back," Scott said, pulling the door closed behind him. "Sorry about that. I'm a youth volunteer at my church and this week it was my turn to hold the youth outing at my house." He shrugged and glanced at her.

Scott couldn't stop shaking with silent laughter. She looked like a sodden feline, indignant toward the bathing. Ruffled and brittle around the edges, but helpless to change the circumstances.

He followed her around the side of the house to the garden area. Then he noticed abnormally large pools of water. His head swung back around toward Debbie for an explanation. She simply pointed to the tiller that sat at an angle on the edge of the garden plot.

Looking closer at the rotors, Scott saw a piece of broken white PVC pipe. Realization dawned. The pipe he had had laid a month ago was cut and in desperate need of repair. The end of her garden had come right up along the pipeline. Six inches off course and she had hit the buried line.

"How?" He gestured at the mess.

"Well, I didn't know you had a sprinkler system," she rushed, stopped, and started again. "The sprinklers came on. I was getting drenched and frustrated, and I guess that is when I got out of my row, hitting the pipe." Her shoulders sagged. "I'll have it repaired right away."

Scott breathed deep. How could he be mad when she looked so distraught? He reached out and cupped her shoulder. The heat of her skin through the wet cotton shirt seared his hand. He reconsidered the action and pulled away, wiggling his fingers in surprise.

"Why don't we just wait to discuss the problem tomorrow afternoon? If you don't dig any more and the sprinkler stays off, there won't be any further damage."

She arched a questioning brow at him and he spun away on a direct path back to the house. "I have company," he threw over his shoulder.

Debbie sat on the back porch swing Sunday afternoon. She had chosen to wear a light blue flowery skirt with a lightweight sweater top for a day of church and relaxation. She sat with her eyes closed, one leg tucked up under her, drifting with the sway of the swing.

Grandma was on the front porch visiting with Myrna Yoder and talking to other neighbors who strolled by. It was a beautiful, warm spring day that begged a body to be outdoors. The small new leaves on the trees were bright green and the tulips were opened to catch every ray of sunshine. Debbie loved the clean air and the clear blue sky that was dotted by an occasional puffy white cloud.

After the workout the tiller had given her, her body protested the slightest of moves. She opened her eyes slowly to find herself under inspection. From the foot of the porch steps a small black squirrel gazed back at her. Having grown up outside town, Debbie still found the black squirrels a novelty. They had their origins in Canada, but had drifted south after being released on the Kent State University campus. Their numbers were now quite thick in Dover.

And they could be greedy little snoops. This one tilted his head from side to side, obviously searching for a dropping or handout. Debbie laughed at it, then stomped her foot to shoo it away. The squirrel stayed still a moment and glared at her, then bounded into the shrubbery.

❧

Scott approached the Julian house with a little sense of dread. He knew he would do himself a favor to stay away from Miss Debbie Julian. She confused him, and his reactions to her mere presence were clear signs that this woman could quickly and easily get under his skin—into his soul. But he wasn't looking for a complicated relationship with an equally complicated individual. He was looking for comfortable friendship, mutual love and respect, a mother of his children, and a partner in Christ. He was willing to wait as long as it took for that woman to come around. He was really in no hurry.

But the vision Debbie created in the white wicker swing with her skirt flowing around her bare ankle and her hair softly framing her relaxed face was enough to stir his desire to know her much better.

He approached the porch quietly. Her eyes were closed and she may have been napping. The only seat available was next to her on the swing. The only other chair held a tablecloth that Maxine was airing. He chose the top step to rest his frame on.

Debbie opened her eyes and didn't show surprise at seeing him. She watched as he took his seat on the step. He observed that she braided a small section of her long, free-flowing hair in a natural—almost involuntary—motion. Perhaps it was a nervous habit. Did he make her nervous?

"How was your church service?" she asked suddenly.

"Uh. . .great," Scott stammered. "Pastor Jim had a wonderful lesson on witnessing. How about yours?"

"Oh, the sermon was something broad about world peace. I didn't follow it very well," Debbie confessed, still twining her hair. "Gran's pastor is a friendly older gentleman, but his tone of voice can really drag on and on."

"Are there other programs you are involved in like young adults' or children's work?" Scott leaned into the conversation. He liked to talk about churches and the work of God's people.

"No. . .it is rather small." She stopped swinging. "I guess. . .really. . .if I had the time to look, I would like to find a little larger church with more life. . .well, you know, activities and excited people." Debbie leaned forward to rest her elbows on her knees, a completed braid brushing her left cheek.

"You're welcomed to visit my church." *Thata way to keep your distance, Robillard.* "It's not huge, but we have lots of young families and programs. I work with the men's group, the youth, and the Sunday school. I even volunteer with visitation every other Wednesday on my day off." Scott wasn't bragging. He really enjoyed his church work.

"Oh, I'd never have time for all that." Debbie leaned back in the swing with a stunned look on her face.

Scott didn't want it to sound like he was comparing himself to her. "Now is the best time for me to be active. I don't have a family, my career is rather predictable, and I still have the energy of youth." Scott patted his knee. "The joints only creak a bit."

Debbie smiled. "Sounds easy for you, but I have found working with the school system can be pretty draining on the body and emotions. I don't need to add that to my free time."

Scott had seen it before—Christians who gave so much to other things that they didn't have enough left over for the Lord. He wouldn't make a case of it. Maybe it was just a sign that her goals weren't the same as his.

"I want to be involved in Christian work, just maybe not every week," Debbie said. "I think I am more of a behind-the-scenes kind of person, like with bookkeeping or cooking. And, I'd like to work on praying more."

Okay, maybe our goals aren't so different. "Well, anytime you want to visit, the church sits on Glen Street, right where the hill peaks. Maxie had talked about visiting my church, too, but she is worried about leaving her church after so many years of dedication to it."

"Leave the church? She never told me that," Debbie said quietly with a sigh.

They sat in silence for several minutes. Debbie had

set the swing in motion again. Scott shifted on the hard wooden porch step. He could picture himself introducing Debbie to his church friends. There were a couple of gals he thought she would really fit in with.

"After I pay for the broken pipe, can we call the garden quits?" she asked in a hushed tone.

"No," he said too loud and too fast. "I mean, why give up on the garden before we even plant the first seed?" *Robillard, this is not the way to give each other space. Why has this garden become so important?*

"Because," she drew out the word, "you should realize that it has already caused more trouble than it's worth." Scott smiled at her flushed face that so appealed to him, and she looked away. "Besides, planting seeds is like making a commitment to seeing them through to harvest. We are both busy people. Do we really have time to nurse a garden?"

Commitment is an interesting word choice, Scott thought.

Four

Scott mulled over Debbie's words as he leaned back against the porch post. "I have been thinking that it is really unfair of me to expect you to do all the work while I benefit from the produce. What do you say to me purchasing some tomato plants and other things for the garden? I'll even help you set them." *I'm willing to commit myself to seeing where this goes.*

Debbie frowned. "You really don't have to. I can explain to Gran that a garden isn't a good idea this year."

"No way. The ground is broken and we are already *committed.*" Scott rose to leave. "By the way, I'll be paying for my own piping."

Debbie couldn't find her voice. She watched his every move as he crossed her backyard to his own back door. Before entering, he shot her a brief wave. She knew she had been caught watching him.

He was full of surprises and she couldn't figure him out. *Lord, I need serious counseling here. I am sorry I don't seem to consult with You until I am in a hard spot, but You know this man's mind and You know I don't have time to play games. Each time I try to remove myself from him, circumstances bring us back together. Please take away this giddy girlish feeling I get every time I see him and help me make it through the growing season like an adult.*

Debbie shoved the swing harder as her thoughts were in turmoil, and she talked to her Lord. *Really, his concern for the garden, and me, must be for Gran's benefit, seeing how they seem to share so much. And now, he has turned the tables so that the garden sounds like his project.*

It was time to prepare for a carried-in dinner at Gran's church. *You know, Lord, he would be a lot easier to ignore if he weren't a single, Christian man.* Debbie trudged to the kitchen to pull out her baking pans.

❧

Two weeks later, after the fear of frost had passed, Debbie spent her Saturday morning planting two rows of green beans, two hills of cucumbers, a hill of zucchini, and a row of leaf lettuce. It didn't take long, and soon she was sitting in the grass planning her next row. She would buy some beet seeds. There would still be plenty of room for six rows of sweet corn. She would put the tall growing vegetable on Scott's end of the garden—probably on purpose.

"Going to have room in there for some tomatoes?"

Debbie jumped. "Oh, hi, Scott. I didn't know you were out here." *If I still had that crush, I would be attuned to his every move.* She was feeling that she had made emotional progress after only seeing glimpses of him for the past two weeks. He did look good, though, standing there holding a tray of young plants.

She hurried to her feet and stepped into the dirt. "Why don't I put them along here?" She pointed out a couple rows in the middle of the plot.

"Good. I'll get a bucket of water and be right back to help." He set down the tray and was off to his garage before she could voice an objection.

She counted out twelve plants. The help would sure make the job go faster. She hoed a hole to set each plant in. Scott returned and started pouring water in each hole.

"Let me put some bone meal around those plants before we pull the dirt up to them," Debbie said, retrieving her box of fertilizer.

In no time they were packing dirt around the last little plant. Debbie swiped the hair away from her face with the back of her hand and leaned back on her heels.

"Uh. . ." Scott tilted his head and pointed to her face. "You have a dirt smudge on your cheek."

Debbie brushed her right cheek.

"No, the other cheek."

She tried again.

Scott gave a deep chuckle. "It's worse now. Here. . ." He gently dusted her cheek with his lean fingers.

Debbie froze, enjoying the contact. Her eyes met his dark gaze. The sun seemed to glow warmer and radiated from his hair. The moment between them felt so natural. . .so right.

Scott's fingers traced down her jaw line. Her gaze was drawn to the thin line of his lips. The air between them was heavy when the screen door on the Julian house slammed, and they both jumped apart at the sudden sound. Debbie found herself unexpectedly sitting in the dirt.

"I think I just rubbed the dirt in." Scott gave a

nervous laugh, then he rose and offered her a hand up.

She hesitated, but allowed his long fingers to wrap around her own. He tugged her to her feet. She quickly pulled away and turned to meet her grandma, her complexion warmed by more than the bright sun.

Maxine Julian called, "Come to dinner tonight, Scott. It has been such a long time since I had you over. I'll make your favorite."

"Which would be. . . ?" Debbie asked.

"Why Scott just loves my fried chicken with mashed potatoes and gravy. Add a side of green beans and top it off with apple pie," Grandma said, rubbing her bony fingers together.

The meal was also one of Debbie's favorites. Did Grandma remember? Debbie avoided it, though, in fear of increasing her waistline, but it would be a great treat.

"I can't wait until we have fresh beans from the garden," Grandma was saying. "There is nothing that compares to fresh vegetables."

Debbie cocked an eyebrow toward the tall man. "So will you be joining us?"

"How could I possibly refuse?"

⁂

Scott had helped her plant corn that afternoon. They worked well together, and he had let her make decisions regarding the garden. Debbie was starting to allow feelings that this was the kind of relationship that could turn into something permanent. It scared her. Was she letting her desires get the best of her, or was she looking at things rationally? Was Scott really the type of man she wanted to spend the rest of her life with?

Debbie was quiet during dinner that evening. She had placed walls around her emotions again. She felt better that way. There really was no reasonable hope for a future with her neighbor, and she couldn't afford to be hurt.

She watched Scott devour six pieces of the succulent chicken, observed his easy comradery with Grandma, and felt out of place. She couldn't blame Grandma for enjoying Scott's warm charm. Debbie figured that Grandma missed her own son, Debbie's father, who was still out in Arizona.

She pushed her pie around her plate. It had lost its temptation.

By the end of the meal, Debbie was confident that an intimate future with Scott was a stretch of her imagination. He was Gran's friend, a neighbor, and not someone Debbie should set her hopes and dreams on. If the Lord were her shepherd, she could trust Him to lead her to the right man, though a better man might be hard to find.

Debbie sorted the pile of college applications and student records on her desk. She had been helping several senior students all Wednesday morning with last minute decisions about continued education. She stretched, feeling her stomach rumble in anticipation of lunch.

Her phone rang and she picked it up using her practiced greeting.

"Hey, Debbie, this is Scott." His voice sounded rushed.

"Scott?" Her eyes widened and her hand flew to her hair, twisting nervously.

"You know, your neighbor."

She laughed. "I know. This is just. . .a surprise."

"Well. . .this is my day off and I noticed some trouble in the garden." He slowed his voice and sounded more thoughtful.

"Trouble? What kind?"

"Just some dogs. They were attracted to your bone meal and, between the two, dug up all of the tomato plants."

"Oh dear." Her mind spun. She could hurry home on her lunch break and replant them before the sun scorched their roots, but she really didn't have time to leave the office and risk getting dirty. A movement at her door caught her attention.

"I really don't know why I'm calling. I already righted the plants." Scott sighed.

The PE coach, Jesse Conner, had stopped at Debbie's door. He held his lunch bag and a can of pop. He pointed toward the teacher's lounge and motioned for Debbie to hang up. His antics were comical.

"I guess I wanted to tell you in case I forgot to call you tonight." Scott's tone sounded dejected. Debbie shooed the coach away and gave Scott her full attention.

"Thanks. Really, I'd much rather be working in the garden today than in this mound of paperwork." Debbie wanted to say more, but didn't know what it should be.

"You know I recently had a memory come back to me. When I was fixing the chain on Maxie's tiller I was remembering the summer I stayed here with my grandparents," Scott said. "I remember now that I worked on a bicycle chain that summer on a girl's bike."

Debbie's breath caught in her throat.

"That was your bike. Wasn't it?"

"Yes," she breathed. *He remembered!* Her most precious memory of that summer and he remembered it. He may not recall her silly plays for his attention, but he did remember the ten short minutes that he made her feel like she and her broken bike chain were the most important use of his time.

A delightful chill tickled her arms. "You have a way of rescuing me from my troubles."

He chuckled. "Well, it's all in a day's work. Now I should let you get back to those paper mounds. Good-bye."

"Good-bye, and thanks again."

Now just where went my determination not to get carried away by this man? He has never given me any indication that he is any more than a friend.

Coach Conner was back in Debbie's doorway. He had probably never left the hallway. "Sounded like a boyfriend."

"That? Oh, not at all." Debbie laughed, though inside she wished things could have been different.

"Then there would be no problem with your accepting a dinner date with me," he insisted.

"Well, I. . .perhaps." Debbie was reluctant to

promise. He really wasn't her type. He seemed very nice, though, and had been petitioning her since her first day on the job. He had no reservations about showing his interest in her.

"We'll set something up as soon as baseball season is over," the coach beamed.

Debbie forced a smile. It was time she moved on from fantasies.

Five

Another Saturday had dawned and promised a gorgeous spring day. Scott stirred a dash of milk into his cup of coffee. He didn't have any office hours this Saturday, so he had prepared a list of things that needed to be done around the old house—a leaky faucet to replace, a crack to plaster, and hardwood floor to polish. None of the activities excited him, and he dallied by the kitchen window with his cooling cup of coffee.

Movement in the backyard claimed his attention. Debbie stood near the rear of her lot looking like a spring flower. Scott hadn't talked to her since Wednesday, when he had made his lame call to her office. He still couldn't believe he had used the excuse of the dogs' mischief to hear her voice.

Scott noticed that Debbie was watching two men set up a tripod. If the thought hadn't been a ridiculous one, he would have guessed they were surveyors. Scott watched the men study a large sheet of paper, then move their tripod closer to his house.

He set his cup down in the sink and hurried out his back door. "Howdy, neighbor, what's up?" he called cheerfully.

Debbie crossed her arms in front of her. "Just a little preparation work."

Scott waited for her to continue. The yard separating them seemed to stretch like a large plain.

Finally she said, "I'm putting up a fence."

"A fence?" His words fell like breaking glass.

"Next fall, after the garden is done, of course."

Scott didn't like calling to her across the lawn in front of strangers. "Debbie, can I talk to you?"

She nodded but stayed rooted to her spot, making Scott go to her. He thought they had been making good progress in their friendship, but this wasn't a good sign.

"What is this all about?" Scott asked. He reached out to touch her arm, but she gently pulled away.

Debbie steeled herself from his touch and his soft, probing gaze. "I need to know how big the fence will be so I can budget it into my finances."

"But why?" Scott looked wounded. "Your house has been here fifty years without a fence."

She shrugged. "It's a corner lot that gets a lot of traffic, and a nice fence will raise property values."

He appeared unconvinced.

"Nothing against any of our neighbors," she said. "It will be a low fence—probably a white picket."

The sound of a shovel hitting stone caused both to turn to the workers. They had uncovered a stone marker in Scott's yard.

"What are they doing?" Scott asked, clearly frustrated.

Debbie shook her head.

"Miss Julian," the older surveyor spoke up, "this

would be the property line." He stood barely six feet from the side of Scott's house. "The line should run straight into that pine grove, but we'll double-check it."

"That's impossible," Scott said under his breath.

Debbie's eyes widened as she followed the surveyor's line to the garden. It appeared that the whole garden was actually on her property and, in fact, Scott's sprinkler line was also in her yard. Scott saw the lay of the line also.

"Didn't you have this place surveyed when you bought it?" Debbie asked, finding it hard to keep the smug tone from her voice.

Scott glared at her. "I didn't feel it necessary when my neighbors were so friendly and helpful. I made the mistake of not planning for future neighbors."

His words had bite and smarted as they made contact. This hadn't turned out like she had wanted. She had planned the fence to keep her messes from ruining his landscaping perfection. She supposed she could admit to herself that it was also a display of independence. They could be neighbors but she would keep the fence between them to remind herself that it couldn't be anything more.

Debbie turned her back to him and walked toward the surveyors. Scott seized her arm and spun her back around. He quickly dropped her arm, but his mouth remained open with no sound coming out. She waited.

"I. . .okay. . .I thought we had made some progress," he stammered.

She stared at him. "Progress at what—a garden?"

"No, because that is clearly on your property now." Scott was obviously fighting the urge to get angry. "I thought we were becoming friends."

"Nothing has changed," she insisted. "We are still neighbors."

"Neighbors?"

"Sure."

"If that is how you want it, then I won't bother you about the garden again. You'll have plenty of goods to share with your relatives." He backed away as if repulsed by the sight of her.

"Scott. . . !" She couldn't believe his cold attitude.

He spun away from her and rounded his garage out of sight. Soon she heard his car start up and leave the drive.

Debbie stayed in the yard until the surveyors had finished. Then she entered the house, glad that Grandma was closeted in her sewing room. She pulled herself upstairs, stewing over each of Scott's words.

Lord, I don't want Scott to be the dream forever out of my reach, and I don't want him to be my enemy. What's wrong with wanting to be civilized neighbors? Lord, I give this situation into Your hands. Show me my failures and help me mend this new mess I have created.

She waited for a peace to come, but it didn't. She sat in her window seat and gazed across the backyard. Scott didn't return home until early afternoon. Then she never saw him in the yard.

❧

Scott drove around town, made an unnecessary stop at

a super store just to walk around, then ended up at the house of his associate pastor. The two men were very close in age and had quickly become friends when Scott had started attending the church last fall.

Over the noisy play of two toddlers, Scott brought up the subject of Debbie to Pastor Jim.

"You're asking me about women?" Jim laughed, then lowered his voice to a whisper. "Don't tell my wife or she'll gloat, but I don't understand women at all."

Scott sighed. "You're no help, man."

"How long have you known her?"

"We first met about thirteen or fourteen years ago, but I couldn't even tell you what she looked like back then." Scott shrugged. "We really only met at the beginning of this month."

"Well, now, it seems to me that it could be like deer hunting. . .no, more like fishing."

Scott laughed at his friend's quest for an illustration.

"You see," Jim said, gaining confidence in his words, "your Debbie is like the fish that nibbles on the bait. She is tempted but she is afraid of being caught. She will put distance between herself and the bait, but as long as you keep some play on the line, she will be tempted back."

Scott tried to picture Debbie as a fish.

"My friend, you have to keep the bait out there," Jim declared, "until she's not afraid of the hook. Woo her, man. Woo her until she is clay in your hands."

Scott gulped.

"But pray. Ask the Lord if she is the one, and if you get the green light, go for it," Jim stated confidently.

"Jim!" a female voice called from the kitchen.

Jim jumped.

"Wash the kids up for lunch, please."

"Yes, dear," Jim promptly answered and smiled at Scott. "Then you can have this kind of wedded bliss to look forward to." He scooped a child up under each arm and trotted off to the bathroom.

Scott stayed for lunch with Jim's illustration running through his mind. Could he afford to do some more fishing? Was Debbie just scared or bad tempered? She had already ruined his lawn and shrunk his property down in size. What next, his house?

❧

Scott prayed all evening, petitioning God for the direction he should take with Miss Debbie Julian. He needed to know if he should be content to live as her congenial neighbor or if the Lord was sanctioning a relationship for them.

Sunday morning his answer suddenly arrived in the middle of the worship service. Scott had been prepared to wait, as God usually took His time revealing His plan to His child. But a peace about his future with Debbie completely surrounded him. It was as if a family member had given him a hug and pointed out the path he should travel.

Sunday afternoon, Scott visited with Maxie from the front walk. He was careful to stay off the Julian property even though he didn't see Debbie in sight. He had determined to test the waters slowly and see if he could coax a nibble. If it were meant to be the way he was envisioning, she would eventually let him get close. And when the timing was right, he would hook a ring on her finger and never let her go.

Six

Wallpapering was the last way Debbie had planned to spend her Memorial Day vacation, but Grandma pleaded that they redecorate the tiny sewing room. Debbie knew that Grandma had given her an extremely fair price on the house, and she felt obligated to work on the projects that her grandmother had been avoiding for the last ten years.

The grueling task of picking out the paper was accomplished on Saturday evening. Debbie compromised with Grandma's passion for big flowers, and they purchased a tasteful floral vine design instead of Debbie's preference for a small stripe. Debbie started some of her measurements on Sunday afternoon. Monday morning she allowed herself to sleep an hour longer than usual, just because it was a holiday, then she dug out the water pan, sponges, a knife, scissors, rulers, and all the tools that might make the papering go smoothly.

The tiny room was right beside the master bedroom on the first level of the house. Debbie set up a card table in the bedroom for her cutting work. She shoved the sewing desk, boxes of crafts and material, a bookshelf, lamps, an ironing board, and a chair all to one side of the room. She quickly primed the old paint job, and just before noon she was ready to hang the first piece.

The piece was nine feet long and needed to curve around a corner and match the straight line with the doorframe. Debbie's two-foot step stool barely allowed her to reach high enough and didn't fit flush against the wall. She wet the paper and stepped up to the top of her stool. The first reach didn't get the paper flush to the ceiling and caused a cramp in her side. She had to relax her arms and lower the paper.

Her second try at fitting the paper left a huge bubble in the top corner and the bottom was hanging three quarters of an inch off. Debbie pounded her fist on the offending bubble.

"How's it coming?" Grandma asked from the doorway, where the furniture allowed a very narrow passage.

"I'm going to have to take this down and readjust it. Hopefully I can still salvage the paper," Debbie grumbled. "It is not a good start. This stool is too short, and I don't have the reach."

"Hold just a minute," Grandma said. "I may have the solution."

Grandma disappeared and Debbie pulled the chair into the corner. She placed one foot on the top of the stool and the other on the back of the chair. She started pulling the wet paper away from the wall. The top third crumpled down on her head, but she kept pulling gently so as not to rip the paper.

When the paper felt loose, she reached up to find the top end. Blinded by paper covering her face, she felt along both sides and down toward her back. Her hand came in contact with something large and warm.

"You look like you could use an extra hand."

Debbie let out a high-pitched scream and teetered on her perch. She had been so absorbed in her project that she hadn't heard anyone enter the room, but she would recognize Scott's voice anywhere. Her balance was failing, but suddenly strong hands grasped both of her sides and steadied her.

"Hold still," he quietly commanded.

Debbie barely breathed as she felt Scott's weight on the stool and the heat from his body against her back. He took the paper from her, and reaching over her, he smoothed the top edge up against the ceiling. Debbie couldn't move. She was trapped between the wall and his blanketing presence.

His arm gently brushed hers as he stepped down from the stool. His hand came to her lower back as she searched for a solid footing. She almost forgot her next task, then hurriedly smoothed the paper the rest of the way down the wall with a large sponge. It was a perfect fit and the bubbles smoothed out with ease.

Debbie turned to thank Scott, but the room was empty. She squeezed out the narrow passageway, and her feet rushed along the short hallway to the kitchen, where Scott and Grandma were chatting. Scott grinned as Debbie braked to an abrupt stop.

She flung a hand pointing back toward the sewing

room. "Uh. . .thanks. The first piece is always the hardest." Her movements were awkward and she felt tongue-tied.

"But what she is trying to say is that it would go a lot easier with two sets of hands," Grandma interpreted smoothly.

"Gran. . . !" Debbie screeched, turning beet red. Her old anguish had returned.

"You're right," Scott answered Grandma, "and I'll stay if I'm needed, but I'll go if Debbie tells me everything is under control."

Debbie opened her mouth to reply, but the words didn't come out as she had planned. "I guess I could use some help. . .only if you have time."

Scott's face lit up with a smile. "Certainly."

"Well. . ." Debbie shrugged, speechless. She spun on her heel and darted back to the close walls of the tiny sewing room. *He sure smells great today.* His scent still lingered along with the pungent smell of wallpaper paste.

Soon he was standing in the doorway. "Just tell me what you need done."

Debbie stared at the rolls of cut paper, the pan of water, and everything that littered the small area. She had no response. She couldn't possibly tell him how she wished he would put his arms around her again and let her enjoy being so close to him.

"Is the next piece cut? Perhaps I can get it started along the ceiling."

Debbie nodded mutely and riffled through her pile

for the precise piece. Finally finding the right one, she rolled it and submerged it in the water for a short time. Slowly pulling it out, she quickly reached the limit of her arms' extension while still having a good two feet of paper still submerged.

Scott reached around her and took the top of the paper while she pulled the rest out of the water. They worked in companionable silence, hanging three sheets of paper with barely five words between them. The paper was going on with little problem because the area they worked on was smooth and had no obstacles.

Soon they reached the window. There was a sharp turn to make around a corner, then a short distance to where they would need to trim around an outlet and the window frame. Scott started the long piece at the ceiling, smoothing the paper until Debbie could reach it with her sponge. Halfway down Debbie was confronted by a crease that refused to budge. She tried smoothing it into the corner, then out toward the seam. It refused to disappear.

"We are going to need to pull the paper loose and work out this crease," Debbie resigned.

"Okay." Scott started loosening the top half.

The loose paper allowed Debbie to maneuver the crease, but when the paper was tight again, she still had a long oval-shaped bubble to wrestle with. She smoothed it with the straight edge of her ruler and was left with several small bubbles. Taking her sponge over the area brought her back to the original predicament of one big bubble.

Scott had stood patiently in the background as she

worked, but now he stepped forward. "May I try?"

Debbie was getting tired and the frustration was wearing at her patience. She tossed him the sponge and moved away.

Scott tried a couple of passes with the sponge, then he moved to her pile of tools. "Do you have a straight pin?"

"Sure. It's a sewing room," was her offhanded answer. She pulled out a narrow drawer in the sewing desk and gently placed a tiny pin in the palm of Scott's large hand.

He worked the bubble into one area, then stuck the pin into the center. Cupping his hands around the perimeter of the bubble, he forced the air toward the pinhole. Instead of air, though, a stream of pasty water shot from the hole and spit directly into Scott's face. He jumped back in surprise, pressing Debbie against the desk in the tight space.

Debbie's breath was briefly knocked from her, but as Scott flailed for his footing, the comedy of the situation hit her. She shook with giggles. It felt good to laugh after the silence and frustrating work of the past hour. Soon she was laughing out loud.

Scott placed a light hand on her shoulder. "Are you okay. I didn't mean to plow you over."

She tried to contain the fit of laughter, but when she looked at his face, a drop of paste dripped from his regal nose and she lost control again. She sank to a sitting position on the floor and held her sides as waves of laughter shook her.

"Are you laughing at me?" Scott knelt beside her.

She took a gulp of air and nodded.

He wiped his face with the tail of his shirt. "I should sue you for poor working conditions." He sighed dramatically.

Laughter gushed from her again, punctuated by hiccups, and soon Scott's deep chuckle joined her as he rested himself on the floor beside Debbie.

"What's so funny?" Grandma asked from the door.

Scott shrugged and smiled. Debbie shook her head, unable to speak through the hiccups.

"Whatever it is," Grandma declared, "I hope it isn't catching." She retreated to a new chorus of laughter, and it was a long time before another piece of wallpaper was hung.

That afternoon when Debbie and Scott finally fitted the last piece of paper near the door of the room, they stepped back in great satisfaction.

"This little room is quite pretty," Debbie said in awe of their work.

Scott nodded. "You could use it as a nursery some day. . .well, since it's near the big bedroom."

They both fell silent. The topic was an awkward one for Debbie to reply to. She bent to gather her tools. Scott started collecting bits and pieces of leftover paper.

"I need to apologize," he said suddenly.

Debbie jerked her head up, confused by his train of thought.

"I shouldn't have gotten upset about the surveying and fencing."

Debbie sighed as she began to realize where the conversation was going.

"You were right," he continued. "We are neighbors and a fence doesn't mean we still can't be friends. Does it?"

Her eyes widened. "Of course not!"

"Good." He visibly relaxed. "Friends." He stuck out his hand.

She tentatively placed her smaller hand within his grasp and watched his fingers engulf her own. His hand felt warm and safe.

"A good job done deserves good food. I've got a German chocolate cake ready," Grandma said from behind them. "Oh, I'm sorry!" Grandma smiled, turning away.

Scott pulled away slowly while his gaze stayed on Debbie's face. "I would welcome some of that cake, Maxie." He took large steps to catch up with the older woman and embraced her in a bear hug.

"Thank you for helping with the papering job," Grandma said, patting the man's face.

"Anything for my gal."

Debbie looked on and once again felt left out of their circle. The old nagging returned to warn her that Scott had no real reason to be friendly and helpful to her if it wasn't for her grandmother. The warmth that had so recently encompassed her now turned to a chill of self-doubt.

Seven

First thing Tuesday morning, Coach Conner caught up to Debbie in an empty hallway.

"Well, the season's over," he said with a distinct note of sadness. "Sure didn't end like I would have liked, but we played good ball."

Debbie smiled and nodded. She hated to admit that she hadn't kept up with the baseball team's record.

"So, how about Friday?"

"Friday?" Debbie asked.

"Yea, our date. We can get some eats and see a movie," he said, bumping her shoulder with his beefy one. "Not much else going on in our little town this time of year."

Debbie reminded herself that she had basically made a promise last week and nodded her consent. "What time?"

"Better make it six," Jeff Conner said and strutted off toward the gym.

❦

Friday came quickly after a week of heavy workload. She had a new wave of SAT and ACT test scores to consult with students about. She counseled with a frantic senior girl who was fearful of not getting into college that fall due to a poor test standing. Then Friday led to some tearful good-byes as the seniors completed their last day of classes. The week had drained Debbie's energy and she longed to close herself up at home for an evening of relaxation.

But Coach Conner was at her door promptly at 6:00 with his 4x4 running along the curb. He treated her to a heavy meal of steak and potatoes at the Texas-style steakhouse. Jeff, as he asked to be called, was warm and friendly, but his favorite line of conversation centered on sports of any variety. Debbie had very little to contribute on the subject.

It was raining after dinner as Jeff kindly helped Debbie up into his large 4x4, then he ran through the list of their movie options.

"Can I request that the movie not be rated R?" Debbie asked.

They agreed upon a comedy with a military setting. It spawned some laughs from Debbie, but she was disappointed in the use of foul language. Glad to see the movie end and aching from the tired strain, Debbie declined Jeff's offer for a nightcap of coffee and doughnuts.

She had him pull up along the side of the house since her key only fit the back door. Jeff hurried around to help her out. She would have preferred ending the evening at the truck, but Jeff took her arm and slowly strolled her through the wet grass up to the porch steps.

"I had a great time," Jeff said. "We should do this again."

Debbie searched for the right words that would let him down gently. She didn't see any point in repeating a date with him. He was a sweet guy, but he didn't show any clear signs of being a Christian, they had little in common, and it just plain didn't feel right. Her gaze drifted to the glow from Scott's front window.

Jeff leaned closer, and Debbie turned in time to offer her cheek for a quick peck.

"Howdy all!" came a loud intrusion.

Debbie was shocked to hear Scott's voice coming from her darkened porch. "Gran, are you there?" she asked.

"No," Scott answered, "Maxie has already gone to bed. It's getting late." He stepped out to where the glow of the street lamp illumined his rigid posture; the porch swing swayed in the shadows.

"Is this your brother, Deb?" Jeff asked congenially.

Scott smirked.

Debbie seethed at Scott's smug attitude. He stood with arms crossed as if he were her personal bodyguard. "Jeff, this happens to be my neighbor, *Mr.* Robillard. He was only here to check on my grandmother and was on his way home."

Scott stood planted on the top porch step.

Jeff looked back and forth between Scott and Debbie. Debbie shifted nervously under the scrutiny of the two men.

"Listen. . ." Jeff stammered as he backed away, "I didn't know. . . I'll see you on Monday, Deb. Have a great weekend." He hurried to his truck and drove away.

Debbie stood in the grass, the dampness seeping through her flat suede shoes.

"Seems like a friendly guy," Scott said.

"Do you often spy on your neighbors' comings and goings?" Debbie retorted. She really didn't mind that Jeff's display of affection had been cut short, but she resented the fact that Scott was prying into her business. He blocked the way up the porch steps, so she remained in the yard.

"I didn't mean. . ." Scott stopped. He was forced to admit to himself that he had purposefully lingered on the porch after coffee with Maxie, knowing that Debbie was out and expected home soon. He had been interested in learning what kind of man appealed to Debbie and whether this relationship had depth that would threaten the future he had hoped he might someday have with her.

"You're right," he finally continued, "I shouldn't have dallied on your porch, and I should have revealed myself sooner. Please accept my apologies and convey them to your friend." Now would have been a good time for him to head home, but he couldn't find the will to move.

He looked down at Debbie where she shifted in discomfort. He watched as her gaze swung around the darkened yard, where long shadows had transformed the inviting backyard into a place of mysterious qualities.

"I hope you had a nice evening," he said on impulse.

She stared up at him in silence.

"You deserve to be shown. . ." he paused, then rambled on, "the love of a good man."

Her eyes widened.

Scott stepped carefully down the steps and passed Debbie. "Good night." The word came out like a whisper.

She didn't change her rigid posture until he was a safe distance across the black expanse of soggy lawn. Then she went directly inside. Scott plodded home under dripping tree limbs; his shoulders dropped in defeat. One step of progress with Debbie always seemed to be met by a step back in the wrong direction. He was getting nowhere moving cautiously. Perhaps he should follow his pounding heart, rush in, and expose his true feelings.

Or, perhaps it was time to get back on his knees and talk with the Instructor.

❧

Debbie stepped into the quiet house and felt her breathing start to settle back to a steady pace. She put the lock in place and peeked out the curtained window in the door. She couldn't explain why she felt so angry with Scott or why his words of kindness moved her to speechlessness. Nothing was making sense anymore, and something had to change.

She turned into the darkened kitchen and for the first time realized Grandma was sitting at the empty table.

"Gran, I didn't know you were still up."

"Why can't you see it, Dandy girl?"

"See what?"

"Are you afraid of him?"

"Afraid of Scott? Of course not," Debbie quickly retorted.

"Why won't you let Scott show you how much he loves you?" Gran asked another question without directly addressing Debbie.

Debbie couldn't believe what she was hearing. She pulled a chair out from the table and sank onto it. "Gran, Scott is your friend. He has often been kind to me, but he is not interested. . .in romance," she choked out.

"Dandy, I always considered you to be one of my brightest grandchildren."

Debbie frowned at her.

"That man's face plainly displays his fondness for you."

Debbie shook her head. "You may want it to be that way. Has he said something about it?"

"Well, no, but he hasn't had to. I know you both well and can see things that you are not willing to," Grandma stated. "And, I know you care for him, too."

Debbie shifted uncomfortably. "Gran," she framed her words gently, "you care for us both, and I think you have let your desire to see something happen between Scott and me cloud your judgment. There is nothing between us and there is no reason why there should ever be."

"God," Grandma said quietly.

"What?"

"God is in both of your lives and He knows each of your needs."

"Yes, Gran, but it doesn't mean He wants us together." Debbie toyed with her fingers nervously. "I don't even know if we have anything in common."

"Your faith is the best thing to have in common," Grandma insisted.

"Have you talked with Scott about this?"

"No," Grandma spoke honestly.

"Have you encouraged him in anyway toward a relationship with me?"

Grandma fidgeted on the hard seat. "Well, I might have contrived the garden mishap. I mean," she paused and smiled, "I encouraged you to place the garden where I was sure you would get into Scott's yard. I knew you would have to meet and solve the problem together. It worked until you had to go and clearly point out the proper boundaries that haven't been considered for at least forty years." Grandma sounded like she was getting herself worked up. "Then I admit to trying to place you two together for meals and projects whenever feasible, but I have never uttered a word to sway either of you until now." Grandma leaned back in the chair having had her say.

⁂

Debbie went directly to her window retreat after leaving the kitchen. *What am I missing?* A guy who had his life in perfect order like Scott couldn't be interested in her. She couldn't even juggle her tumbling emotions. *It is like I haven't learned from the mistakes of childhood. I have let myself get stuck on one guy and have placed all my expectations on him. I just know he is going to disappoint me.*

Sure he will.

Only the Lord is constantly there for me.

She talked back and forth to a small voice within her. Her conscience or the Holy Spirit, she wasn't ready to say. She was only assured that the answer would be found in prayer. She reached onto her desk for the Bible she had regrettably not touched all week.

She read and prayed in the glow of an antique-styled lamp until well after midnight. She fell into bed with a certainty that she was loved. Her heavenly Father loved her more than anyone else could. He had her best interests in consideration. She would wait on His lead.

It would not be easy, but first thing in the morning, Debbie knew she had to apologize to Scott. She had let her own insecurities and fears have authority over her actions. If there really was something to Scott's affection, as Grandma had said, then maybe Debbie was too afraid to acknowledge it. No matter what the future held, she had a past to right.

Eight

Debbie fixed another cup of tea and dressed it up with sugar and cream. She kept her vigil at the kitchen window, looking out at the backyard. The evening's rain had given this Saturday morning a clean, polished shine. The day promised many wonders, but Debbie was only intent on one thing, one person.

Watching her neighbor's back door reminded her of when she had been just eight years old and spending the fall weekend with her grandparents. She had joined a group of mischievous children who thought they could prove themselves as grown up as the teenagers if they successfully toilet papered a tree. The Robillards' tree was chosen only for the fact that it was in a side yard that was quickly obscured by evening shadows. The children accomplished their task before bedtime and parted feeling proud.

But Grandma had been wise to Debbie's whereabouts. She dropped casual questions and soon Debbie was crying out her story, no longer the brave little vandal.

The next morning Grandma marched Debbie to the Robillards' back door and Debbie had apologized to Mrs.

Robillard. She spent over an hour gathering all the paper she could reach and had plenty of time to think.

None of the other children involved had been reprimanded, even though Debbie had willingly given up the names of her partners. Grandma and Mrs. Robillard had chosen not to pursue the issue and none of the other children came forward on their own. Debbie had cleaned the yard alone, and Mr. Robillard had kindly finished what she could not.

It was a lesson that she would long remember. The labor involved in cleaning the yard was nothing compared to the disappointment Debbie had witnessed in the eyes of the adults she cared greatly for. She valued her relationships and now she had unwillingly driven a wedge between herself and her new neighbor. She never meant to hurt Scott, but her defense mechanism kept throwing darts.

Her gaze was drawn to movement at Scott's garage. He ambled into the backyard carrying a hoe. She watched as he checked over his rhododendron bush, cleaning off the fading blossoms. With slow, deliberate steps, he made his way to the garden plot and gradually circled the perimeter. He stopped at the young tomato plants and gently cut around the base of each with his hoe.

His fluid movements mesmerized Debbie. She watched until the tomatoes were finished, and Scott moved on to tiny heads of green weeds between the rows of newly sprouting lettuce and beets. She collected her composure and left the house.

Scott looked up at Debbie's approach but continued

his work down the row. Debbie stopped at the grape arbor and examined the tiny leaves sprouting from the mature vines. Was it painful when those buds burst open?

Scott zipped through the remainder of the row and was soon only a couple of steps from Debbie's side. He leaned back and stretched with exaggerated movements. "Beautiful day," he bellowed.

Debbie watched him carefully. . .shyly.

Suddenly Scott was actively cleaning his shoes and hoe of dirt and talking at a rapid pace. "What are you doing this afternoon? Wouldn't this be a great day for a picnic? There are still trees in bloom over at Tuscora Park. We should take some time to enjoy it."

Where was Debbie's voice? Was this a display of Scott's affection or an attempt to apologize for his spying behavior of the night before? She couldn't interpret the signs. *Now what do I do, Lord?*

"I have some paperwork I should get done, but perhaps Gran would enjoy some time out," Debbie offered.

"Ah, leave Maxie out of this. Saturday is her day to go and play with the old girls. They'll either be shopping, playing dominoes, or pigging out at a buffet," Scott refuted. "Call it a time-out or call it a date, but I'd like to treat you to a playful afternoon."

Debbie was shocked. Scott was talking so fast that she didn't have time to react. He sounded like he had had a caffeine overload. Silently she searched for a proper response.

"Okay," he said after pausing a moment. "You can do your paperwork this morning, then I'll pick you up around 4:00. We'll have an early picnic dinner by the pond and enjoy the evening there. It is predicted to be quite pleasant this evening." His broad smile left no room for arguments.

Debbie nodded mutely, no longer trying to speak. Saying something now might spoil the moment, and she didn't trust her voice.

"Don't worry about the garden," Scott instructed. "I'll pulverize these weeds in no time while you take care of your personal business." He stepped back into the garden soil and attacked a new row. Though his movements were energetic, he was careful to avoid the area where seeds of green beans were still sprouting.

When Scott said no more and she still had no thought to voice, she drifted back to the house. She avoided going directly in and walked around the side yard to the front porch. There were some families out working in yards. A father and son were washing their minivan across the street.

The sun thoroughly warmed Debbie and her mind pictured Scott in the backyard. She still couldn't figure out what had overcome Scott to behave so radically, but perhaps this was a sign from God that she should give a relationship with Scott a chance.

It wasn't quite how she had desired to be approached by her knight in shining armor. Her knight would have wooed her with sweet words and romantic gifts. Scott was riding in on a charger and expecting her to canter alongside. But out of the two, she knew that Scott was the one she could be friends with, and friendship was the best place to start a romance.

❦

By 4:00 Scott had pulled his Buick around to the front of Debbie's house. She watched from the window as his feet danced up the walk.

Grandma had stayed curiously in the background all day, and Debbie was able to accomplish a surprising amount of bills, laundry, and cleaning. Grandma left around 2:00 with a group of five friends and Debbie had the whole house to herself. She had taken care to pick a comfortable, but attractive casual outfit for the evening. Her navy twill slacks were creased and slimming while her lightweight cardigan covered a wide-necked T-shirt of baby blue.

Scott appeared to have a little better rein on his enthusiasm and met her with a playful grin. Completely the gentleman, he helped her into her side of the car before taking his place behind the wheel. He filled the ten-minute drive to the park with mostly one-sided conversation about the weather and the community.

"Are you hungry?" he asked as he parked his car near the community hall and snack bars.

"Not really."

"Good, then we'll leave the picnic supplies here, and I challenge you to a round of putt-putt."

"Oh, I'm not very good."

"You're in luck, I'm pathetic," he said, leaving the car. He opened her door and helped her out. "Thankfully I have a great drive and can hold my own on a regular course."

Debbie struggled to keep up with his long strides as he led them across the park to the ticket booth. He secured two clubs, balls, and a score pad for them and insisted that Debbie be the first to putt.

They relaxed and kept their conversation focused on the game. Debbie managed to do quite well, keeping her score just below his. Then they came to the loop. Golfers were expected to putt their balls onto a metal track with enough force to send the ball around the loop and out the opposite side. Debbie's first try came right back to her at the starting point. So did her second and third tries.

Scott rooted her on. "Put more force into it."

Debbie whacked the ball with double the energy. The ball winged to the top of the looped track then popped out and disappeared into the bushes at the left side of the green.

Debbie groaned while Scott laughed. He got down on his knees and felt under the scrubby little bushes for her ball. "It went in here, didn't it?"

"I think so."

Scott stood and looked all around the bushes. A line of golfers was forming behind Debbie. Scott gave up. "Here, use mine." He placed a neon green ball in her palm.

This time Debbie's shot was perfect. The ball made the loop and stopped within a foot of the cup. She had an easy, one-stroke putt from there. Handing the ball back to Scott she said, "The ball made all the difference."

But the golf ball didn't have the same effect for

Scott. His first attempt missed the track, his second was too weak and rolled back, then his third shot was strong and zipped through the loop. It sailed over the hole, smacked into the wooded edging, bounced back, and dropped into the cup.

"Wow! Did you see that?" Scott leaped over to Debbie and hugged her in his excitement.

Debbie's breathing was choked by his overwhelming closeness. He held her a moment longer than necessary, then pulled back in slow motion, his gaze locking on her eyes. She felt suddenly shy as she recognized a tender warmth in his eyes. She dropped her lashes.

"Clear the course," yelled a teen with a bad attitude.

Scott retrieved his ball and led Debbie up the path. Debbie finished the eighteenth hole with her only hole-in-one, giving her a score that was just three under Scott's. He pouted playfully as they turned in their equipment.

"Okay, now what can I beat you at?" he said while surveying the area. The park was beginning to fill up with families. Young children loved the small Ferris wheel, the swings, a mini train, and, of course, the carousel. "How about the batting cages?"

Debbie moaned, "Do I have to?"

"No," Scott smiled. "I'll call a truce if you promise to ride the carousel after our picnic."

Debbie brightened. "I haven't done that kind of thing in years. I'd love to."

Scott grasped Debbie's hand where it hung at her side and pulled her back toward the car. They unloaded their picnic paraphernalia and took it to the edge of the pond. Scott picked out a spot that hadn't been littered by the resident ducks and spread out an old quilt. It was worn and frayed, but the double wedding ring pattern was clearly visible in a variety of colors.

"Is this something your grandmother made?" she asked as Scott set out plates and plastic food containers.

"I really don't remember. My only recollection of the quilt is that my grandparents carried it around in their car during winter in case they ever got snowbound."

"Well, it is charming."

"Yes." Scott was looking at her again, and Debbie felt a warmth not attributed to the setting sun spread through her limbs. "Do you mind. . ." he hesitated, "if I tell you that for weeks I have found you to be quite charming?"

Debbie felt like a corralled group of wild horses had just been released in her stomach.

"I don't want to play games with you, Debbie, but neither do I want to scare you," he said as he reached out to smooth a strand of curls behind her ear. His hand stroked her cheek. "I want you to know that I want to be your friend and to know you much better."

The adoring look in his eyes chased away her fears and defenses. Grandma had read him right, and Debbie knew she trusted his words. Her face spread with a serene smile. She was deliriously happy.

Silently, Scott drew her face toward his own. Across the quilt pattern that represented the bonding of two souls, he kissed her tenderly once, then twice.

❧

For the first time, Scott and Debbie really talked. They discussed family and friends. They exchanged ideas about their mutual faith and goals for the future. Debbie even had a confession to make. Scott was being so open with her that she decided that she needed to get past the roadblock that had been discouraging her from a relationship with him.

"Scott, can I tell you something?" Debbie timidly asked. "You may find it rather silly."

"You can tell me anything." His gaze was tender, and he adjusted his position on the quilt so that he was just a bit closer to her.

"You may not remember that I was around my grandparents' house thirteen years ago when you spent the whole summer with your grandparents, but I was and I remember a lot about you." Debbie shifted nervously, playing with the patches on the quilt. "I had quite a crush on you. You were the focus of my entire summer, and I longed for your attention."

"Ah, I'm sorry, Debbie. I do remember fixing your bike, though. It was an ancient thing."

"My grandmother's."

"But you really were better off not to have me chasing you in return. I was pretty self-absorbed back then, and I wouldn't have appreciated how special you are."

Debbie laughed in spite of herself. "When we met a few weeks ago, I was still so embarrassed by my behavior as a teen. I couldn't believe you didn't remember that. I was sure that my ridiculous plays for your attention would have had a lasting impression."

Scott reached out to cup her chin. "Maybe it is better that I don't remember, because it doesn't really matter about the teen you were. I want to get to know who you are now." His hand traced the features of her face, recording each detail. Debbie leaned into his caresses.

The shadows of approaching night were deep before they packed up the remains of submarine sandwiches, macaroni salad, potato chips, and brownies. Scott had confessed to buying most of it at a deli, but he had assembled the sandwiches and baked the brownies from a boxed mix.

They set their sights on the carousel now, and once again, Scott claimed her hand in his warm clasp. There was a long line of parents and children waiting for the spinning carousel to stop and let them on. Debbie pointed out the gray and red horse she wanted to ride.

When the carousel was ready for a new load, Scott was quick to secure Debbie's horse. He helped her step up and swing her long leg over the little horse. Then Scott climbed on the white horse beside hers. Debbie smiled at his proud posture on the white steed, but didn't voice her thoughts about a knight riding a white stallion. It was a silly thought. Mythical knights didn't exist, but a few lovable, God-fearing men still did. Scott was among that kind, and as long as he kept his focus on Christ, she knew she could be secure in her love for him.

The carousel slowly began to spin. Scott chuckled and hummed an old cowboy tune.

Debbie studied him with an endearing smile. *Love?* Did she really feel that strong emotion? There was no physical fire about to consume her but a warm glow that assured her what they had started today was the development of a lasting bond, a comfortable companionship, and, yes, a mature love.

Debbie leaned her head back as the carousel turned faster and faster. This childish entertainment was liberating. Scott held his palm out to her and she placed her hand in his. It was a natural fit.

They rode the carousel twice, then conceded that it was time to go home.

❧

The house was dark and quiet as Debbie preceded Scott into her kitchen. Debbie called for her grandmother. When there was no answer, Debbie said, "She must be getting ready for bed; it *is* getting late."

"Why don't you check your messages while I put on some coffee?" Scott said, indicating the blinking red light on the answering machine. "There are still some brownies left." He moved comfortably around the kitchen, finding what he needed.

"Where are your coffee filters?" Scott asked, and Debbie showed him while she waited on the tape to rewind.

Then a professional sounding voice spoke clearly through the machine. "This message is for Debra Julian. Please call this number at Union Hospital concerning your grandmother."

Debbie thought her heart would stop and she reached

for Scott. He folded his arms around her quaking shoulders. "It will be all right. Call them back and get an explanation."

"I assumed she was here." Debbie moved to check Grandma's bedroom just to be sure. Then she made the dreaded call. She clutched Scott's hand as she listened intently.

"The nurse who made the call is no longer on duty," Debbie reported to Scott, "but this nurse said Gran is there and stabilized. She has been admitted for at least overnight. The nurse couldn't tell me what was wrong."

Scott pointed to the answering machine. "There is another message that you didn't listen to."

Debbie pressed the play button. "Hi, Debbie, this is Myrna Yoder. I'm at the hospital. Maxine is having stomach trouble and it sounds like food poisoning. Now, the girls and I ate from the same Chinese buffet, and so far we are fine. Well, anyway, you'll want to get down here and bring Maxine some toiletries for an overnight stay. See you soon."

Debbie breathed a little easier as she rushed to collect the things Grandma would be needing. Scott drove Debbie to the hospital without her having to ask him. She wanted him near while she faced the unknown. She prayed the whole way on the short drive. This was much too early to lose the vibrant matriarch.

Grandma had already been placed in a room. Debbie flew down the hall to find her dozing in a hospital bed. The other bed in the sterile room was empty.

"Gran," Debbie spoke quietly and felt Scott come

to her side, placing his hand on her shoulder. "What happened, Gran?"

"Dandy?" Maxine Julian opened her eyes that were dulled with pain and medication. "Ah, and Scotty, too." She smiled.

"What has the doctor said?" Scott probed.

"Bad food." Grandma grimaced. "Probably the shrimp, since I'm the only one who likes it."

Scott pulled up a chair for Debbie and she sank gratefully into it.

It was a long wait until the doctor made his last round of the night and assured them that Grandma could easily be released by 7:00 the next morning. Grandma appeared to nod off after midnight while Scott and Debbie talked quietly.

"So, you've heard about my exciting evening; are you going to tell me how your evening was?" Grandma suddenly spoke with her eyes still shut.

"Uh. . ." Debbie didn't know how to tell Grandma that she was right about Scott's regard for her.

"I think your Dandy likes me," Scott answered.

Grandma chuckled. "And you like her. I know."

"So, I would have permission to uh. . .say, court your granddaughter?" Scott asked.

"Wouldn't think of stopping you," Grandma said in a tired voice.

Debbie leaned over and kissed her grandmother's cheek. She and Scott watched in silence as Grandma drifted into a relaxed sleep. Then in the glow of a small lamp in the stark hospital room, Scott leaned down to whisper in Debbie's ear.

"I think I love you."

Debbie gasped. "I think I love you, too!"

"Praise God," Scott whispered.

Epilogue

Debbie filled a bucket with what would be the last of the summer's tomatoes. The early September sun was not as direct as August's had been, and the garden's remaining plants were withering in the chilled nights.

It had been a wonderful summer. Debbie had enjoyed having long days to work alongside Grandma and long evenings to spend with Scott. Grandma had seen to it that he had eaten dinner with them almost every night, even though Debbie teased that he was being spoiled. The garden had flourished under the joint efforts of Scott and Debbie, and they had had plenty to share with Debbie's parents, who came home for several weeks before loading their motor home and setting off toward Maine for a fall foliage trip.

Debbie and her grandmother had started attending Scott's church, and already they both had found places to become involved. Debbie enjoyed the singles' group and had made new friends. She survived an energized week of vacation Bible school and even signed up to assist with the children's puppetry program.

Things were falling into place in her life, and one of the most important of those things was walking across the yard toward her at that moment.

"Did you leave school early?" Scott asked as he leaned down to gather some small red tomatoes.

"No, you must have had long office hours today."

"It has been a long week," he admitted. "You and Maxie going to can these?"

"Certainly! Gran makes wonderful soups from her tomato juice."

They filled Debbie's bucket and still had tomatoes to pile in the grass.

"Can we plan a date for tomorrow evening?" Scott said.

"I can't. Tomorrow is the women's retreat up in Canton, and it won't be over until late."

"Oh." He sounded truly disappointed as he cleaned a bush of all its tomatoes. "I'll be right back." Scott scrambled up from a hunched position and hurried through his back door.

Debbie was ready to haul tomatoes to the house when he returned. Scott reached awkwardly for her hand, and she failed to see that he had something serious on his mind. She joked with him. "Do you want to help me get the dirt out from under my nails?"

Scott gave her an exasperated, lopsided grin. Then taking a deep breath, he spoke. "I had more romantic places in mind, but I started thinking that since this garden is where we met and how our relationship got started, I should do this here."

Debbie frowned at him. "What are you talking about? Are you okay?" His fingers quivered around her left hand.

Scott made a frustrated shake of his head and plugged on. "I asked the Lord back in May—very soon after I met you—to show me if you could be the one I have been waiting for. It didn't take long to feel that God had given me permission to love you." Scott looked lovingly at Debbie's confused expression. "In fact, I was almost giddy about it on the morning I asked you to Tuscora Park, because I already knew I loved you and couldn't wait for you to know it, too."

Debbie sighed. She was so blessed to have him care for her. His hair was tousled and she smoothed it with her free hand.

"Debbie?" His tone caused her to meet his gaze. "We have managed to become good friends by sharing this garden plot. Do you think we could consider sharing all of our future gardens?"

Her eyes widened. His words held deep meaning.

"Debbie. . .dear Dandy, would you marry me?" he asked. Slowly he pulled a golden ring from his pocket. The diamond stone was simple in cut but dazzling in beauty.

Once again he had made her speechless, but she didn't need words. She smiled and leaned into him. Their lips met and she promised to love him through thick and thin for as long as God should grant them life.

Let us not become weary in doing good,
for at the proper time we will reap a harvest
if we do not give up.

GALATIANS 6:9

REBECCA GERMANY

"Becky" is the fiction editor for Barbour Publishing and manages the editorial process of the **Heartsong Presents** series. She grew up just twenty miles from where the publishing company is located. Her lifelong love of reading and history has made this the perfect job for her. Single and sharing a home with her parents on the family farm, Becky has begun her own writing career with three published novellas.

Stormy Weather

Tracie Peterson

One

Gina looked at the instructions in her hand for the tenth time. "Official Grand Prix Pinewood Derby Kit," one side read. The other side had "Contains Functional Sharp Points" as its title.

"What in the world are functional sharp points?" she asked, looking down into the questioning eyes of her eight-year-old son. "Do you know what this means, Danny?"

The boy shrugged. "Mr. Cameron didn't say. He just said all the Cub Scouts were going to race them some Saturday."

Gina nodded and turned back to the kit. A block of wood, four nails, and four plastic wheels stared back up at her, along with the confusing instructions. "And we're supposed to make this into a car?"

"A race car," Danny corrected.

"Did your scoutmaster say how you were supposed to make this into a race car?" Gina asked, pushing back limp brown hair.

"You have to cut it into the shape of a car and then paint it. He said to have your dad call if he had questions. I told him I didn't have a dad, and he said moms could call him, too."

"I see," Gina said. Three years of widowhood had left a great many holes in her life, including a father to assist Danny in times of crisis. And this was definitely a crisis. The Cub Scout pinewood derby was, according to the date at the top of the page, only a couple of weeks away and she'd not yet gotten up the courage to carve on the chunk of wood, much less produce a finished race car. Looking from the instructions to the kit to her son, Gina felt an overwhelming desire to lock herself in her bedroom until after the pinewood derby race had passed.

"I guess I'll call him," she muttered and went to the list of phone numbers she kept on the refrigerator. Of course, the refrigerator was also covered with a multitude of other papers and pictures, which made her task even more difficult. By Gina's calculations the memorabilia and paperwork added a good twenty pounds to the already well-worn fridge door.

"Cub Scouts," she muttered, fanning through the precariously placed information. Cub Scout letters were always on blue paper. Telaine Applebee, the mother of twin boys who always managed to outperform all of the other Scouts, had created their den's newsletter. She thought by putting it on blue paper it would make parents more organized. She could hear Telaine, even now, her high-pitched voice announcing the newsletter like a prize at one of those home-product parties.

"And look," she'd nearly squealed with pride, "it's blue! You'll always know it's Scout information, because it's blue like their uniforms." Only it wasn't blue like their uniforms but a sugary shade of sky blue that seemed to match Telaine's perfect eyes.

Gina sighed. It wasn't that she didn't like Telaine. She did. Telaine was a wonderful woman and Gina would give just about anything to be as organized. But looking at Telaine and seeing her perfect life was like looking into a mirror and finding all your own inadequacies.

"Here it is!" she declared, forgetting about Telaine and the thought that no doubt her twins had already completed turning their wood blocks into race cars.

"They'll probably be featured on the front of *Great Mechanics,*" she muttered and picked up the receiver.

Dialing the phone, Gina noted that Danny seemed oblivious to her feelings of inadequacy, but that was the way she wanted it. To share with her eight-year-old the fears and loneliness of being a widow seemed an injustice of grand proportion. Danny just stood there staring at her with such hope—like he expected her to have some magical formula for changing wood into cars. How could she disappoint him when he believed so strongly in her ability to make things right?

The number she'd dialed began ringing and Gina immediately tensed. What would she say? How could she explain that she'd let the project get away from her and now it was nearly time for the race and she hadn't even begun to help Danny put it together?

"Hello?"

The baritone voice at the other end of the phone immediately commanded Gina's attention. "Yes, is this Mr. Cameron, Cub Scout leader for den four?"

"Among other things," the man replied in a tone

that betrayed amusement.

Gina smiled to herself and took a deep breath. "Look, we've never met, but my son is one of your Wolf Cubs. No wait, I think he's a Bear Cub or a Bobcat. Oh, I forget." The man laughed, making Gina feel uncertain whether he was laughing at her in a nice way or because she'd just managed to sound like ditz of the year. "I'm sorry," she muttered and tried again. "This is Gina Bowden, Danny's mother."

"Ah, your son is a Bear."

"Especially in the morning," Gina countered.

The man chuckled. "Well, I can't vouch for that, but on Tuesday night, he's definitely a Bear. What can I do for you?"

Gina looked heavenward and rolled her eyes. *Take me away from the monotony. Give me a reason to put on mascara. Teach me what to do when the sidewalk opens up with cracks big enough to swallow small children or when the dryer won't dry but just dings at you like you should know what that means.*

"Hello?"

The masculine voice broke through Gina's thoughts. "Sorry, it's been a bad week," she said softly shaking her head. "This is the problem. I'm looking at this pinebox derby stuff—" Hysterical laughter erupted on the end of the line, causing Gina to pause. "Is something wrong?" More laughter. "You are the Cub Scout leader I'm supposed to call if I need help, aren't you?"

The man collected himself. "Yeah, but it's pinewood derby, not pinebox. We aren't racing coffins out there."

"You might as well be," Gina replied, then laughed at her own mistake. "I'm afraid if I start in on this thing that's what it'll resemble. Come to think of it, it already resembles that. And just what are functional sharp points?"

"Would you like me to come over and help you and Danny?"

Gina sighed. "Mr. Cameron."

"Gary. Call me Gary."

"Okay, Gary, I would be very grateful if you would come give us a hand. I'm a widow, and although I've tried to be father, mother, taxi driver, Little League coach, and general all-around good sport, I've yet to master woodwork." She paused for a moment, then remembering that strange "check engine" light in the van, she added, "Or car mechanics."

His chuckles warmed her heart. "I have talents in both areas. Do you have time to work on the car right now?" he asked.

Gina smiled, unable to resist. "Which one?"

"Let's start with the wooden one and work our way up," Gary countered.

Gina breathed a sigh of relief. Just thinking about not having to be responsible for the functional sharp points was making it much easier to face the day. "Sure, come on over. The address is 311 Humboldt."

"Be there in ten minutes."

Gina hung up the phone and looked at her forlorn child. "Mr. Cameron is coming right over." Danny's face brightened. Glancing down at her sweat suit, she added,

"I'm going to go change my clothes so I don't look like a bag lady. You let him in when he gets here."

Seven minutes later, while Gina was just pulling a brush through her hair, Gary Cameron was ushered into the house by Danny. She could hear their animated conversation as she came down the stairs.

"Hey, Mr. Cameron, I'm sure glad you could help me make my car."

"No problem, Sport. Where's your mom?" It was that wonderful voice. That wonderful masculine voice. Gina paused at the door just to listen, fearful that if she crossed the threshold too soon, she just might break the spell of the moment. She needn't have worried. Danny broke it for her.

"She's upstairs changing her clothes. She didn't want to look like a rag lady."

"A rag lady?" Gary questioned.

Gina stood six feet away in complete mortification. Gone was the feeling of satisfaction that had come in fixing her hair and putting on makeup. Gone were the plans of appearing in total control and confidence.

"That's *bag* lady, and Danny you really should learn the better part of discretion." The boy shrugged and Gary laughed. Gina felt self-conscious and glanced down at her sweater and jeans.

"You look nothing like a bag lady." He smiled, and Gina noted tiny crow's-feet lined the edges of his eyes. He was obviously a man who liked to laugh. He extended his hand and formally introduced himself. "I'm Gary Cameron."

Holding his gaze a moment longer, Gina felt her pulse quicken. She put her hand in his and felt warm fingers close around hers. "I'm Gina."

For a moment neither one moved, and Gina felt hard-pressed to force herself to be the first to break the companionable silence, but finally she did. "I left the mess on the kitchen table."

"Let's get to it then," Gary said with a smile. "The sky is starting to cloud up and, knowing springtime in Kansas, we could be in for almost anything. Part of our work will need to be done outdoors so as to save you from extra cleanup."

Gina nodded. "It's this way." She walked to the kitchen, Gary following close behind her with Danny at his side. She pointed at the mess. "Nothing like waiting until the last minute," Gina apologized, bending over the pieces, "but I kept thinking sooner or later I would figure out what to do with it." She gazed up mischievously. "I came up with a few ideas, but none of them seemed to benefit Danny or the derby."

Gary held up a small, red toolbox. "We'll have you on your way before you know it. We can carve it out today, and if Danny is willing to work hard at sanding it down, I can come back over and we'll work on it some more tomorrow."

"We go to church tomorrow," Danny declared.

"So do I," Gary replied. "But I was thinking maybe the afternoon would work out for us."

"Won't your wife feel neglected?" Gina asked without thinking.

"My wife and son were killed in a car accident four years ago," Gary said matter-of-factly.

"I'm sorry. Danny's father died in an accident three years ago. His car was hit head-on by a drunk driver."

Gary picked up the car kit. "Lot of them out there."

Gina studied the sandy-haired man for a moment, and when he looked up and met her gaze, she suddenly knew that here was a man who understood her pain. Here was a man she could relate to. The look he gave her made Gina tremble at the faded memory of feeling young and loved and happy.

"So would tomorrow work out for you?" Gary asked as though they hadn't just shared a very intimate moment.

"It would be fine with me. What time?"

"How about whenever you're finished with lunch?"

"Why don't you just come for lunch and stay to work on the car?"

Gary smiled. "Sounds great."

"My mom's a good cook," Danny told the man. " 'Cept when she burns something."

Gina tousled his hair. "Which is nearly once a day because some eight-year-old demands that I come see what new creation he's built in the backyard."

"She burned the macaroni and cheese, today," Danny announced. "Do you want to see the pan? Mom says it looks like—"

"Danny, I think Mr. Cameron would prefer not to hear about our shortcomings. How about you sit down and let him get started with that. . .that. . .

thing," she interrupted, looking sadly at all the bits and pieces.

Gary laughed. "Your mom's right. We need to get a move on. We'll want to do our cutting outside, and those clouds are getting darker by the minute." Then he turned to her and flashed a quick smile. "Lunch sounds great. Church is out at noon, so, say I come here directly after?"

"Perfect," Gina replied.

Sitting down to the table, she was relieved when Gary picked up the conversation and began to explain the process of carving out the race car. She felt almost exhausted from their first encounter and needed the neutrality of woodwork. It wasn't long until Danny and Gary settled on a plan and were off to the backyard to start sawing away at the block of wood.

Watching from the kitchen window, Gina couldn't remember the last time she'd had this much fun. She and Danny had remained rather isolated after the accident, but now she honestly felt ready to deal with people again. Oh, it wasn't that she didn't have friends. She had several she felt comfortable enough to spend time with. But for the most part, it was go to church on Sunday, home-school Danny through the week, and go to Scouts on Tuesday nights. Well, Danny went to Scouts. Gina usually sent him with Telaine and her boys and used the quiet evenings to get personal matters done that she couldn't accomplish with Danny in tow.

Telaine had been sympathetic to her needs and, because of her continual ability to be organized even in the face of adversity, Telaine had honestly helped Gina to get through the last three years. But now, Gina felt it was time to throw off her isolation.

It was funny how spending an afternoon with Gary Cameron had helped her to realize that she was ready to get on with her life again. She felt rather like a flower, opening up to the sun. Hadn't God promised He'd turn her mourning into laughter? At this she heard Danny's giggles and saw that Gary was bent over examining something in Danny's hand.

It was the rain that finally drove them into the house. Lightning flashed and thunder shook the windows, but the storm moved through quickly and the trio seemed perfectly content to ignore it as Gary explained how to sand the wood smooth.

The afternoon passed nearly as quickly as the storm, and Gina was almost ashamed when Danny complained of being hungry. She'd completely forgotten to feed the child lunch after the macaroni and cheese fiasco.

"I could use something, myself," Gary said, putting away his coping saw. "How about we go have a hamburger?"

"Can we, Mom?"

Danny's hopeful expression seemed to match the one on Gary's face. Gina grinned. "French fries, too?"

"And onion rings!" Gary declared as though closing an important business deal.

"And maybe a banana split," Danny added.

"Yeah," Gary agreed.

"Let me get my purse," Gina said, but Gary stopped her before she could move.

"My treat," he said in a voice that was nearly a whisper.

Gina could only nod. It'd been so long since anyone had offered to pay their way or treat them to anything. "Let's go."

⁂

Later, with half-eaten burgers on the table and Danny off to climb the restaurant's playground equipment, Gina found herself companionably settled with Gary. It was amazing that a chance encounter with Danny's scoutmaster could leave her feeling as though she'd finally found all the answers to a lifetime of questions.

When Gary reached out to cover her hand with his, she bit her bottom lip and looked deep into serious blue eyes. "This seems unreal," she whispered.

"I was thinking the same thing," Gary replied.

Gina swallowed hard. "You can't possibly understand, but I haven't even been out with anyone since Ray died."

"I can understand. I haven't dated since Vicky and that was high school. I never thought I'd have to do it again, and when she and Jason died, I decided I never would. But there's something about this," he said, looking off to where Danny was happily climbing the wrong way up the slide. "I suppose it sounds cliché, but I don't want it to end. I've been alone for four years and now, all of a sudden, it seems unbearable to go even one more week this way."

"I know," Gina said softly. "I figured I would just handle things on my own. That together, Danny and I could face anything and be just fine. Then Danny started saying things that made me realize how selfish I'd been in hiding away. He misses having a dad around."

"I miss being a dad," Gary said, turning to look at her. His gaze pierced Gina to the heart. "I miss being a husband, too. I don't have any interest in the singles' scene or one-night stands."

Gina swallowed hard. "I can't believe I'm saying all this—it really isn't like me to just open myself up like this. But, sometimes, when Danny's asleep and the house is all quiet, I'm almost afraid the silence will eat me alive." She paused for a moment to collect her thoughts. "Other times, like when the car won't start and I haven't a clue what's wrong or when Danny needs a race car carved out of wood, I feel too inadequate to meet the demands of being a single mom."

"It always hits me when I go out to eat, like this," he said, breaking away from the trancelike stare to look where Danny was happily playing.

Gina glanced at her watch and realized it was getting late. She should be making some comment about going home. But she didn't want to. She thought back on the years of emptiness and knew she didn't want to let this opportunity pass her by. It might seem crazy to have such strong feelings on a first date, and not even a real date at that, but something in her heart told her to take a chance. *Please God,* she prayed silently, *don't let me make a fool of myself.*

Gary spoke again, breaking her thoughts. "There are all these couples and their kids and a single man sticks out like a sore thumb. But I come anyway. And that's why I continue as a scoutmaster. Sometimes it's just nice to hear the laughter."

"We laugh a lot at my house," she said softly.

Gary looked at her with registered understanding. "I'm pretty good at fixing cars, and you've already seen what I can do with wood."

Gina smiled. "And I'm sure the house would be anything but silent with you around."

"So where do we go from here?" Gary asked quite seriously.

Gina felt her pulse quicken. He was interested. He felt the same way she did. She gave a light cough to clear her throat.

"I guess we'll have to let God decide the distant future, but for now we have a date for tomorrow. Dinner at my house."

Gary nodded. "Can I bring something?"

She wanted to laugh and tell him he was already bringing the most important missing ingredient in her frustrating life, but she didn't. "Just yourself," she replied with a smile, then remembered the pinewood derby car. "Oh, and some paint."

"Paint?" he questioned, his mind clearly not following her train of thought.

"For the car," she replied.

"Of course," he said nodding. "Danny said he wanted red and I just happen to have a can of cherry red gloss in my garage."

Two

Sunday dawned overcast and humid. Gina looked from the skies to the half-dressed little boy at her side and sighed. "Looks like another stormy day," she told him, reaching down to button his dress shirt.

"Are we still having s'ketti for lunch?" Danny asked hopefully.

"You bet," Gina replied, helping him tuck the shirt into his pants. "There. Now you look absolutely charming. Every little girl in Sunday school will notice how handsome you are."

"Oh, Mom," the boy replied, his expression very sober, "I can't be worried about that right now. I got lots of time to get a girlfriend and get married. First I want you to get married."

Gina smiled and knelt in front of her son. "I know you want that. And for once in a very long time, I think I want it, too. I think we should both pray about it and trust God for the answer."

"I think Mr. Cameron would make a good husband for you. He's strong and he knows how to fix cars and you don't know how to fix cars," Danny said seriously. "Mr. Cameron also told me that you have a smile that's like sunshine."

Gina felt herself blush. "Oh, he did, did he?" Could it be the heart of a poet beat within that Cub leader facade? "Well, we will just have to see what happens. Now come on or we'll be late for church."

They pulled into the church parking lot just as thunder rumbled low. It continued rumbling off and on throughout Sunday school and church, but always it seemed to hang off in the distance. Gina gave it very little thought, however, as she hurried Danny into the van and headed for home.

She felt as giddy as a schoolgirl going on her first date. A man was actually coming to the house. A handsome man who was interested in her for more than just the pinewood derby.

"Danny, get changed right away and come help me in the kitchen," she called as Danny disappeared into his room. She hurried into her own room and tried to figure out what to wear. She was just reaching for a sleeveless cotton blouse when the weather radio sounded a warning alert. Reaching for the button that would let her hear what the latest weather update revealed, Gina kicked off her shoes and pulled at the zipper in her skirt.

"This is the National Weather Service office in Topeka," the male voice announced. "The Severe Storms Forecast Center in Kansas City, Missouri, has issued Tornado Watch #237 to be in effect from 12:30 P.M. until 6 P.M. This watch is for an area along and sixty miles either side of a line from St. Joseph, Missouri, to Council Grove, Kansas. Some of the counties included in the watch are. . ."

"Great," Gina muttered. "Just what we needed." The man was continuing the routine speech, giving the names of counties to be on the watch for severe weather and telling what a tornado watch entailed. To Gina, who had lived in Kansas all of her life, the information was something she could quote line for line, including the pattern of counties as they were given for a specific area. But even as she mimicked the weatherman's announcement, Gina took the matter in complete seriousness.

"Danny, we're in a tornado watch," she called out. "Make sure you have your bag ready." Danny's bag consisted of treasures he wanted to protect in case they had to make a mad dash for the basement.

"Did you put new batteries in my flashlight?" Danny questioned at the top of his lungs.

"Check it for yourself," Gina replied, slipping on comfortable khaki slacks.

"Wow!" Danny hollered back. "It shines really bright now. Just like when it was new."

"Well, pack it in your bag and take it downstairs," Gina instructed.

Going to the window, Gina glanced out to check the skies. Nothing appeared overly threatening. There were heavy, gray clouds off to the west, but otherwise it actually seemed to be clearing in their area. She knew this could be both good and bad. Cloud coverage usually kept the temperature down and since higher temperatures seemed to feed the elements necessary for stronger storms, she would have just as well preferred the clouds remain.

Deciding not to worry about it, Gina clicked the radio off and grabbed her own bag of precious possessions. Her bag, more like a small suitcase, contained important household papers and photos that were irreplaceable. Usually when the storm season began, she simply took the case downstairs and left it there; but this year the weather had been fairly mild through March and there hadn't been any real need to worry about it.

Trudging downstairs, Gina found Danny already in the basement. The basement was small and unfinished, but Gina had tried to make it homey for situations just like this. She had put in a small double bed for those times when the storms seemed to rage all night long. It had come in handy last year when the season had been particularly nasty. There were also a table and chairs and several board games she and Danny could play if they wanted to keep their minds off the storms.

There were also more practical things. Under the stairs, Ray had enclosed the area for storage and for protection if a storm was actually bearing down on them. They had heard it was the strongest place for shelter and so it was here that they would take their last line of defense. Gina had placed a supply of batteries, candles, matches, and bottled water on a narrow section of shelving that Ray had built for just such a purpose. There was also a battery-operated television, and Gina stored her extra linens and blankets here as well. The only other thing was an old mattress that had been propped against the wall. Ray had always told her that if a tornado was actually headed for them, they would pull the mattress down on top to help shield their bodies from the possibility of flying debris. They'd never had to use it, but Gina was ready and it made her feel safe just knowing that it was there.

She knew her friends often laughed about the cautious manner in which she dealt with storms, but she still had nightmares about a time when she had been young and a tornado had devastated the farm she'd lived on. After seeing firsthand what a tornado could do, Gina knew she would never take the matter for granted.

"Mom, are we gonna have a tornado this time?" Danny questioned, securing his bag under the game table.

"I sure hope not. Why don't we say a little prayer just in case." Danny nodded and Gina bowed her head. "Dear God, please keep us safely in Your care, no matter the weather, no matter our fears. Let us remember that You hold us safely in Your hands."

"Amen," Danny said loudly. "Can we eat now?" He looked up at her with a mischievous grin.

"I still have to boil the pasta," she told him. "Let's get upstairs and you can set the table while I see how the sauce is doing."

"Don't forget the bread."

"I won't," she told him, giving his backside a playful swat.

They worked silently, Danny setting the table with the good dishes and Gina trying to imagine what it would be like to have a regular Sunday meal with a man at her table. She tried not to make too much of it. She wasn't one of those women who couldn't cope in life without a man at her side, but she did realize how much nicer it was to have the companionship of another adult. Especially a male adult.

She had just pulled the bread from the oven when the front doorbell sounded. "That's him!" Danny yelled from the living room.

"Well, let him in," Gina replied and hurried to drain the pasta. She arranged spaghetti on each of their plates and had started to ladle the sauce on top of this when Gary came into the kitchen, a two-liter bottle of cola in his arms along with a bouquet of flowers.

"I brought flowers for the lady of the house and drink for all," he announced, giving her the flowers with a sweeping bow.

Gina laughed. "They're beautiful, but you really shouldn't have."

Gary sobered, his blue eyes seeming to darken as he beheld her. "And why not?"

Gina couldn't think of any reason and simply shrugged. "You're just in time. I only need to slice the bread."

"Let me," Gary said, putting the soda on the counter. He immediately glanced around for a knife.

Gina handed him a slender knife and pointed him in the direction of where she'd placed the bread to cool. Just then the unmistakable sound of the weather radio shattered their companionable silence.

"Danny, please run up to my room, unplug the radio, and bring it down here," Gina ordered. Danny, knowing the seriousness of the matter, took off in a flash and quickly brought her the radio.

Gina punched the button in time to hear that a tornado warning had been issued for Morris County. "A tornado was spotted on the ground five miles west of the town of Wilsey. People living in and around the areas of Wilsey and Council Grove should take immediate cover."

"And so it begins," Gary said, trying to sound lighthearted about the matter.

Gina nodded and continued listening to the information. "It sounds like the storms are moving our way, but not very fast. Maybe we'll have time for lunch before we have to concern ourselves with anything too serious."

"I'm sure we'll be just fine," Gary replied. He held up the bread like a prize. "This is ready."

"Well, let's eat then," Gina declared, bringing the plates of spaghetti to the table.

Gary offered to give the blessing and when he did, Gina felt tears come to her eyes. Ray used to pray over the meals in a similar manner, and hearing Gary's voice only served to bring back the memory in a bittersweet wave.

Caught up in the memory, Gina didn't even realize Gary had concluded the prayer until Danny asked if he could have some bread. She pulled herself together and looked up with a smile.

"Of course you may," she told her son and watched while Gary handed him a slice.

Gary had just begun to tell them tales of his own days as a Cub Scout when the radio went off once again. This time, it seemed, another storm had popped up in Wabaunsee County just to the west of them. It was only a thunderstorm warning, but both Gary and Gina knew how dangerous these things could be.

Danny ate with great enthusiasm, apparently oblivious to the look that flashed between Gina and Gary. The weather was making it impossible for Gina to eat, but she tried to give the pretense in order to keep Danny calm. Gary smiled reassuringly until another tornado warning, this one issued for towns much closer to their own, sounded on the radio.

"You do have a basement, right?"

She nodded, feeling better knowing that if she had to endure a bad storm, she would at least have Gary's company through the worst of it.

"Danny and I are all prepared."

"Why don't we just move our dinner downstairs?" Gary suggested. "Then we can more or less ignore the radio and just have a good time. We can even work on the car down there, although I wouldn't want to paint it there. The fumes would probably make us all goofy by the end of the day. In fact, with the humidity the way it is, I wouldn't suggest painting it today anyway. We can work on the axles and wheels and add the weights. I even brought a scale to make sure it's regulation weight."

Gina nodded as the radio once again sounded the

alarm. "I guess we could move everything downstairs. The basement isn't finished or very nice to look at, but I do have a table and chairs down there. And you do have an after-dinner activity. . . ."

"Then lead the way," Gary said, jumping to his feet. "Danny, you grab up the bread and take your silverware. Gina, you bring your plate and Danny's—oh, and don't forget your silver. I'll bring the rest."

Gina liked the way he took charge and only paused long enough to grab the weather radio as she headed downstairs. They might as well have it with them to know what was going on, even if they didn't have to worry about taking cover. Of course, it was always possible a tornado could plop down nearby and then she would want to get under the staircase, but that wasn't something she wanted to think about just now. She wanted things to be calm and for the storms to go away, and she nearly laughed out loud as she made her way down the basement stairs. How dare stormy weather interfere with her date with Gary!

"This is a real adventure," Danny declared as Gina put his plate on the table. "We're having fun, aren't we, Mom?"

Gina forced a smile. "I think you have the right attitude about it. When life gives you a storm, look for the silver lining."

"Or the basement," Gary called out as he made his way down the stairs. His arms were filled and Gina hurried to help him. "I'll be right back," he told her as he put his plate on the table. "I'm going to get our drinks and napkins—and my little red toolkit."

Within a few moments he had returned, and as he took his seat at the ancient plastic-top table, the radio announced additional tornado sightings. Gina felt herself tense. She didn't realize how evident it was, however, until Gary reached over and gave her arm a gentle pat.

"You have a nice cozy place here," he said, glancing around the room.

"We had to spend all night down here last year," Danny told him between bites of food. "We even home-schooled down here."

"Oh, so you're home-schooled," Gary replied. And with that he set the conversation in full swing and soon even Gina was caught up in explanations of how home-schooling worked and what she tried to accomplish. Danny related wonderful field trips they'd taken and how he even joined the soccer team at the local YMCA.

She was so engrossed in the conversation that when the tornado sirens actually went off and the radio weatherman announced that a tornado had been sighted not ten miles from where she lived, Gina was completely surprised.

It was only then that she noticed the rain beating down on the basement window. The window well was already filled with about two inches of water. Lightning flashed and thunder roared right behind it, betraying the fact that the storm was right upon them.

Gina tried to take a deep breath in order to calm herself. She silently prayed for courage and calm in order to keep Danny from being afraid, but already she could read the fear in his eyes. When he left his place at the table and came to her, Gina wordlessly pushed back from the table and took the boy onto her lap. Eight was a difficult age for a child, especially a boy. They needed independence and rough soccer games and all-night camp-outs with their friends. But sometimes they still needed their mothers' laps and hugs that reassured them that all would be well.

Gina wrapped her arms around Danny's trembling body and kissed his forehead. "We're in God's hands, Danny," she whispered.

Gary reached over and stroked Danny's back. "Don't worry, Sport, it'll be over before you know it." He spoke to Danny, but it was Gina's eyes he looked into.

Gina drew strength from his calm demeanor.

"Why don't we play a game?" Gary suggested.

Danny peaked his head up. "Which one?"

"Hmmm, I don't know, how about—"

Just then a roaring boom of thunder shook the whole house and the lights went out. The room was dark except for the flashes of lightning that seemed to come one right on top of the other and penetrated through the small basement windows.

"How about Blindman's Bluff?" Gary said with a laugh. "We won't even need blindfolds."

Gina laughed, amazed that Gary's presence could give her so much peace. God had known she would need help, and even though the storm raged overhead and the electricity had been knocked out, she realized she wasn't half as afraid as she might have been had she and Danny been alone. Sometimes it was just easier to bear the storms of life when you had someone to stand beside you.

❧

By evening the storms had calmed and the weather had turned peaceful. The electricity had even been restored, and Gina noted that everything still appeared to be in one piece as they moved back up from the basement. The radio droned softly from the kitchen, announcing the forecast for the evening to be clear.

Gina walked Gary to the front door and laughed. "Well, it wasn't exactly how I figured our first date would go."

Gary stopped in mid step and looked at her seriously. "This wasn't a date."

Gina swallowed hard. Had she misread him? "It wasn't?"

"No," Gary said, shaking his head. "You don't take eight-year-olds on romantic dates. I have something special planned for our first date. You doing anything on Friday night?"

Gina grinned, feeling a sense of elation wash over her. "That depends on what you have in mind. I was going to clean out the refrigerator and wash my hair. Can you top that?"

Gary gave her a look that made her want to melt into a puddle at his feet. "I think I can manage to beat that out. How about I pick you up around seven and we go out for a nice grown-up dinner and then take a walk at the lake?"

Gina tilted her chin up while she considered her options. "Hmmm, that's a tough choice. Dinner with a handsome man and a romantic, moonlit walk or burying myself in condiments and soapsuds." She watched a grin spread across his face. "I guess the fridge can wait."

"Good. Seven o'clock sharp," he said. "Oh, and if you're free on Saturday, we can paint the car. That should give us plenty of time to detail it out for the race."

"Sounds like a winner to me," Gina replied.

She watched him climb into his car and didn't stop watching until he'd backed out of her drive and headed off down Humboldt Street. *This was definitely the start of something exciting,* she thought. *Please God, let it be real.*

Three

Gary showed up at seven o'clock sharp. He looked down at his navy suit and red-patterned tie and hoped it would meet with Gina's approval. He hadn't felt this nervous since. . .well. . . since the last time he'd showed up for a first date. Taking a deep breath, he punched the doorbell and waited for Gina to answer.

"God, don't let me push too hard or act out of line," Gary prayed aloud. Just then Gina opened the door and the vision took his breath away. She smiled a smile that went all the way to her blue eyes. . .and to his heart.

"Good evening," Gary said, struggling to control his breathing.

"Good evening," she replied.

He faltered. Should he compliment the way she looked? Should he say that the cream-printed dress looked particularly nice—that he liked the way she'd styled her shoulder-length brown hair? His mouth felt dry.

"Ah. . .um. . .you look really great," he stammered.

She looked down briefly, then returned her gaze to meet his eyes. "Thank you, you do, too."

His mind went blank. What was he supposed to do now?

Gina stepped back from the door. "Would you like to come in for a minute. I just need to check on something upstairs, and I'll be ready to leave."

"Sure," Gary replied, following her into the house. He waited while she went about her business, wishing he felt more at ease. *This shouldn't be such a big deal,* he told himself. But it was a big deal.

It seemed strangely quiet without Danny's rambunctious voice, and Gary figured this would be as good a way to break the ice as any. "Where's your son?" he called out.

"Staying with the Applebee twins," she replied, coming back down the stairs, securing her right earring. "He was very excited to be able to have a sleep-over at their house." She lowered her voice to a whisper and added, "They have two horses and some chickens, don't you know."

Gary laughed. "Yes, and a dog who's got a litter of six-week-old puppies as I recall."

Gina nodded. "So are you ready?"

"I thought I was."

This caused Gina to pause and look at him rather sternly. "Is there a problem?"

Gary thought she almost looked alarmed, as if he might back out of their date and ruin the evening. "I'm nervous," he finally admitted.

She grinned. "Me, too. I thought I'd pass out when I opened the door."

This finally broke the tension, and Gary smiled. "That makes two of us. Why are we acting like this?

We're grown adults and we've been through all this before."

"Yes, but not with each other," Gina replied.

"True, but that shouldn't matter."

Gina gave him a look of disbelief. "But of course it matters. You haven't learned my hideous secrets yet. You don't know how I look when I wake up in the morning or how I keep house or cook—with the exception of spaghetti."

"Which was fantastic," Gary interjected. "And exactly what secrets could you have that would make the prospects of spending time with you any less attractive?"

"I don't know, but there are bound to be some. You know how it can be. I remember arguing with Ray over stupid little things."

"Like what?"

"Like not leaving dirty clothes all over the floor but rather in the hamper," Gina began.

"A horrible secret to be sure," Gary teased. "Okay, what else?"

"Well, we used to clash when it came to vacations. I liked to go to quiet places far removed from the tourists. Ray liked to hit all the tourist traps."

"Anything else?"

"I like to read in the evening when Danny goes to bed."

"Hmmm," Gary said, stroking his chin, "Did that habit come about before or after Ray died?"

Gina blushed. "Well, I have to admit, it came about after."

"So. . .if you had something better to do, you might reconsider?" Gary questioned, a mischievous expression on his face.

"I might."

"Well, I just don't see a problem. I'm a very flexible man. I like most foods, love to travel and try new things, but am just as happy to sit still and do nothing. I have given myself a lot of consideration, and I just don't think I have too many flaws that will interfere or create a conflict with our personalities."

Gina smiled. "In all seriousness, we don't know much about each other."

"That's why we're dating," Gary replied. "And I'm starving, so can we continue this conversation at the restaurant?"

Gina nodded. "I was beginning to think I should just warm up some leftovers."

Gary took hold of her arm and maneuvered her toward the door. "Not that I wouldn't enjoy another sampling of your cooking, but I've got special plans for tonight."

He liked the way she looked up at him, her eyes wide with curiosity, her expression betraying her anticipation. She brought back all the excitement of his youth, and suddenly he believed in love at first sight.

❧

Dinner passed in pleasantries and memories of Danny and days gone by. Gary enjoyed listening to Gina talk about her childhood and tried to imagine the brown-haired beauty as a tagalong child in pigtails.

"I've often thought I'd like to move back to the country and live on a farm again," Gina told him.

"Honestly?" Gary questioned. "I've considered such a thing myself."

"You're just saying that to impress me," Gina teased.

"No. I'm serious. I think a farm could be a lot of fun."

Gina laughed lightly. "It's also a lot of work. Things don't just take care of themselves. I'm always trying to explain that to Danny. Especially when he nags me for a puppy."

"I've no doubt that's true," Gary replied. "I didn't mean I wanted to actually run a big farm. Plow the fields and plant and harvest. I doubt I'd be any good at that and if that's what you had in mind, then maybe we have reached our first clash of personalities."

Gina shook her head. "No, I don't desire to go back to that headache. But I love the way the air smells in the country. The ground freshly plowed, wheat when it nears harvest, the scent of the trees after a summer rain. . ."

Gary smiled and nodded, then his smile faded as he caught sight of someone across the room. He tried to regain control of his emotions, but Gina was too quick for him.

"What's wrong?"

Gary tried to figure out what to say. He didn't want anything to spoil their evening. But, because the man he'd spied was now walking toward their table, Gary knew his wish wasn't going to come true.

Tensing, he took a long drink of his iced tea and waited.

"Hello, Gary."

Gary looked up at the same time Gina did. "Hello, Jess," Gary said rather stiffly.

"I think this is the first time I've seen you out with a woman since Vicky died," the man replied, his voice clearly hostile.

"Gina, this is Jess Masterson. My father-in-law."

Gina reached out her hand, but Jess clearly ignored her. "I suppose you haven't heard yet, but there's going to be a rather sticky issue brought up before the city council."

"And you're no doubt behind it," Gary replied, not even bothering to hide his hostility.

Masterson smiled. "As a matter of fact, I am."

"So why is this sticky issue something you needed to bring up at my dinner?"

The older man shrugged. "Because it has to do with your pet project of Scouting."

"Scouting?" Gary shook his head. "What in the world are you talking about?"

Masterson glanced around the room, noted his party and waved, then turned to Gary and Gina. "I'm strongly pushing to drop all funding for Scouting given by the city."

Gary felt unquestionable anger surfacing. "And what did the Scouts do to offend you?"

"They're an elitist group. They force those who join to participate in religious indoctrination. I'm suggesting," he paused and smiled, "or rather demanding, that the Scouts eliminate any ties to 'God' in their organization or the city will have to discontinue its support. There's that whole separation of church and state thing, you know."

Gary clenched his jaw tightly, and before he could speak, Gina replied, "I'm sorry you feel that way, Mr. Masterson. I'm afraid if they removed the funding from Scouting it would make it more difficult, but I doubt it would do away with the local organization. Even if you could remove a focus on God and country from Scouting, it wouldn't change anything. Scouting is not part of the church or government. We joined voluntarily because we honor the values of Scouting. No one is forcing anyone else to join."

"No, but they are forcing taxpayers to help support the organization. That isn't acceptable when it's such a selective organization."

"And do you speak for the majority, Mr. Masterson, or for a select few?" Gina countered.

Gary wanted to applaud her bold attitude, but he knew that sooner or later Masterson would drag her to the ground over the issue. He started to interject his own thoughts on the matter, but Masterson spoke before he could answer.

"I speak for the law of the land, Miss—"

"Mrs. Bowden," Gina replied.

Masterson scowled as he threw Gary a look of disgust. "Dating married women, Gary?"

Gina slammed down her fork at this. "I am a widow, Mr. Masterson. Not that I think it's any of your concern, but because you are a very rude man I will clear the matter before you continue to prejudge the situation. I am also the mother of a Cub Scout. I fully support the Boy Scouts of America and their desire to put God at the center of their organization. Perhaps if more people put God at the center of their lives, this would never be an issue. However, because you are so intent on bringing up issues of separation of church and state, perhaps you should research the origins of those issues and read for yourself that while our forefathers had no desire to allow government to organize or prohibit religious affairs for the people, Thomas Jefferson wrote quite eloquently of the need for Christian values in government."

"He also wrote of the need to have a revolution every twenty years," Masterson retorted.

"And perhaps we should," Gina replied hotly. "Perhaps if we'd had a revolution the first time someone suggested the elimination of God from the foundations of our society, we wouldn't be in the situation we are today."

"You are naive, Mrs. Bowden."

"And you are out of line, Jess," Gary said, getting to his feet. "I came here for a nice quiet dinner, not for a political-religious debate. I suggest you join your party and allow us our privacy."

Jess Masterson's dark eyes seemed to narrow on Gary as if he were sizing up his opponent. "I simply thought you'd like to know about the situation."

"You could have called me at home. You know the number."

Masterson looked as though he'd like to say more but simply nodded and quickly walked away from the table. Gary watched him rejoin his own group before taking his seat. The evening had been quite successfully ruined as far as he was concerned.

Calling for the check, Gary hoped he might be able to salvage at least part of their date by going on the romantic walk he'd promised. But as they reached the parking lot, a light rain began to fall and his plans were thoroughly thwarted.

But Gina came to the rescue.

"Well, why don't we forget about the walk and go back to my place instead? I have a couple of movies I checked out from the library and I could fix us some popcorn." She slid into the car and smiled. "Or we could just sit and talk politics."

Gary let his anger fade. "I think the first part sounds good."

Coming around to the driver's side, Gary felt as though he should somehow try to explain Jess Masterson and his anger. When he climbed behind the wheel, he sat silently for several seconds, trying to figure out how best to begin.

"I'm sorry for that," he finally said, not even bothering to start the engine. "Jess has been angry at God ever since Vicky and Jason died."

"He blames God rather than the drunk who hit them?"

"Vicky didn't die right away, and Jess, who was always a bit mixed on his feelings about God and

Christianity, began to pray as he'd never prayed in his life. He pleaded with God to save Vicky. She was an only child, you see. And with Jason already dead and Vicky so severely injured, Jess wanted to grab at any lifeline being offered."

"But she died anyway," Gina whispered.

Gary turned to look at her. The compassion and understanding in her expression made him want to take her in his arms. She knew that pain and longing. "Yes, she did. After nearly thirty-six hours of fighting for her life, Vicky died. Jess went ballistic, and Cissy, Vicky's mom, collapsed into my arms in tears. Cissy was a strong believer; so was Vicky. Jason was only four, but he loved to go to Sunday school and church. Cissy and I got through by turning to God, but Jess alienated himself from God and rejected the whole line of comfort. He said if God cared so much He would never have allowed Vicky and Jason to die in the first place."

"I think that's a pretty normal response," Gina replied. "I remember feeling rather hostile, myself. I knew God was still there for me, but I wasn't sure I wanted His kind of comforting. After all, He could have kept Ray alive and He didn't."

Gary nodded. "I know. I felt that way, too, at least initially. God brought me past that point, however."

"Yes, He did that for me as well, but," Gina said quite seriously, "I wanted to come past that point. I wanted to let go of Ray and the accident and the anger of blaming the man who killed him—blaming anyone. Jess Masterson doesn't appear to be a man who wants to get beyond those things. How does his wife deal with him?"

"She died last year. Cancer," Gary replied flatly.

"Poor man," Gina said, shaking her head. "He must have been devastated."

Gary's heart warmed at Gina's compassion for the man who'd just so angrily berated her. "You're a special lady, Gina Bowden," he said softly, reaching out to touch her cheek.

Gina held his hand in place with her own hand. "I guess this date turned out to be rather revealing, after all. I'm not sorry for what happened. I hope you won't be, either."

Gary took a deep breath and let it back out. She had such a calming effect on him. He smiled. "No, I'm not sorry. I'd pay good money to see you take Jess to task again the way you did in the restaurant. I don't think he expected that out of you."

Gina grinned. "Like I said, it's been a very revealing evening."

"Revealing but not very romantic," Gary said almost apologetically.

"Well," Gina said, removing her hand from his, "the night's still young."

Four

Saturday dawned in complete pandemonium. Telaine called early to say that Danny had been begging to come home since six that morning. It seemed to have something to do with the fact he was going to work on his pinewood derby car with Mr. Cameron. Then, after assuring Telaine that it was all right to bring Danny home before the agreed upon nine-thirty, Gina had to face the fact that her dryer had given up and was now completely useless.

It had been some time since she'd hung clothes outside, but after wiping down the lines, she went to work and actually found she enjoyed the task. It brought back memories of childhood, when all of their clothes had been line-dried. She remembered how sweet their things had smelled after being outside in the sunshine.

She had just managed to empty her laundry basket when she made out the unmistakable sound of someone pulling into her front driveway. No doubt it was Telaine with Danny. Then a feeling washed over her. *Surely Gary wouldn't be coming at this hour,* she thought, looking down at her watch. It was only just now eight-thirty. She felt her pulse quicken.

She hurried through the house, leaving the empty basket in the laundry room, and had just reached the front door when someone knocked loudly from the other side. Opening it, Gina found herself face-to-face with a delivery man and a huge bouquet of flowers.

"How beautiful!" she exclaimed, taking the flowers in hand.

"Mrs. Bowden, will you sign here?" the man requested.

Gina smiled, smelled the flowers, and nodded. "Who are they from?" she questioned as she took the pen he offered.

"There's a card," the man replied. "That should tell you everything you need to know."

She nodded again and handed the man his pen. "Wait a minute and I'll get your tip."

"No need, ma'am. I've already been tipped sufficiently for this delivery."

With that, he was gone. Gina closed the door slowly and savored the aroma of hothouse flowers. She put the glass vase on the kitchen table and opened the card. After sitting up until midnight talking with Gary, she had little doubt that the flowers were from him.

But they weren't.

My sincerest wish is to be forgiven for my rude behavior. If I offended or otherwise caused you pain, I am sorry.

Jess Masterson.

"Well, I'll be," Gina whispered, looking at the card again to make certain she'd read it correctly.

The bouquet was clearly an expensive one. Gina didn't even recognize some of the flowers included in the arrangement, but the size alone made her well aware that the cost must have been considerable. Leaving them on the kitchen table, Gina threw another load of clothes into the washing machine and then returned to start some baking. She wanted to bake a batch of Danny's favorite cookies. Chocolate chip with nuts.

"Mom! Mom, I'm home!" came a yell as the front door flew open with a resounding bang.

"I'm in the kitchen," she called to her son.

"Mrs. Applebee says to tell you I was good," Danny declared coming into the kitchen. "I got to ride the horse and play with the puppies. Those puppies are sure cute and one of them liked me a whole lot. Do you suppose we could have one? Where's Mr. Cameron?"

All of this came without Danny drawing a single breath or pausing long enough for a comment or answer from his mother. Gina looked at the rambunctious boy and laughed. "He's not here yet. No we can't have a puppy right now. I'm sure they were very cute, however, and I'm glad you got to play with them and ride the horse," she replied in reverse order of his delivery. "I'm also glad you were good for Mrs. Applebee, although I can't imagine it was good that you got her up at the crack of dawn to come home."

Danny's enthusiasm remained high. "They have to get up early to feed the animals," he told her simply. "I didn't wake anybody up. The rooster did that." He came up to Gina to see what she was doing. "Are you making something I like?"

"I sure am. Chocolate chip cookies with pecans."

She had thought it impossible for Danny to look any happier. "All right!" he declared and practically started dancing around the room.

Just then the doorbell rang. "Mr. Cameron!" Danny exclaimed, heading at a full run for the door.

Gina knew he was probably right. A part of her wanted to run for the door at the same time, but instead she held back and mixed in the final ingredients for the cookies.

"Hello, Danny" she could hear Gary say from the front room. She felt flushed just thinking of the way his voice excited her. Last night had been wonderful, in spite of Jess Masterson. They had talked and shared their hearts on so many things. Gary believed in the power of God to move those pesky mountains of life, and he seemed the perfect counterpart to her own beliefs.

"Mom's making cookies," Danny told Gary as they came into the kitchen. "Can we paint the car today?" he questioned eagerly.

"I don't see why not," Gary replied. "Why don't you go get it?" Danny gave a little cheer and hurried off to his room, while Gary turned his full attention to Gina. "Good morning."

She spoke about the same time he spied the flowers. "Good morning. I see you've noticed my morning surprise."

Gary nodded. "Is it your birthday?"

She laughed. "No. They're from Jess Masterson, complete with apology. Here," she said, picking up the card. "Read for yourself."

Gary took the card and shook his head. "You must have made some impression on the old man. I've never known him to apologize to anyone."

"Well, I have to admit, I was stunned. I thought the flowers were from. . ." She paused, realizing how pretentious it might sound to admit the truth.

"From me?" Gary said, fixing his gaze on her.

Gina licked her lips and felt her face grow hot. "Yes," she finally managed to say.

Gary laughed. "I would have, but I ran by the bookstore this morning and then, well, to be honest—I forgot. The place was in chaos. We're having a sale today and there were some last-minute changes."

Gary had told her all about his bookstore, Cameron Christian Books and Gifts. Gina was fascinated to know that after many years of patronage to the store, she'd never once met or seen Gary, the owner. "I really didn't expect you to bring flowers. I just figured they were from you because I didn't know who else would have had any interest in sending them."

Gary sobered. "It sure isn't like him."

"Well, if you have his number, I'd like to call him later and thank him for the flowers. And, to accept his apology."

Gary reached out and touched one of the blossoms. "I just wonder what he's up to."

Gina frowned. "Does he have to be up to anything?"

Gary shrugged. "Unless he's changed; and after seeing him last night, I don't think that's happened."

"I think we should give the man the benefit of a doubt," Gina replied, wiping her hands on a nearby dish towel. "After all, the Bible says we're to forgive if asked."

Gary seemed to consider her words for a moment. "I just don't like it, that's all. I know Jess Masterson too well, and I'm worried that this is just his way of trying to manipulate you."

"Why would he care what I thought?" Gina asked, her temper starting to get the better of her. That Gary would act so callously and be so skeptical about his father-in-law's apology really bothered her.

"Here's my car!" Danny declared, bounding back into the kitchen.

He was totally unaware of the tension and Gina intended to keep it that way. "I'm sure you and Mr. Cameron want to get to work right away. You can either work in here or out on the patio; the choice is yours."

"Outside!" Danny declared.

"Yes, I think that would be best since we'll be spray painting," Gary agreed. He looked at Gina for a moment, his expression apologetic, then turned to Danny. "Do you have some newspapers?"

"I've been saving them just like you told me to do," Danny replied with great pride.

"Good, then go spread them on the patio table and we'll get right to work."

Danny nodded and took off through the laundry

room and out the back door.

"Look, I'm sorry," Gary said to Gina.

"Are you really, or should I doubt your apology as well?"

"Touché," Gary said, stuffing his hands into his pockets. "I guess I acted out of line."

Gina grinned. "It's all a part of that 'getting to know you' stuff. I just didn't want to think that when my apologies were necessary, you'd believe them less than sincere."

Gary nodded. "Point well taken."

Later that evening with Danny happily preoccupied with a naval battle in the bathtub, Gina picked up the telephone in her bedroom and dialed the number Gary had left for Jess Masterson.

"Hello?" a gravelly voice sounded.

"Mr. Masterson?"

"Yes."

"This is Gina Bowden. I wanted to thank you for the flowers and the apology."

There was silence for several seconds before Jess Masterson replied. "Well, I did feel bad for acting so rudely. I appreciate your willingness to look the other way."

Gina wasn't sure she agreed with his wording, but she didn't want to create yet another scene by challenging his statement, especially when she wanted to ask him more about his stand against the Boy Scouts. "May I ask you a question?"

"Certainly," Masterson replied.

"I wondered why you were so set on fighting this thing out with the Boy Scouts. I mean, I know firsthand there is a lot of local support for Scouting. I suppose I'm just curious as to why you would ruin a good thing for everyone else just because you're angry at God."

"Who said I'm doing it because I'm angry at God?" Masterson retorted, his voice betraying his anger. "I suppose that was Gary's analysis."

"Well, isn't it true? I mean, what does it matter to you if the Boy Scouts make it an issue to honor God and country?"

"It matters that they are treating others unfairly by demanding an allegiance to God."

"I fail to see how it is unfair. No one is forced to join the Boy Scouts. It isn't a requirement in order to be educated in the public school system. It isn't necessary in order to be able to vote or serve in government or other forms of public service. It is an elective club, rather like your country club, Mr. Masterson."

"But my country club doesn't interfere in my religious beliefs. I may still join the country club so long as I adhere to the rules of the club and pay my dues."

"It's no different for the Scouts," Gina countered. "We adhere to the rules. Rules about being honorable to God and country. Promises to do our best, to help other people. Oh, and we pay dues that are a whole lot less exclusive than the dues you pay to your country club."

Masterson was silent for several moments. When

he spoke, it so surprised Gina that she could do little more than agree to his idea.

"I'd like to come over and talk about this in more detail. Perhaps you could arrange for Gary to be present as well."

"When?"

"How about tomorrow?"

"We have church in the morning, but the afternoon would be fine. Say around three?"

"Thank you, that would be fine," Jess replied. "I'll see you then."

"Oh, do you have the address?" Gina questioned, forgetting about the flower delivery.

"Yes, it was in the telephone book. That's how I arranged for the flowers."

"Of course," Gina said, feeling rather silly. "Until tomorrow then."

As she hung up the phone, she heard the unmistakable sound of water being drained from the bathtub. Danny had apparently finished with his bath. She stared at the telephone for a moment, wondering why Jess Masterson would make it a point to come all the way over to her house to talk about his fight against funding for the Boy Scouts.

"I'm ready for bed," Danny announced from the doorway. Once again he'd failed to dry off before putting on his pajamas, and Gina wanted to laugh out loud at the way the material clung and bunched.

"Come here," she said with a grin. "Let me get you untwisted." She turned him around and found the entire back of the pajama top was caught up around his shoulders, leaving most of his back bare.

She adjusted his shirt, then prayed with him, and finally kissed him soundly before tucking him into his bed down the hall.

"Mommy," Danny said sleepily, "do you think if you and Mr. Cameron get married, I could call him Dad? I mean, do you think Daddy would mind?"

Gina felt her throat grow tight. "Honey, Mr. Cameron and I are just friends right now. I don't know if God would have me marry him or not, but I'm sure that's a question we don't need to worry about right now."

"I want to call him Dad when you get married," Danny said, not seeming overly concerned with Gina's words. "I'm going to pray and ask God to 'splain it to Daddy in heaven. I don't want to hurt his feelings."

Gina kissed him on the forehead. "I think Daddy will understand perfectly," she told her son. "Now get some sleep. I love you very much."

"I love you, too," Danny said yawning loudly. "And Mommy?"

"Yes?"

"I had a lot of fun today."

She smiled and tousled his hair. "I'm glad. I did, too."

There was a comfort in knowing he was safe and happy and healthy. A comfort that Gina wouldn't trade for anything in the world. Not companionship with Gary or any other man. She wanted to remarry and give Danny a father, but it had to be right. It had to be the right man and the right time. He had to be someone she could love and respect and someone who would love her and Danny as if they had belonged to him from the start. Gary had made a special place in both their hearts, but Gina knew it was important to be careful.

Back in her own room, Gina stretched out on her bed and picked up her book, a wordy intellectual piece on New Age religions. Telaine had suggested it, but Gina found it rather dry and boring. Putting it aside, her mind turned to Gary's comments on whether she read because of a lack of anything else to do. She smiled. Of course, he was partly right. She loved to read, however, and would find time for it whether she was married or single. But this time of night had always belonged to just her and Ray.

She allowed her mind to run back over the memories of her marriage. She was happy as a wife and mother. She couldn't imagine wanting anything more out of life. She didn't mind that other women wanted it all—careers, travel, children, husbands—even politics. But she was happy with things being simple and noninvasive. Even now her modest home was paid for, and she had Ray's life insurance money in the bank, which paid their living expenses. No boss called her to come in when she had something else planned with her family. No political scandal brewed outside her door while the world waited for her to make a wrong step. No one knew or cared who Gina Bowden was. It had become a comfortable anonymity.

Would a relationship with Gary change that? She

thought of his involvement with the community. His bookstore. His Scouting leadership. She had learned only that morning that he was heavily active in his church and couldn't help but wonder how that might change things for her and Danny should their relationship grow more serious.

Five

Gary didn't like the idea of Jess Masterson arranging to speak to Gina. He couldn't imagine what possible good it would do. Did the old man think to persuade her to join his cause? Furthermore, he still found it of concern that after nearly four years of absolutely no communication, Jess Masterson had also requested that Gary be present.

Pulling into Gina's driveway, Gary was just about to switch off the car when the radio announced that the area was once again under a tornado watch. *Good old Kansas weather,* Gary thought as he shut off the engine and made his way to the house.

"You're early," Gina said, greeting him before he could even ring the doorbell.

"I know," Gary said. "I guess I wanted to make sure I got here first."

"Didn't want to leave me at the mercy of the angry councilman?" Gina teased.

"Something like that."

"Well, come on in. I was just cleaning up in the kitchen."

"They've just put us in another tornado watch."

Gina nodded and picked up a dish towel. "Yes, the

weather alert radio just went off. Danny's putting his things downstairs."

"You're acting a bit prematurely, aren't you?" Gary was more than a little aware of Gina's preoccupation with storms.

"As a Scout I would think you'd approve. 'Be prepared!' Isn't that the motto?" She picked up a glass and began drying it. "We don't just sit in the basement the whole time we're in a watch. We just make ready so we can go about our business until the time comes that we need to go to the basement. The last thing I want is to have Danny running around here like some sort of frantic ninny, trying to gather up things important to him and make his way to the basement."

"But the things aren't important," Gary pressed. "Are you sure you aren't teaching him to value possessions more than life?"

Gina continued drying the glass even though Gary could see it was already dry. He'd pushed her too hard, and now she was no doubt angry at him. But to his surprise, Gina put the glass in the cupboard and picked up another.

"I suppose," she finally said, "that it might look that way to you, but it's not. Danny knows the things are unimportant. Property can be replaced and memories will live forever in your heart and mind. Being responsible for his bag of treasures is one way he feels he has some control over the situation. My mother used to do this with me and it helped a lot.

"My parents' farmhouse was built at the turn of the

century, so we had to go out into the weather to get to the storm cave and it always scared me. So, my mother decided to do what her mother had done when she was a child and give each of us kids an old pillowcase to put a few of our favorite things in. When the weather looked threatening, she'd have us take our stuff down into the storm cave. That way we had a vested interest in the cave and it was more than just some place to get to when the storms came." Gina put the glass in the cupboard and leaned back against the counter. "I like to believe that I'm helping Danny have some control over his environment. He focuses on what he can do to be ready rather than stewing about the upcoming storm."

Gary nodded. "That makes sense. I'm sorry if I sounded out of line."

Gina smiled and continued drying dishes. "A lot of folks go around doing nothing about the weather. They feel that God will protect them, and of course, He protects us all. But I feel it's important to take precautions. After all, people have been killed in these storms."

The way she looked as she said that final sentence made Gary wonder if she'd lost someone she loved in a storm. "You sound like you know better than some."

Gina nodded. "A good friend of mine died when I was thirteen. She used to laugh at my fear of storms. She and her mother teased me and said it wasn't Christian the way I fretted about things. They lived about a mile north of us and one spring a bad storm system went through and a tornado hit ground about a quarter mile southwest of our farm. I'd just come from helping Dad turn the cows out into the pasture in case things got bad. We could see it bearing down on us, and Mom and the others were already making a mad dash for the cave. I was so scared I could hardly move. The roar was bad enough, but the sight of that thing. . ." Gina shuddered and grew silent for several moments.

Gary got up and went to her. He felt bad for having made her relive such a nightmare. Gently, he pulled her into his arms and hugged her close. "You don't have to tell me any more."

Gina seemed not to hear him. "It destroyed our farm and it kept going north, where it destroyed my friend's farm, too. Only they hadn't bothered to take shelter. They weren't paying attention to the weather, and we were too far away to hear any warning siren blown in the city. The house collapsed on top of them." She began trembling.

"Shhh," Gary hushed her and stroked her hair. "It's all right."

Gina looked up at him and tried to smile. "I'm sorry. Sometimes it's still so hard to remember."

Gary cupped her chin with his hand. He looked for several seconds into her eyes. Without a doubt he had fallen in love with this woman. And now, seeing her so vulnerable and weak, he loved her even more. He wanted to protect her—to keep her safe from anything that might harm her.

She watched him with an expression that implied concern and curiosity. He hesitated only a moment, then lowered his lips to hers. Just then, the weather radio sounded, startling both of them nearly out of their wits. Gary laughed and Gina pushed away to punch the radio on. As she did, the tornado sirens started up.

"Guess we don't have to ask what the radio has to say," Gary declared, grabbing the radio and pushing Gina toward the basement stairs.

"Where's Danny?" she questioned, seeing that the basement light was off.

"I'll find him," Gary assured her. "You get downstairs." He handed her the radio, then went off in the direction of the living room.

"Danny!" he called, looking around the room. Seeing no sign of the boy, he bounded up the stairs, the constant blaring of tornado sirens in his ears. "Danny!"

The boy came streaking down the hall. "Dad!" He threw himself into Gary's arms. Neither one said anything about Danny's usage of the word *Dad*.

"Come on, Sport. Your mom's already in the basement," Gary said, lifting the boy and carrying him downstairs.

As Gary reached the bottom step, he made out the sound of knocking on the front door. Opening it, Gary came face-to-face with a stunned Jess Masterson. "Come on, Jess," Gary commanded. "Basement's this way."

The older man nodded and followed Gary. Gary felt the rapid beating of Danny's heart as the boy clung to him tightly. He longed to comfort the child, but the most important thing was to get them both out of harm's way. Gary hadn't needed to look for long at the greenish-black clouds that he saw overhead when he'd opened the door for Jess. He knew the signs were all there. The color of the clouds. The puffy fullness—indicating wind. They might well be in for it this time.

They made their way down the stairs with Gina grabbing Danny out of Gary's arms before he even reached the bottom step.

"Oh, Danny," she said, holding him tight. "I was so worried about you. Where were you?"

"I went to your room," Danny said, his lower lip quivering. "I thought you were there."

Gina hugged him close. "We're all right now, Danny. We don't have to worry. Did you say a prayer?" she questioned, taking a seat at the table.

"I think we were both saying prayers," Gary interjected, trying to lighten the mood. Outside the rain had picked up and the unmistakable sound of hail pounded down.

Gina nodded and Danny popped his head up. "I prayed." He paused only a moment and added, "Look, Mom. We found this guy at the door."

Gina looked up and smiled. "Ah, Mr. Masterson. So glad you could join us."

Gary looked over to meet Jess's expression. "You timed that just right."

"I was rather concerned," Masterson replied. "I

could see that storm coming up fast and wondered if I'd even get here before the rain started."

The lights flickered and Gary looked at Gina. "Flashlights?"

She nodded. "Danny, go get your bag and get your flashlight ready." The boy seemed to calm at this and nodded. He slipped off her lap and Gina smiled at Gary. He knew what she was thinking. Giving Danny an action, something to occupy his mind, had given the boy a sense of renewed strength.

Gina got up and went to the stairway enclosure. Opening the door, she handed out a battery-operated lantern. "I picked this up the other day. They were having a sale and I figured it would be—"

B – O – O – M!

Thunder shook the house so hard that for the briefest moment before the lights went out, Gary could see Gina's expression of sheer panic. He switched on the lantern, and Danny turned on his flashlight. By the time they could see each other again, Gina had pulled her facade of calm into place. Gary admired that she wanted to appear strong for her child, but he worried about her.

"We may be here for a spell," Gary said, motioning to the table and chairs. "Might as well have a seat, Jess."

The older man nodded and took a seat. Gina did likewise. Gary noted that Danny was already busy rummaging through his bag, apparently oblivious to the drone of the weather updates and the raging storm outside. He was safe and he knew it. He knew it because routine told him it was true and his mother's calm assured him that all was well in spite of the storm. Gary could easily see that even Gina was calming.

"So, Mr. Masterson," Gina said with a smile, "you wanted to talk with Gary and me?"

Jess chuckled. "Yes, well, I wanted to better explain my position regarding the Boy Scouts."

Danny perked up at this. "Are you a Boy Scout?" he questioned, pulling something out of his bag and coming to the table. "I'm a Cub Scout. Do you want to see my pinewood derby car?" His hopeful expression seemed to penetrate Jess Masterson's resolve.

"Sure, son," Masterson said, exchanging a quick glance with Gary before turning to the boy. "Let's see what you've done there."

"We've been working for about two weeks on it," Danny told him. "See how fast the wheels go?" The little boy ran his hand against the wheels and watched them spin.

"They do indeed go fast," Masterson agreed.

Gary listened in silence as the boy explained how they were going to have a race on the following Saturday. Danny's enthusiasm was so contagious, in fact, that when he invited Jess Masterson to be his special guest at the derby, the old man surprised them all by accepting.

Gary shook his head and walked to the window well in order to see if he could make out anything. It was usually on the back side of a thunderstorm that tornadoes made their deadly path. He glanced to where Jess Masterson was nodding to something Danny had said. Compared to his father-in-law, tornadoes were predictable.

Six

Well," Gina said as she met Gary at the door to the church community center, "it looks like clear skies for the derby."

"After last Sunday's storm," he replied, "I'm ready for clear skies from here on out."

Gina laughed. "Me, too. Thanks for helping me clean up." She could still see the mess of downed tree branches in her mind.

"No problem. Pity you don't have a fireplace."

"I'm just grateful we didn't have any more damage. I heard that the tornado touched down near a housing development on the west side of town. Destroyed about six houses."

"I heard that, too. We were fortunate no one was killed," Gary said softly.

"Yes," Gina said nodding. The thought made her shudder, and she turned quickly to watch Danny rush by her, his Cub Scout hat sitting rather cockeyed and his necktie twisted in the back. She compared his haphazard appearance with that of Gary Cameron, who stood before her wearing the adult uniform as if he were born in it. She realized all at once that he was watching her study him. Feeling her face grow hot, Gina looked away to where the boys were playing around the derby's inclined track.

"Is Jess here yet?"

"Nope, not yet. I still can't believe he agreed to come today."

"I know," Gina replied. "He hardly said two words to me after Danny latched onto him during the storm."

"Me either. I tried to call him once during the week, but I only got the answering machine. You do realize the council meets next Thursday night?"

Gina nodded. She knew Gary was worried about Masterson's plans for the Scout funding, but she also knew he was troubled by more than just that. Reaching out, she touched his arm. "What are you afraid of?"

His eyes widened for just a moment before he regained control. Then, as if deciding she deserved his honesty, Gary's expression softened. "I just don't want to see anyone hurt. Especially that little boy." He nodded to where Danny was proudly showing off his car. "I've come to care a great deal about him."

Gina smiled. "I have, too."

"Do you know he called me Dad?"

"When?" Gina questioned, remembering Danny's request to call Gary Dad if and when they married.

"During the storm. It was when I found him upstairs. He was terrified and he called me Dad."

Gina nodded. "I don't doubt it for a minute. He cares a lot about you, and. . ." She hesitated to continue.

"And?" Gary questioned, taking hold of her hand as if they were the only people in the room.

Gina licked her lips. "And he asked me if he could

call you Dad after we got married."

Gary's expression revealed surprise, almost shock. Gina tried to pull her hand away, fearing that she should never have mentioned the "M" word.

Gary held her hand fast and asked, "What did you tell him?"

"That he needed to give it time and let God show us the direction to take."

"And has He?"

"Has who—what?" she asked, feeling her senses overcome by the way he was looking at her. He seemed to reach into her soul with his eyes. Her mouth felt cottony and her hands began to tremble.

"Mr. Cameron! Mr. Cameron!" one of the Bear Cubs was shouting from across the room.

Gary grinned as if sensing his power over her. "We can discuss it later. But," he said, pausing to lean closer to her, "I think God's already shown me plenty. The path seems very clear, and if I have my way about it, we'll be making derby cars for years to come."

"Danny won't be a Cub Scout forever," Gina teased.

Gary winked. "No, but it'll take a while to get all his brothers through Cubs." With that he walked away, leaving Gina to stare after him. *His brothers! Gary was implying—*

"Hello, Gina."

Gina turned to find a very casually dressed Jess Masterson. "Hello, Mr. Masterson." She felt both regret and relief that Masterson had chosen that moment to show up.

"Now I thought we agreed that you were going to call me Jess."

Gina gave him a slight smile and eyed him as one might when considering a rattlesnake. *Caution!* Her mind seemed to warn. "I'm glad you could come, Jess," she offered.

He smiled. "I know you are making an effort where I'm concerned, but really I'm not such a bad guy."

"Why don't we take a seat. It will take a while for the leaders to get everything ready. We might as well make ourselves comfortable."

Jess nodded and followed her to a gathering of empty chairs. "I don't want you to hate me, Gina."

Gina realized how very reserved her actions must have seemed to the older man. Asking God for guidance, she took a seat and turned to Jess. "I don't hate you," she began. "I don't understand you, but I don't hate you."

Jess looked at her in a rather puzzled manner. "What don't you understand?"

Gina folded her hands and looked at them as though they were the most interesting things in the world. "Why would a grown man set out to ruin the pleasure of children? Why do grown-up politics have to creep into everything in life?" She forced herself to look at Jess. "I believe in my heart that you are doing this for two reasons."

Jess looked rather surprised. "Do continue."

Gina swallowed the lump in her throat. "I think first of all you're angry at God for not saving Vicky. I can understand that. God knows I was angry at Him after Ray died. See, my husband died in a car accident like your daughter. A drunk driver hit him broadside and killed him instantly."

"I'm sorry," Jess said, stiffening in his chair. "I didn't know."

"I think you want to get back at God, but we both know that won't work," Gina continued. "Secondly, I think you want very much to hurt Gary because he lived and Vicky and Jason died." Jess paled and looked rather shocked. But Gina didn't give him time to answer. "You and Gary could have gained strength from each other, but instead you somehow hold him responsible."

"I don't suppose Gary bothered to tell you, but Vicky and Jason were only in that car because they were on their way to pick him up from a late night of inventory work at the bookstore," Jess said rather haughtily.

"Yes, I know," Gina replied. "And my husband was on his way home to me after a business trip. Should I blame myself? Was it my fault he was killed? Better yet, maybe I should blame Danny; after all, Ray was in a hurry to get back to us because Danny's birthday was the next day." She paused and looked him square in the eye. "Or was it the fault of the drunk behind the wheel? And beyond that, do I blame God because He took away someone I loved, when it was God who gave him to me in the first place?"

"Ah, the old, 'The Lord giveth and the Lord taketh away,' " Masterson replied. This time anger was clear in his voice.

"Blessed be the name of the Lord," Gina finished.

"Meaning what?" Jess's eyes flashed in rage.

Gina reacted without thinking and placed her hand on Jess's arm. "Meaning, God is still God whether we blame Him or praise Him. Meaning God is still in charge even when we think He has somehow forgotten our zip code. Meaning God was with our loved ones when those drunks crossed their paths, and He was there when they breathed their last breath on earth and took their first steps into heaven."

Jess's expression remained fixed and rigid. "You can believe that way if it brings you comfort."

Gina smiled and squeezed his arm. "It does, Jess. It honestly does. Just knowing I don't have to bear the weight alone is more comforting than any kind of retaliation I can think of. You can go ahead with your plans against the Boy Scouts, but it won't change the fact that Vicky and Jason loved God." She paused and looked him in the eye, hoping she wasn't about to go too far. "It won't change that your wife loved Him either."

"What do you know of my wife?"

"I know what Gary told me. How she stood fast in her faith in spite of Vicky and Jason's death."

"She turned to God, but not to me," Jess said, and this time his voice sounded tired—resigned.

"She always had God, but maybe when she lost you, God became even more precious."

Jess's eyes widened in surprise. "How dare you say

something like that! You didn't know her. You don't know me."

Gina released her hold on him and smiled. "Maybe I know you better than you think. I've been hurt just like you. I've lost people I loved, and I pushed away the love of others because I feared ever feeling that emptiness again. Jess, you go ahead and do what you think you need to do, but it won't change how you feel inside right now. I just want you to remember that."

"Mr. Masterson!" Danny exclaimed. "You came!"

The man eyed Gina for a moment, then turned to greet Danny. "I told you I'd be here and I'm a man of my word."

"Come see my car," Danny said, reaching out to take Masterson by the arm.

Gina forced a smile, Masterson's words echoing in her head. *"I'm a man of my word,"* he'd said, making it both a threat and an affirmation.

❧

The afternoon passed in noisy exultation. Gina laughed to watch the boys line the pinewood derby track. It was hard to imagine that something so simple could give such pleasure. From time to time, she also caught sight of Danny with Jess Masterson. The man seemed completely caught up in the moment, and Gina actually found herself glad he'd come.

The awards were handed out and Danny enthusiastically received the award for "Best Design." She smiled, knowing that if Gary hadn't bothered to take the time to help the child, Danny would have been racing a block of wood. She smiled, wondering if they had an award for the "Most Boring Design." No doubt she could have helped Danny win that one.

When the celebration was over, they gathered their things, and while Gina helped Gary, Danny was busily talking to Jess Masterson. She headed over to rescue the man, but as she drew close enough to hear their conversation, she halted in surprise.

"I had a very nice time, Danny. Thank you for inviting me. I'd almost forgotten what it was like to be young."

"I'm glad you came," Danny replied, entwining his fingers with Masterson's. "I need a grandpa and you need a boy so you won't forget about being young. Maybe you could ask my mom about coming over all the time. You could even come to church with us."

Jess Masterson looked up to meet Gina's fixed stare. She thought she saw the glistening of tears in the old man's eyes. She knew for certain there were tears in her own eyes. When Masterson appeared to be at a loss for words, Gina rescued him.

"Danny, come give me a hand with the chairs." She smiled at Jess. "You're always welcome at our house," she said as if to answer the unspoken question in regard to Danny's statement. "And at our church."

"Thank you," Jess replied. "I need to go. Will you tell Gary good-bye for me?"

"Of course," Gina replied. She watched the man leave, wondering what the future would hold and whether or not he would accomplish his goal of removing funding from the Boy Scouts. Either way, she knew he was struggling to find his way out of sorrow and loneliness, and depriving the Scouts of city money wasn't going to change a thing.

Seven

Gina and Gary nervously took their seats at the city council meeting. Neither had spoken to Jess after the derby, and neither knew what kind of scene they would have to endure tonight. But, they had prayed about the situation and had agreed to trust God for the outcome. It would be hard on the Scouts to lose the help of the city, but it wouldn't put an end to the organization.

The meeting was brought to order, and after the rhetoric of various reports, the issue of Jess Masterson's proposal was brought to the attention of the council. Jess, who'd arrived late and had barely taken a seat before the meeting started, cleared his voice and shuffled some papers in his hands.

"If it pleases the council," he began, "I'd like to withdraw my proposal. I would also like to propose the council disregard anything I've said over the last few months." He grinned rather sheepishly and added, "I'm not sure exactly what all that might entail, but I'm certain it was probably less than well thought out."

Silence held the room as Jess continued. "I'm afraid my judgment has been altered by the recent events of my life. Some of you know I lost a daughter and grandson in a car accident. Then last year I lost my wife of forty years. Those aren't the kinds of things a man easily deals with. I'm afraid I didn't deal well with them at all."

Gina felt tears come to her eyes and did nothing to try to hide them. She smiled at Jess when he looked her way—hoping—praying that her expression offered reassurance.

"Instead of my original proposal," Jess said, nodding slightly at Gina, "I'm offering something else." He picked up a stack of papers and handed them down the table to the council. "My resignation."

There were gasps of surprise in the audience, but no one was as surprised as Gary and Gina.

"It's time I retired and did some of the things fellows my age have earned the right to do. There's a little boy out there who told me the other day he needed a grandpa. He also said that I needed a boy to remind me about being young." Jess grinned. "I think he was exactly right."

Gina tightly gripped Gary's hand. "This is unbelievable," she whispered. "I thought it was impossible for us to change his mind."

"I don't think *we* did," Gary countered. "I think Danny did."

Gina nodded. "He sure took to Jess. I guess I just never realized all the missing aspects in Danny's life. It's like he has holes in his life I never even suspected were there."

"Well, we need to get to the business of filling in those empty places, don't we?" Gary said softly.

Gina felt her breath quicken. She knew what Gary was implying. It was time to make a commitment. "Maybe we could leave the meeting?"

The council was already going through the motions of dismissing Jess's earlier proposal and accepting his resignation. As soon as the vote was complete, Gary grabbed Gina's hand and pulled her up with him. They made their way to the back door, and Gary had already opened it when Gina stopped. Turning, she caught sight of Jess watching them. Smiling, she did the only thing she knew would clearly explain her gratitude. She blew him a kiss. Jess Masterson couldn't have looked more shocked had she shaken her fist at him, but then a tiny smile crept across his face.

Gary pulled Gina into the hall, his own expression rather stunned.

"What's the matter?" Gina questioned. "You look as though you've seen a ghost."

"Vicky used to always blow Jess a kiss good-bye whenever we got ready to leave. I guess seeing you do that just now. . .well. . .it just surprised me."

"I'd say it surprised you both," Gina replied, fearful that she'd caused more harm than good. "I hope I didn't upset him."

"From the expression on his face, I think he was touched," Gary said, raising her hand to his lips. "I know I was."

Gina felt overwhelmed by the emotions coursing through her heart and mind and soul. *God always had a way of breaking down doors,* she thought as Gary led her to the car.

They picked up Danny at the Applebees' farm, then made their way to Gina's house. Danny chattered at full speed, telling about the puppies and how much he wanted one. Gina quickly realized that any private discussion she and Gary had hoped for was now out of the question.

Gary must have realized it, too, because after they arrived home, he told Gina he needed to run some errands and couldn't stay. Disappointed but understanding, Gina bid him good-bye and watched as Danny gave Gary a big hug. Perhaps it was better this way. She needed to talk to Danny about the future and help him through any questions he might have.

As soon as Gary was gone, she turned to her son. "We need to talk," she said quite seriously.

"Did I do something wrong?" Danny asked, his face contorting as he appeared to consider the possibilities.

"No, silly," Gina said, tousling his hair. "Come sit with me on the couch. I want to talk about us. . .and about Gary."

Danny nodded. "Are you going to get married now?"

Gina laughed. "Nothing like jumping right in, eh? Well, we might as well talk it through. Would you like for me to marry Gary?"

"Yes!" Danny replied enthusiastically. "I want him to be my dad."

Gina nodded. "I know you've said that before. But I want you to realize how things might change for us."

Danny sobered. "Okay."

"Having a dad around will be a lot of fun for you. You will be able to do things with him while I do other things, and then there will be times when we have fun all together. But if I marry Gary, you will also have to mind him. Do you understand that?"

"Sure," Danny replied as if what she'd said was a given fact. "I mind him at Scouts already. Mom," he said reaching out to hug her, "I want a dad. I promise I can mind."

Gina felt her heartstrings plucked in a most evident way. "I know you can. I want you to have a dad, and I think Gary would make a great dad and a good husband. I think God has finally shown me that we would make a good family."

Danny let out a yip of excitement. "I'm gonna have a dad and a grandpa!" He got up from the couch and danced around the room.

Gina laughed at his enthusiasm. "Danny, come back here. Nothing is settled yet. Gary and I haven't even talked about getting married. I mean, not really. We need to talk about it first, and then we need to give ourselves plenty of time to make plans and get to know each other better. I need for you to know him better, too."

Danny threw himself into her arms and looked up at her. His baby face was fading more and more each day, and in its place had grown a boy's hopeful expression. "How long will it take?"

Gina laughed again and tickled Danny lightly under his arms. "Not long. Not near as long as it's taken to find the right person for the job."

❧

Gina had fully expected Gary to call her later that night, and when he didn't, she felt an emptiness inside that her newest fiction novel couldn't fill. Then when Gary didn't call on Friday or Saturday, Gina thought perhaps she'd done something to offend him. She thought back to her actions reminding everyone of Vicky and worried that she'd created a major mess of things.

Sunday found her and Danny just going through the paces. How empty it seemed without Gary. It was as if a vital part of their lives had been suddenly taken from them. It reminded her too much of how she'd felt after losing Ray. Finally, on Sunday night she broke down and gave Gary a call.

But he wasn't there. His answering machine clicked on and asked her to leave a message, but that was the only sound of his voice that Gina had. Going to bed that night, she tossed and turned fitfully. What was happening? Had Gary given up on the idea of making a commitment to her and Danny?

Monday morning, Gina awoke more tired than when she'd gone to bed. Going through the familiar routine of home-school studies and daily chores did nothing to help calm her fears. Gina had just managed to finish cleaning the bathroom, while Danny worked on multiplication facts, when the telephone rang.

"Mrs. Bowden?" a decidedly aged voice questioned from the other end of the line.

"Yes?"

"This is Nora down at Cameron Christian Books and Gifts."

Gina felt her body tense. Why should this woman be calling her? Had something happened to Gary? She could still hear the voice of the police officer who'd come to tell her about Ray's accident.

"Is something wrong?" Gina questioned, praying silently for strength.

"No," the woman assured. "Well. . .that is. . .I hope you'll forgive me, but I've neglected my duties and now I fear I've been the cause of making you worry."

"I don't understand," Gina replied softly.

"Gary asked me to give you a message last Friday and I totally forgot."

Gina felt relief wash over her. "A message?"

"Yes. Gary wanted me to tell you that he needed a few days of prayer for a special situation. He thought you'd understand. He took off for a three-day weekend. I expect him back any time, but I was supposed to let you know last Friday. I hope you'll forgive me."

Gina was so happy to hear that nothing horrible had happened to Gary that she would have overlooked any mistake the woman might have laid claim to. "That's all right, Nora. I understand how these things go." Gina listened as the woman apologized once again, then thanked her and hung up with renewed enthusiasm for the day.

Danny brought his paper to her. "I'm finished. Can I have a recess break?"

Gina smiled. "Sure thing. Oh, and that was a

woman who works at Gary's bookstore. She said she forgot to call us last Friday and tell us that Gary was taking a short trip away from town."

Danny's face brightened. "So he's coming back?"

Gina nodded. "Yes, I'm sure he will. Now you go play and I'll call you in about fifteen minutes. We still have social studies, but then we'll be done."

Danny hurried out the back door, while Gina followed in order to check on the clothes hanging on the line in the backyard. Silently she thanked God for Nora's call. She looked heavenward, noting the building clouds. It looked like the weather might once again grow threatening. Glancing at her watch, Gina saw that it was nearly three o'clock. Their worst storms took place in late afternoon and early evening. If she was fortunate, the clothes would have time to dry before the rain set in.

By five o'clock, Gina was hurrying to pull the clothes from the line. The area had been put into a severe thunderstorm watch, and from the look of the weather radar on television, storms were popping up all around them. The unmistakable darkness of the clouds to the south gave Gina little doubt the storms would soon be upon them as well.

She fixed them a light supper while Danny played quietly upstairs. The first sound of thunder rumbled in the distance, and Gina silently prayed for safety from the storm. "Danny!" she called, putting two plates on the table. "Supper!"

Danny came bounding downstairs, his storm bag in

hand. He put it by the basement door and looked up at his mother. "I brought this down just in case. I don't want to be stuck upstairs again if the sirens go off."

Gina frowned. She didn't want her son so paranoid that he couldn't go about his business when storms came. Sitting down to the table, she took hold of his hand. "Danny, we don't have to be afraid of the stormy weather. God is watching over us. He will take care us, no matter what happens. You believe that, don't you?"

Danny's eyes were wide as he nodded. "I think so," he said doubtfully. "But sometimes people die in storms. You told me about your friend."

Gina gently stroked his hand. "I know. Sometimes bad things do happen. Sometimes storms destroy homes and lives. Sometimes people are hurt by other storms in life, as well. But, Danny, I promise you—God has it all under control. He won't leave us to go through it alone. The Bible says He will be with us always."

"But sometimes you get afraid," Danny said quite seriously.

"Yes," Gina nodded. "Yes, I do. But that's when I forget to give it to God. The times I get afraid are those times when I try to take care of everything myself. When I try to be in charge—instead of letting God be in charge. Understand?"

Danny nodded. "But you said that we should be prepared."

"And we should. We should use the knowledge God has given us to help take proper care of each other and of our things. But we don't sit in the basement all day, every day for fear that a little rain cloud might send us a tornado. It's the same way with other things in life. When the threat of bad things comes, we have to do what we know is right in order to get through those times. Sometimes we get hurt—"

"Like when Daddy died?" Danny interjected.

"Yes," Gina whispered, her voice heavy with emotion. "Like when Daddy died. But God brought us through that. He showed us that we were still loved by Him and that we would always be loved by Him. He's taken good care of us, hasn't He?"

"Yup, and God sent us Mr. Cameron."

Gina smiled. "That's right, He did."

The weather alert radio blared out its warning tone, interrupting Gina's conversation. Giving Danny a reassuring smile, she went to the radio and pressed the button. The thunderstorm watch had been changed to a tornado watch after two separate storms had produced small tornadoes in the surrounding area. She was still trying to listen to the details when someone rang the front doorbell.

"Danny, go answer the door, please," she told her son.

She finished listening to the report as Danny ran for the door and came back beaming from ear to ear, Gary Cameron following right behind.

"Looks like we're in for it again," Gary announced. "I don't like the looks of those clouds."

"Mom said God will take care of us," Danny offered.

"I agree totally," Gary replied as lightning flashed.

There was little doubt that a storm of great intensity was nearly upon them. Gina tried to maintain her composure. "Danny, go ahead and take your bag downstairs and then we'll have lunch."

"Can we eat in the basement again?"

Gina laughed and cast a quick glance at Gary. "I don't think we have to go that far. At least not yet. Remember what I said about not being afraid of the storms?"

"But I thought it was fun eating down there," Danny countered, picking up his bag. "It was like an adventure."

"Well, I suppose if you really want to. . . ," Gina said, her voice trailing off.

"Come on, Sport," Gary said, picking up his plate. "I'll get you settled downstairs, then come back up and convince your mother that it will be a lot of fun. We'll even play a board game or two."

Danny cheered and headed down the stairs.

"I thought we didn't want him to be paranoid about storms," Gina said in a barely audible voice.

"We don't, but like I said, those clouds didn't look good. Besides, when I come back upstairs, I have some important questions to ask you and I'd like to do it without an audience." He winked at her, then bounded down the steps before she could reply.

Gina felt her heartbeat quicken and her hands go clammy. Did he want to ask her what she hoped he would ask? Had he thought through all the complications in their lives and sorted through his feelings to know that marriage to Gina was the right move to make?

By the time he returned, Gina was leaning casually against the kitchen counter. She tried her best to look disinterested and nonchalant but knew she was doing a miserable job of it. "So what did you want to ask me?"

Gary smiled and leaned against the jamb of the basement door. "How do you feel about having more kids?"

"I've always wanted more children," she said quite seriously. "How many did you have in mind?"

"Three, maybe four?"

Gina bit at her lower lip as if considering the matter. "I think that's workable. What else?"

"Houses and living arrangements," he said flatly. "I prefer to think of us both starting over. A new house in the country is what I have in mind."

Gina tried to keep from smiling, but she couldn't help it. "I know a good real estate lady. Anything else you want to ask me?"

"That just about does it," Gary said. Then without a single word, he crossed the room and swept her into his arms. "I've missed you more than I ever imagined possible." His mouth came down on hers and Gina melted against him in absolute rapture. "I love you, Gina Bowden," he whispered, pulling back only long enough to speak.

Gina tightened her hold on him and let her kiss be her agreeing comment on his declaration. Without warning, he pulled back and grinned. "Marry me?"

She laughed, and as she opened her mouth to speak,

the weather alert radio sounded. Both of them broke into laughter as the weatherman announced the need to take cover from the strengthening storm.

"Ah, Kansas stormy weather," Gina mused, allowing Gary to hurry her to the basement door. "Grab the radio, will you?" She turned on the top step to await him.

"Sure thing," he replied, reaching back to the counter.

He quickly retrieved the radio and gave her a gentle push to start her down the steps. "There's never a dull moment around here," he declared.

"I warned you, our house is anything but quiet," Gina replied.

Gary smiled at Danny, who started to babble about the sirens and his good idea to eat lunch in the basement. "We're having another adventure, aren't we, Mom?"

"That we are. Say, how would you like it if I made this an even better adventure?" Gina questioned.

Both Gary and Danny looked at her, but it was Danny who questioned. "How?"

"By letting you in on a great surprise," she replied, enjoying her son's curiosity and Gary's puzzled stare. "Gary just asked me to marry him, and I'm just about to say yes."

Danny cheered and jumped up from the table to hug his arms around Gary's waist. "I knew you would be my new dad. I just knew it!"

Gary looked down at Danny for a moment before returning his gaze to Gina. "She hasn't said yes, yet, Sport."

Danny pulled back. "Say it, Mom. Say it so Dad

knows you mean it."

Gina laughed in spite of the weather outside. "Yes," she said simply. "Yes, I will marry you, Gary Cameron."

Danny cheered again, but this time Gary joined him and lifted him high in the air to toss him up in joyful celebration. "She said yes, Sport! That makes it official." He caught Danny and held him against his shoulder and held open his other arm to Gina.

"Now we can be a real family." The pleasure in Danny's voice was clear.

Gina laughed and came quite happily into Gary's embrace. "A real family," Gina murmured and silently thanked God for the miracle He'd given her. Even stormy weather couldn't spoil the moment.

Epilogue

A year later, on a clear April evening, Gina and Gary were married in the church where Gary had grown up. Gina loved the people and the wonderful way she'd been welcomed into their family, but most of all, she loved Gary and the way he loved her and Danny.

"You look rather pleased with yourself, Mrs. Cameron," Gary whispered in her ear as their guests gathered around to see them cut the wedding cake.

"I am rather pleased, Mr. Cameron," she replied, giving him what she hoped was a rather sultry look.

Gary raised a single brow and Gina thought she saw sweat form on his forehead. Grinning, she leaned against him ever so slightly. "You're looking a bit stressed, my dear." She held up the knife. "But we mustn't disappoint our guests."

"Just remember," he whispered against her ear, "I wanted to elope."

Gina felt a shiver run from her head to her toes. His warm breath against her neck was nearly enough to make her drop her facade of composure. "We're supposed to. . .ah. . . cut the cake together," she stammered.

Gary took hold of her hand and closed it around the knife's handle. "The quicker we get to it, the sooner we can leave on our honeymoon," he teased and laughed out loud as Gina quickly plunged the knife into the cake.

The reception was a tremendous success and Gina's

heart was warmed by the sight of her son and Jess Masterson sharing company and having a wonderful time. Jess had acted as Gary's best man, while Danny stood up as Gina's only attendant.

"I'm surprised you held the reception in the church basement," Telaine Applebee said, coming to give her best wishes to Gina and Gary. "They have a perfectly wonderful reception hall upstairs. I don't think anyone's used this area in years, at least not for a wedding."

Gina exchanged a quick smile with Gary before answering. "Scout motto."

Telaine looked at her oddly. "Scout motto?"

"Be prepared," Gary countered.

"Yes, I know what the motto is, but what does that have to do with the reception being in the basement?" Telaine asked.

"Gina figured we'd outwit any chances of stormy weather," Gary replied with a grin.

"That's right," Gina replied. "It took me long enough to find this man, I wasn't going to risk losing him in a mad dash for the basement."

Everyone around them laughed at this, while Gina felt Gary's arms close around her from behind. "There wasn't a chance of you losing me," he whispered only loud enough for Gina to hear. "Storms or calm, you're stuck with me for life, Mrs. Cameron."

Gina leaned against him and grinned. "Good thing. See, there's this pinewood derby coming up in two weeks and. . ."

TRACIE PETERSON

Tracie, one of **Heartsong Presents'** most popular authors, is author of over thirty inspirational fiction titles. As a Christian, wife, mother, and writer (in that order), Tracie finds her slate quite full. Tracie resides in Topeka, Kansas, with her husband and their three children. First published as a columnist for the *Kansas Christian Newspaper,* Tracie resigned that position to turn her attention to novels. Besides several romances with **Heartsong Presents** and Barbour Publishing, she has titles co-written with Judith Pella as well as single titles published by Bethany House. Tracie also teaches workshops at a variety of conferences, giving talks on inspirational romance, historical research, and anything else that offers assistance to fellow writers. She has also recently signed on as freelance acquisitions editor for **Heartsong Presents**.

Bride to Be

Debra White Smith

Dedicated

. . .to my friends,
Amy Matthews Moreillon, her husband Paul,
and my friends Mike and Stacy Steel.

One

Amy Matthews looked into the most incredible pair of brown eyes she had ever encountered—the kind of eyes that held a hint of vulnerability and made a woman want to move closer. They belonged to one of her customers. He was standing across the invitations counter with his smiling fiancée attached to his arm. Why did the best ones always have to be engaged?

"M–may I–I help you?" Amy stammered, glad she had actually found her voice. It had escaped her shortly after the tall, distinguished man entered.

"Yes, my fiancée and I wanted to begin planning our wedding," he answered, then smiled toward the attractive woman at his side. His fiancée returned the smile. And while it was companionable, the smile lacked the passion Amy often witnessed between prospective brides and grooms.

Amy figured the dark-haired man was in his late thirties or early forties. The occasional streaks of gray in his thick hair witnessed to his maturing manhood. He was also a gentleman, if his demeanor indicated his character. As her appraisal lengthened, Amy's knees began to waver.

Never had she reacted to a man like she was reacting to this one. She didn't even know his name, for pity's sake. Perhaps she had indulged in too much of the chocolate mocha coffee that her business partner, Stacy Steel, made this afternoon. Given her juvenile reaction, Amy wondered if chocolate mocha might be a dangerous combination. The gourmet coffee's mellow smell still teased her senses and added the aroma of a wedding reception to the displays of china, wedding attire, and flower arrangements.

"This is Bride to Be, isn't it—the wedding shop?" the woman asked with a polite, inquisitive expression.

"Y–yes." Her face warming, Amy averted her gaze and nervously shuffled the miscellaneous papers and bridal books that cluttered the counter. She had been staring. Staring in shock. However, the man stared back with a thoughtful glimmer in his own eyes. But Amy figured her expression had been more of the "doe in the headlights" variety.

Desperately, she tried to control her shattered thoughts. For years, Amy had prayed for "Mr. Right." And at thirty-five, she had begun to despair that he would come along. Most of the men she had dated either left her cold or weren't committed Christians or were only interested in a physical relationship. Last year, Amy realized in all her dating she had been trying to help God with His work. Finally, she decided to let Him lead her to her mate. Nonetheless, Amy still despaired. Much of her prayer life was consumed with "Please, God, please, I don't want to grow old alone. I want a husband and children." The cliché, always the bridesmaid but never the bride, took an ironic twist with Amy—she was always the bridal consultant but never the bride.

As more silence stretched between her and the clients, Amy knew she must escape. Escape or explode. Her friend and partner, Stacy Steel, often told Amy she would know when she met Mr. Right. Could the way Amy felt be the "knowing"? Not that Amy believed in love at first sight. What she was feeling definitely wasn't love. It was more like a volcanic explosion. But her explosion had a bitter twist. Could Amy's Mr. Right already be engaged? Her stomach turned in nausea. Still, she shuffled papers and prayed for an escape.

Amy heard Stacy approaching from the back of the shop. "May I help you?" she asked firmly, casting an odd look at her closest friend. As usual, her tall, lithe partner exuded her take-charge persona.

"Yes, we were wanting to plan our wedding," the erect, plump woman replied. "We've heard great things about this little shop. I understand you take care of everything, including the catering. Are you the owner?"

"You're right, we do take care of everything. And yes, I'm one of the owners. The other owner is Amy Matthews."

By the time Stacy finished her reply, Amy was halfway to her tiny office. She stomped past the displays of wedding gowns and tuxedos along the back wall and tried to tear her emotions away from the scene behind her. At last, Amy collapsed into her office chair, buried her hands in her face, and bit her trembling lips.

This couldn't be happening. She had never behaved in such an adolescent manner. Perhaps she was simply overstressed. Overworked. Even though Rusk was a small Texas town, people came from all over east Texas to procure the services of Bride to Be. The idea of one location taking care of every aspect of a wedding appealed to more and more people. What Bride to Be didn't provide themselves, they subcontracted.

Exhausted. Yes, Amy must be exhausted. Plus, she had stayed up late last night watching the final scenes from *Gone With the Wind,* her all-time favorite movie. Therefore, she started the day in a romantic mode. Upon her 9:05 arrival, Amy even opened Stacy's office door and said, "Wher*ev-uh* will I go? What*ev-uh* shall I do?"

Stacy, a dark-haired beauty, had comically rolled her eyes and said, "Don't tell me, you've been watching *Gone With the Wind* again."

"How*ev-uh* did you guess?" Amy placed her hand on her chest and fluttered her eyelashes to excess.

The gesture elicited an exaggerated groan. "It's going to be a long day."

Little did Stacy know she had been a prophetess. It really was going to be a long day for Amy. Or maybe even a long year. After staring into those brown eyes, Amy wondered if they would haunt her the rest of her life. At once, she realized she didn't even know his name. Amy sat upright.

Feeling like a sneak, she crept toward her office door and opened it the width of a thumbnail. Stacy, willowy and charming, was apparently being her witty self. The couple frequently laughed as they began looking through the various catalogs. This secretive point of observation gave Amy ample opportunity to scrutinize the pair. Desperately, she tried to reason herself out of her initial reaction to the man. But the longer she watched him, the more certain she was her reaction had precious little to do with reason and everything to do with intuition.

To add grief to her heightened emotions, Amy became convinced that the two were not in love. Her initial assumption had been correct. They consulted each other like two friends who were in a business partnership, not like two lovebirds ready to be married. They made a handsome couple. His dark complexion contrasted with her fair hair. He wore a dark suit. She wore a fashionable, red suit, which was cut to hide a marginal weight gain. They looked really nice together.

But they didn't belong together.

In the two years Amy had owned Bride to Be, she had seen several couples who exhibited the same behavior. Most of them were forty or over and seemed to be marrying for companionship. Some had never married and decided to make the best of it with a friend. Amy could have married several times on those terms herself. But friendship, companionship would never be enough for Amy. She wanted the passion wrought only by true love.

So she had waited.

As she continued to soak in every nuance of the attractive stranger, Amy felt as if her long wait for Mr. Right were being thrown in her face. She wasn't by any means ready to marry this man, but he seemed to be the type of man she would consider a prospect.

As if he sensed her watching, he glanced over his fiancée's bent head and straight toward Amy's office door. Without realizing it, Amy had allowed the door to inch open the width of her face. The stranger stared full into her eyes.

Amy's stomach lurched.

She didn't blink.

She didn't breathe.

She didn't move.

Something she recognized stirred in the depths of his eyes. She realized she recognized that something because it was what she was feeling. Amy knew in that instant she had arrested his attention as much as he arrested hers. Never the type to draw a crowd of men, Amy always considered herself attractive in an understated sort of way. Her tall, athletic frame, hazel eyes, and sandy hair weren't exactly supermodel material. But given this man's appraisal, Amy felt like a supermodel. For the first time in her life, she felt beautiful. Truly beautiful.

The blond fiancée asked him a question, and he bent an attentive ear to her.

The moment broken, Amy clicked her office door shut and collapsed into her chair. Closing her eyes, she took deep, deliberate breaths as her prayers for a husband began to mock her. This had to be some kind of cruel cosmic joke.

❧

Paul Moore left Bride to Be with Jill's hand firmly in his. He clung to the hand in an attempt to convince himself he was doing the right thing. Jill, known to her colleagues as "Ms. Personality Plus," chatted excitedly about the wedding plans they had just initiated. Somehow, Paul couldn't quite conjure up the excitement he saw in Jill's candid blue eyes.

Abstractly, he glanced toward the town square on which sat the Cherokee County courthouse. Surprisingly, everything was the same. The dogwoods in full bloom. The rows of cars parked around the courthouse. The new spring grass. The smell of an afternoon rain still lingering in the air. After that encounter with the owner of the bridal shop, Paul had expected the whole world to be tilting.

He hadn't felt that sort of attraction since he was in college. The first time he met Vivian. They married six months later. Paul assumed that sort of thing only happened once in a lifetime. Had he been wrong?

"What do you think?" Jill asked as they stopped beside Paul's trusty red minivan.

"Huh?" How many times had Paul heard that same clueless expression from one of the high school boys who had been sent to his office for correction? "Huh. . . duh. . .I don't know." But Paul had no idea what Jill had said. Unexpectedly, he experienced a surge of sympathy for those teenagers "doing time" in the principal's office.

"You weren't even listening!" Jill playfully slapped his arm.

"Sorry." Paul produced a penitent smile.

Once Jill was in the van, Paul took the driver's seat. "Now, what were you saying?"

"Oh, nothing. I wondered if you would like for me to cook for you and the boys. I've cooked roast for you enough. I thought this time I'd try a casserole the boys like. What's their favorite?"

"Oh, pizza, hands down."

"Pizza isn't a casserole."

"It's the *only* food to them."

"Well, the time has arrived for you guys to stop all that pizza and start some casseroles and salads."

"Yes, ma'am."

Jill was so forgiving. No pressure. No aggravation. No insistence. Such an easy companion. Many women would have taken a good five minutes to examine Paul's lack of interest in the original conversation, but not Jill.

Paul smiled in grateful admiration for the woman he had chosen to be his lifetime mate. Their families had known each other for years. She would be a good wife to him—and a good mother to his junior high boys. Although they were putting up a resistance to Paul's marrying their math teacher, they desperately needed a mother. And Paul was ready for a wife. Even five years after Vivian's death, Paul still tenderly re-membered her.

But he had to move forward. The time had come to begin a new chapter in his life.

Yes, he was making the right decision. Not exactly in love, Jill and he shared a mutual respect. A deep friendship. A relationship with the Lord. They would make a good life together.

Still, the image of Amy Matthews teased his mind. But at age forty, Paul reminded himself he was a mature man who couldn't act on every attraction he felt. Paul had made his commitment to Jill. He would stand firm by that commitment.

Two

Well, I must say, I have *nev-uh* seen you act like that before. I'll admit he was attractive, but good grief, Amy, don't you think you overreacted?"

Her face still in her hands, Amy peeked through her fingers to see Stacy leaning against the door frame, arms crossed, a teasing light in her gray eyes.

"Oh, go do something in your own office. Mine's too crowded."

"No, really, what gives?" she asked more seriously. "Are you sick or something? You acted like you might be about to faint. There's been a spring flu going around. . . ."

Amy studied her friend and soon realized Stacy had no idea her first words were the correct ones. She had been merely teasing. Stacy really thought Amy was ill. It would have been very easy for Amy to allow Stacy to think that falsehood. But the two friends had been through too much together for Amy to try to hide her emotions. There was no reason for her to hide them. Stacy was like her sister.

"I'm not sick." Amy slumped back in her chair and looked up. A new spider web claimed a spot in the room's upper corner. She immediately stood, opened the storage closet, retrieved the broom, and brushed away the offending tangles. "Whether or not you meant what you said first, you were closer to the truth." With a humorless smile, she turned candid eyes to her friend.

Stacy did little to suppress a surprised giggle. "You're kidding, right?"

"No, I'm not kidding."

"Are you sure you're okay?" Stacy didn't try to hide her shock. "You've never acted this way before." She waved her hands for emphasis. "You've never been the type to fall into instant relationships."

"I didn't say I'm ready to get married today. I just meant that he seemed to be the kind of man I'm looking for. Meeting him just took me off guard."

"But you don't even know him."

"He acted like a gentleman, and something in his eyes says he has character."

"Yeah, those dreamy brown eyes had all sors of *character,*" she said with a smirk. "And I guess his infectious smile didn't influence you either?"

At once, Amy was more exasperated with Stacy than she ever remembered. The two had been friends since high school. They both grew up in Rusk, attended the same college, and pursued degrees in business administration. Both were only children and had long ago claimed the other as a sister. As with most people who work side by side, they occasionally got on each other's nerves, but this anger Amy felt went far beyond a case of nerves.

"Would you stop it!" she snapped. "Do you think I like feeling this way? He's already engaged, for pity's sake. When you met Mike, he was footloose and fancy-free. Now you've been married five years! What do you know about how it feels to think you might spend your whole life single? Then, when I meet somebody who I think might be a candidate, he's already taken! You have no clue how frustrating this is!" Amy's voice had risen with each of her words. Her eyes were misting, and the pain she masked with hard work and a cheerful demeanor began to spew from her soul like bitter bile.

Stacy's eyes widened in sympathetic dismay. "I'm sorry. I had no idea. . . ," she rasped.

Still holding the broom, Amy clutched it as if it were her only link to sanity. Already, she regretted her outburst. She hadn't dealt fairly with Stacy. "I'm the one to be sorry." She rubbed her forehead.

Never one to hold a grudge, Stacy shrugged her shoulders in dismissal of the whole ordeal. "It's okay. But I had no idea you were still struggling. Why didn't you *say* something?"

Sighing, Amy slumped back into her chair and worried with the seam in her denim skirt. "It's not something that's easy to talk about, you know." She directed a sad, lonely smile to her partner. "When you got married, I was thrilled and hopeful that I'd be next, and, if you want the truth, a wee bit jealous. Don't get me wrong, I was delighted for you. But at the same time, I desperately wanted to be as in love as you and Mike."

Stacy remained respectfully silent.

"By this time in my life, I assumed I'd have a husband and a couple of kids. But here I am, thirty-five, unmarried, and let's face it, my biological clock is ticking. If I'm going to have kids, I need to be doing it. But instead, I'm helping everybody else and their brother arrange marriages, with no prospects in sight for me. And, quite frankly, Stacy, it's a lonely existence."

"But your life is so full—"

"Yes, and I crawl into bed at night alone. I want to know what it feels like to make love with my husband at midnight and wake up in the circle of his arms and share a home with him every day. Is that too much to ask?" The room seemed ready to explode with Amy's volatile emotions.

"No, it's not too much to ask," Stacy said, her eyes brimming with tears. Dear, sweet Stacy, always compassionate. Amy often wished she could be half as tenderhearted. "But I thought when you stopped dating last year that you had really come to terms with being single."

"I thought I had, too." When she stopped dating, Amy told Stacy she was turning the whole thing over to God, letting Him be the one to lead her to her husband. Now her own words mocked her. Had she really relinquished the dream to be a wife and mother? Would she be able to completely release it? Would she ever get to a point that God's will was more important to her than her own dreams?

"Did you get his name and address?" Amy asked

wearily.

"What?" Stacy, obviously confused by Amy's sudden reversal in perspective, wrinkled her brow.

"Mr. Wonderful." Amy smiled at her own term. "Did you get his name and address? Does he live in Rusk?" She figured he didn't. In a town with a population of only five thousand, Amy would have most likely seen him by now. Nonetheless, she wanted to keep their encounters to a minimum. Amy would avoid his side of town if he did live in the area.

"Yes," Stacy answered sympathetically. "But he's only been here since August. About eight months. His name's Paul Moore. You know, the new high school principal."

With a silent nod, Amy suppressed a groan. Yes, she had heard of him. Her mother, a high school English teacher, had mentioned their new Christian principal and wanted to introduce Amy to him. In past years, Marie Matthews had tried several times to play matchmaker with Amy. Each time ended in a fiasco, so Amy had long ago drawn a firm line and stopped agreeing to any of her mother's schemes. Despite Marie's continual hints of "He's such an attractive widower with two delightful boys" and "I really think the two of you would hit it off," Amy had remained firm with "No more blind dates, Mom. I'm sorry."

What a twist of irony! The one time Amy resisted her mother, the dear, sweet woman had been right.

"Are you going to be okay?" Stacy asked.

Another late customer entering saved Amy from

having to answer. At this point, she did not feel that she would be okay. Amy saw with renewed clarity that the only avenue to "okay" was going to be a complete relinquishment of her dream to God. This afternoon had proven to her that her relinquishment last year had been nothing more than mere lip service. She still clutched her dream, and presently, she didn't know exactly how to release it.

❧

The next day was Saturday, and Paul got up early for his weekly trip to the grocery store. His boys, Brice and Dayton, knew the Saturday schedule. They always slept late. When they got up, Paul would be home with this week's supply of six gallons of milk, five dozen eggs, four loaves of bread, a case of sodas, eight frozen pizzas, and the list went on from there. Paul remembered his own mother grumbling about the amount he and his brothers ate in adolescence. He passed his voracious appetite on to his boys. Recently, Paul had purchased an oversized refrigerator to hold all the food they needed. Otherwise, Paul would have made continual trips to the grocery store to replenish the groceries. Thankfully, he had gotten the shopping down to once a week.

Upon entering the store, he wondered if Jill was really prepared for cooking for two teenagers and an active man. Last night, her casserole had been scrumptious. But as she set it on the table with a proud flourish, Paul exchanged a knowing glance with his boys. When Jill left the dining room to retrieve the salad, Paul whispered, "We'll get burgers later." Despite the boy's aversion to Jill, they had inhaled the layers of cheese, hamburger meat, and tortilla chips. Nonetheless, the small casserole hadn't even taken the edge off their hunger. After they left Jill's, Paul had driven them through the local hamburger joint and ordered enough burgers and French fries to feed Jill for a week. Paul finally faced the fact that before he married Jill, he would have to drop a few hints about the size of her meals. This was the third time she had cooked for them as a family and the third time they had ended the evening with burgers.

But despite her lack of boy-knowledge, Jill was great. He had continually reminded himself of that since late yesterday afternoon. Every time he remembered Amy Matthews spying on him from her office, Paul forced her from his thoughts and reminded himself that Jill was great. Paul grabbed the nearest shopping buggy, and, to the elevator tune of "Do You Know the Way to San Jose?" he began his weekly chore. But as much as he focused on peanut butter and bread and which frozen pizzas to buy, Amy's "girl next door" freshness haunted him. She wasn't even the kind of woman who normally attracted Paul. He usually went for blonds. Vivian had been blond. Jill was blond.

Jill. Jill. Jill. He needed to keep his thoughts with Jill. She would be his wife in two months. Paul couldn't be disloyal to her. She was a fine Christian woman. After his boys got used to the idea of a new mother, she would be so good for them. Paul couldn't hurt her. He wouldn't hurt her. He was committed.

He would simply have to expunge the memory of that electrified moment with Amy Matthews from his mind. He didn't even know her. How could he have reacted to her so strongly? But hadn't he experienced the same thing with Vivian?

Impatient with himself, Paul tossed several frozen pizzas into his buggy. He was supposed to be a mature, forty-year-old man, not a fickle teenage boy who went into orbit with every attractive female he encountered. *Good grief, get a grip on yourself!*

Scowling, Paul wheeled his cart from the frozen food department and toward the dairy section. This early on Saturday morning, he usually had the store pretty much to himself. But a woman in a blue suit was standing near the milk. "Excuse me," he said, politely reaching for this week's supply of six gallons of milk.

"Oh, of course," the woman replied, glancing up at him.

Paul wanted to disappear. It was her. He had lived in the small town for eight months without encountering Amy Matthews. Now he had encountered her on two subsequent days. The milk forgotten, Paul silently stared at her. And yesterday's emotions flooded him, only stronger this time.

Once again, she scrutinized him in round-eyed shock. "Hi," Amy finally said in a choked whisper.

"Hello," he rasped back.

"I. . .I was just out buying cream for our coffee at work. I guess I'm a little picky, but I like real cream," she rushed as if she were required to provide an explanation.

A flush of red crept up her cheeks to enhance her light application of makeup.

"Oh. Well, I buy groceries every Saturday morning. My boys drink about six gallons of milk a week."

"My mother told me you had two teenagers."

"Your mother?"

"Yes. Marie Matthews."

"Oh. Marie Matthews is your mother?" *Smooth, Paul. How'd you get to be a high school principal, anyway?* he wondered. "The English teacher?"

"Yes."

"It's a small world."

"No, it's just a small town."

"She mentioned several times that she wanted to introduce me to her daughter, but. . ." Why had Paul blurted that truth? As Amy's slight blush turned scarlet, he wanted to bite off his own tongue. "I'm sorry," he muttered, his apology covering far more than the fact that he had spoken words better left unsaid. He was sorry he had resisted the introduction. He was sorry he had gone and gotten himself engaged to someone else.

"It's okay," Amy uttered, but the pain in her eyes said it was far from okay. "She kept trying to get me to agree to an introduction, too."

Amy felt exactly what he felt. There was no reason for either of them to pretend. There was something between them that went far beyond understanding, far beyond words. Their souls somehow connected in a way only God Himself understood. Not that Paul fancied himself in love with her. But there was a recognition of a man who sees a woman he could very easily fall in love with. Madly in love. The kind of love that rocks the universe. And it all came to nothing because Paul was engaged.

An instrumental version of a pop tune from the seventies began playing in the store. Many times, Paul had sung along with the sentiment of "It's Sad to Belong to Someone Else When the Right One Comes Along." Today, the tune made him ill.

"Well, I need to get to work," Amy finally said, her trembling voice not matching the businesslike mask she had hidden behind. "Stacy will be wondering where I am."

"Of course."

Without picking up the cream, she rushed away and turned down the nearest aisle.

Amy wanted to cry but refused herself the luxury. This was ridiculous. She was an accomplished businesswoman. A true professional. She steered her car into the parking place near her shop. Paul Moore was a client. That was all. She must get over this. . .this. . . whatever that made her speechless every time she encountered him.

Amy knew that, despite what they both felt, Paul Moore was the kind of man who stood by his word. He was already engaged. Amy was certain he wouldn't break that promise. He apparently felt something for his fiancée or he would have never proposed. Even though Jill and Paul weren't passionately in love, they shared the love of one friend for another. He wouldn't toss that aside on the chance that a relationship with Amy would materialize into true love. Once Paul and Amy got to know one another, this initial attraction might well die an ugly death. They had only just met, Amy reasoned. The thoughts she had about Paul possibly being "Mr. Right" were beyond irrational.

As she rested her head against the steering wheel of her compact car, Amy contemplated prayer. But she drew a blank on how to pray. It seemed there was a giant steel wall between her and God. Deep in her troubled soul, she knew only one prayer would demolish that wall—the prayer that told God she desired His will for her life more than she desired her own agenda. But Amy was truly terrified that if she agreed to being single the rest of her life, God would sentence her to exactly that. A life without a mate. A life of no children. A life of loneliness.

Three

One month later, Amy drove into the parking lot of the Jacksonville Public Library. Jacksonville was the next town north of Rusk. Even though Rusk had a library, Amy had chosen the Jacksonville library because she feared encountering Paul Moore.

After the grocery store episode, it seemed Amy saw Paul almost every other day. If he wasn't in Bride to Be with his fiancée, Amy would see him in town. At the gas station. The post office. Even at the scenic Rusk State Park. Within a month, Amy labeled herself "Amy Anxiety." She was so worried that she would see him everywhere, Amy became paranoid about the whole ordeal. Wherever she went, before getting out of her car, she had started scanning the scene for any traces of his red minivan or him.

The thing she couldn't figure out was how she had missed meeting him before now. Perhaps she had encountered him in town but hadn't really seen him until that face-to-face confrontation in Bride to Be.

With a sigh, she got out of her compact car and trudged toward the library. Amy had decided to immerse herself in books during her spare time. Perhaps a few good mysteries would help her rid her mind of images of Paul. At this point, she was so desperate she would have read the phone book.

Head lowered, she plodded toward the library's glass doors. April's spring breezes had been swept away by May's still, hot days. On her afternoons off, like today, Amy wore her walking shorts instead of long pants. Along with the rest of east Texas, she looked forward to June, when she could enjoy an afternoon dip in the community pool.

"Bet you can't beat me," a boyish voice called with the opening of the library's glass doors. Amy looked up to encounter two man-sized boys hurtling out of the library and straight into her path. They were so caught up in their juvenile laughter that they didn't see Amy until it was too late.

Desperately, she tried to side step them, but just as she removed herself from the path of one, the other one banged into her. Her purse went one way, and she went the other. Accompanied by a surprised grunt, Amy flopped onto the concrete in a disgraceful heap. Her backside ached. Her elbow burned. Her ire rose.

The wide-eyed boys stood nearby in helpless silence.

Amy was ready to firmly tell them to act their age when another voice spoke her own words.

"I told you two to *walk* to the car. Do you know the meaning of the word 'walk'?"

Amy looked toward the voice and suppressed a groan. It was him again. Paul Moore. Would she never be free of him? She glanced back to the gangly boys, both younger versions of their father. These must be the "delightful boys" Amy's mother had mentioned. They didn't seem so delightful.

"We're sorry," the boys muttered.

Awkwardly, Amy got to her feet, and Paul offered his gentlemanly assistance. "I'm terribly sorry," he said as Amy regained her footing.

"It's all right. Really." Even though she desperately tried to avoid eye contact, it seemed Amy was doomed from the start. Impulsively, she looked up into his eyes.

Dreamy brown. That was how Stacy described his eyes. Stacy was right. Helplessly, Amy held his searching gaze while, in her mind, she begged him to look away. For she had no power to break the moment. She was ensnared, dazed, mesmerized.

This sort of thing didn't happen in real life. Or rather, it wasn't supposed to happen in real life. But then, in real life, Amy should have been married long ago—with a couple of kids, a cocker spaniel, and a tomcat. As their gaze continued, Amy observed all the emotions she was feeling as they flitted through Paul's eyes.

Why did life have to be so complicated?

At last, Amy rasped, "I. . .I was just. . .just coming to the library to check out some m–mystery novels." Why she felt the need to tell her mission was beyond comprehension. Perhaps there was nothing else to say. And, as when they met in the grocery store, an explanation of her presence seemed the easiest conversation.

"I was helping the boys with their science project," he said.

The two spoke so softly, they could have been exchanging the most intimate details of their lives.

"I'm sorry," she said, referring to the fact that she couldn't seem to stay out of his path.

His indulgent smile created a twinkle in his eyes. "You shouldn't be. The science project isn't really that bad."

"No, not about that," she replied, trying unsuccessfully to suppress her own smile. "I just meant that. . . that. . ." She hesitated in an attempt to carefully choose her words, then blurted, "I mean I'm not following you everywhere you go. Honest. I didn't know you were here. I actually came to the Jacksonville library to—" As her face warmed, Amy stopped herself just short of telling Paul she had been trying to avoid him.

"I know what you meant," he said, his voice hollow with sadness.

And Amy knew without voicing her feelings, Paul did indeed understand, perhaps because he felt the same.

"Er. . .Dad?" one of the boys interrupted.

Amy groaned softly. "I forgot all about them," she muttered under her breath.

"Yes?" Paul said, and the moment was broken.

"We don't want to interrupt but. . ." The older boy spoke while his younger brother supplied the giggling. "Our karate class—"

"Oh yes, the karate. I forgot." Paul checked his watch. "We're already ten minutes late. And then, we're supposed to meet Jill—" Paul cut himself off as a guilty look scurried across his face.

Amy was amazed that he should feel guilty. After all, Jill was his fiancée. Nonetheless, something in her wanted to scream, "How could you? You're supposed to be meeting me!" But that was irrational. Completely irrational. He was engaged to Jill, not her. He would marry Jill, not her. He would share his life, his joy, his dreams with Jill, not her.

"Well, I've got to get my mystery novels," she said and brushed past him. At this point, Amy needed about twenty novels. This was only Friday, and it was going to be a long weekend.

As the library door closed behind her, she heard one of the boys release a long wolf whistle. Furtively, she glanced to see the other one punching his dad in the arm in companionable banter. What must those two think?

"So, Dad, who was *that*?" Dayton asked, his fourteen-year-old voice cracking on the last words.

"Nobody. It was nobody," Paul muttered, desperately wishing to change the direction of the boys' thoughts. "Hurry up, now, we're late as it is."

All legs and arms and blue jean shorts, they tumbled into the minivan.

"Guys don't look at 'nobody' the way you looked at *her*," Brice, the self-appointed giggler, interjected with a new supply of laughter.

Paul directed what he hoped was a discouraging scowl their way, then began the short drive to the martial arts class. Each of the boys looked more like Paul than Vivian. Tall. Dark hair. Brown eyes. For that, Paul was eternally thankful. After breast cancer claimed Vivian five years ago, Paul didn't think he could have withstood having a son, or especially a daughter, who strongly favored his wife. Looking at the child would have been nothing short of torment.

After Vivian's death, a good three years lapsed before he stopped feeling like his insides had been ripped out. A fourth year passed before Paul began to realize he should rebuild his life. The move to Rusk last summer had been part of the rebuilding. A new job. A new location, closer to his parents. A new outlook on life. A new wife on the horizon. For the first time since Vivian's diagnosis, everything seemed to be going Paul's way.

Then he met Amy.

Silently, Paul vented a frustrated prayer heavenward. *Why couldn't You have put her in my life before I proposed to Jill?*

"I like her better than Jill," Dayton said. "Why don't you ask her out?"

"Yeah," Brice echoed. "Why don't ya, Dad?"

"How can you say you like her better?" Paul challenged as a surge of obligatory loyalty for Jill awakened within. "You don't even know her. Besides, I've made a promise to Jill. I can't go and break my engagement just because. . .because—this isn't like it is with you guys when you break up with a girlfriend. It's different with adults. Everything is more serious." Dayton and Brice's dislike of Jill both puzzled and annoyed Paul. His boys weren't usually the vindictive sort. But something about Jill aroused an aversion in them that surpassed Paul's understanding. Perhaps they were simply resentful of their all-male domain being invaded by a female. But if that were the case, why were they suggesting he date Amy?

❧

As Amy drove over the rolling, green hills back to Rusk, hot tears spilled onto her cheeks, trickled to the corners of her mouth, and dropped off her chin. A pile of disorganized mystery novels claimed the passenger seat. Amy hadn't even looked at the titles when she grabbed an armful of books from the mystery section. All through the checkout process, she had blinked against the tears that now flowed unchecked. Tears of frustration. Tears of loneliness. Tears of sorrow.

At last, Amy entered Rusk, and without planning it, she drove toward her church. The church board had recently voted to leave the prayer room open for anyone who needed to pray. Amy needed to pray today. She hoped the room wasn't occupied.

Within minutes, she entered the dimly lit room that contained an altar, a simple cross above it, and a few chairs sitting here and there. Thankfully, she was the only occupant. Without preamble, Amy collapsed at the altar, draped herself over it, and allowed the sobs to rack her body. When her grief had ebbed enough for her mind to form words, she began the lamenting that had chased her all the way from the library.

"Why, God—why are You doing this to me? *You* know how badly I want to marry and how much I would like to get to know Paul Moore! Why are You allowing this man to be everywhere I am? I feel as if You've dangled my dream before my eyes and then told me I can't have it. Please, please, please stop this torment. I can't take this any more. Can't You see how lonely I am? Don't You care that I desperately want to get married?"

Even to her own ears, Amy's prayer sounded a bit unfair, but this was exactly how she felt. Why should she mask her feelings with her Creator? He knew her every thought anyway.

And after that prayer, her thoughts were troubled. It seemed her mind kept wandering back to that same, disturbing point. If she were to have peace, Amy was going to have to relinquish her dream of marriage to God and be perfectly content to live out her entire life without a spouse. Her chest tensed as a tug-of-war raged within.

Amy didn't want to relinquish her dream to God. She wanted to embrace her dream. Wasn't that what dreams were for? But was her dream God's will for her?

Grabbing a nearby tissue, Amy saw for the first time in her life that she had never consulted her Lord on His plans for her. She had simply made what she considered reasonable choices in her life, and so far they had worked out well. The college she attended had offered her a sports scholarship. "Why not," she had reasoned. Her father had offered her free rent on the downtown store space that was now Bride to Be. "Why not," she had reasoned. Stacy had offered to invest in half the stock of Bride to Be as a full partner. "Why not," she had reasoned.

At once, Amy wondered if any of her dreams, if any of her accomplishments, if any of her reasoning, had been in God's master plan for her. That brought her back to her purpose for coming to the chapel. Was marriage in God's plan for her? Or was she destined to grow old alone?

"Please, God, please," she whimpered. "I don't want to be single anymore. If Paul isn't the man for me. . . please. . .I want a husband."

Four

I don't want to hear your excuses! I don't care whose idea it was! If you ever, *ever* put a king snake—or any kind of snake for that matter—in any teacher's desk drawer again, I'll. . .I'll. . . Do you realize that I'm the principal of the high school? Do you know how this looks? Do you understand how much you've upset Jill?"

Paul peered into his rearview mirror at both his sons. They each shamefully hung their heads. In his exasperation, Paul loosened his tie and let out an infuriated growl. What a Monday!

"It was just a dumb ol' king snake," Brice mumbled.

"He wouldn't have hurt her even if he'd bitten her," Dayton added.

"And why did you chose a red and yellow and black king snake?"

Neither spoke.

"I'll tell you why! Because the thing looks like a coral snake! When Jill saw it, she thought it was poisonous."

"But we were looking for a grass snake when we found that one—just a plain ol' green grass snake—we didn't start out with the idea to use a king snake," Brice said begrudgingly.

"Who cares! Now, you and your two friends have

gotten yourselves suspended for three days—and I might add that I don't blame the principal in the least." At this point, Paul had to decide what he would do with his boys the rest of the afternoon and the following three days. It was presently one o'clock, and Paul had to return to his office.

"Where will we stay until school is out?" Dayton asked, as Paul steered toward home.

"Right now, I'm taking you home."

"Can we stay at Grandma and Grandpa's the next three days?" Brice asked hopefully.

It was Paul's only choice. His aging parents lived an hour south of Rusk on the family farm, and the boys loved their trips to the farm. For all he knew, they probably found the king snake during their weekend visit there. The only problem with their staying with his parents was that three days with two indulgent grandparents, a great swimming hole, and plenty of homemade ice cream wasn't exactly Paul's idea of punishment for a couple of boys who would stoop to terrorizing a teacher.

Poor Jill. She had been so pale she looked like a corpse when Paul picked up the boys at Rusk Middle School just after lunch. With a strained smile, she graciously agreed to Paul's invitation to dinner that night. He had left a large roast in the slow cooker that morning. After Brice and Dayton's escapade, Paul was shocked she accepted the invitation. If she backed out of the marriage, Paul wouldn't blame her. Not in the least. But that was probably exactly what his sons wanted. Gritting his teeth, Paul was more determined than ever to marry Jill. That is, if she would still have a man who had fathered two obnoxious boys. He would call her later.

"Tonight after supper, I'll take you to the farm," Paul relented. "But there's no swimming allowed. And no ice cream. And. . . ," Paul added as an afterthought, "while you're there, you'll clean out the barn—horse manure and all."

As if on cue, their eyes rounded in horror. "But—" they began simultaneously.

"No 'buts.' If you don't get through by the end of your three days, you get to finish on the weekend. So don't think you can be lazy and get out of it!"

To punctuate Paul's words, a foreign sound erupted from the minivan's motor, the vehicle lurched, and Paul deftly steered it to the shoulder. "Great," he muttered under his breath. "Just what I needed." Frustrated beyond words, Paul put the van in park, turned off the key, and rested his forehead against the steering wheel. The boys didn't say a word, and Paul figured they were afraid to voice any question whatsoever. They knew as well as Paul that when it came to mechanical devices, their dad was less than adequate. Paul had a gift for dealing with people, for administration, and teaching that dazzled most, but mechanics remained a mystery to him.

As Paul contemplated his wretched situation with two mischievous juveniles and a broken down vehicle, his mind began to wander to a scene from his own youth—the year he and Wally Sinclair put Wally's pet rat in old Mrs. Dement's purse. She had done the jig for what seemed like thirty minutes near the teacher's lounge. Every time they had a class reunion, he and Wally would secretly snicker about their antics. Even as grown men, they still chuckled when thinking of that gray-haired teacher hopping around like a kangaroo. Her neat hair, always in a bun, dangled around her shoulders before the rat made its terrified exit. Even now, the whole scene brought a smile to Paul's lips. The poor woman. It was a wonder he and Wally hadn't given her a heart attack. When the dust settled, the two boys had been suspended for a few days. And his father made him clean out the same barn. No wonder that punishment had entered his mind so readily.

But where his own practical joke always left him smiling, Dayton and Brice's snake episode infuriated him. With a chuckle at himself, Paul rubbed his eyes and reached for his cell phone and the phone book. He would call a wrecker and deal with the other problem later.

A light tap on the window interrupted his perusal of the phone book. Paul looked up to encounter Amy Matthews grinning at him. The wind tossed her hair around her shoulders in a most alluring manner. And Paul was reminded of one of those television advertisements where an attractive, athletic woman is running along the windy beach, her hair teased by the breeze. At first, Paul thought perhaps his stressed mind had conjured Amy up. With the day he was having, a round of hallucinations would fit right in. Paul blinked hard only to discover that Amy was not a hallucination.

"Roll down the window," she said.

Mutely, Paul obeyed.

"I. . .uh. . .noticed a red minivan and thought it was you. What happened? Did you break down?"

"Yes. You wouldn't happen to know anything about how to fix cars, would you?" Paul produced a teasing smile.

"Yes, as a matter of fact, I do," Amy replied smugly.

"What?" He never anticipated that she would answer his question in the affirmative.

"Pop the hood. Let me have a look. It might be something really simple. You never know."

To the accompaniment of Brice and Dayton's cheers of approval, Paul pulled the hood release and slid from the driver's seat. Silently, Amy observed the motor, and Paul observed her. If he were totally honest, she had haunted his dreams since their chance encounter at the library two days before. Amy Matthews would never make it in a beauty pageant, but she was the epitome of wholesomeness. She would fit right in at his parents' farm—on a horse, in the garden, among the trees. Neither Vivian nor Jill would ever fit at the farm. Amy was completely different from both the women with whom Paul had enjoyed a serious relationship. Perhaps that was part of Amy's appeal. She struck a cord in him that he didn't even know existed.

With a wry little grin, Paul figured Amy would never have freaked out over the king snake. She probably would have picked the thing up and conducted a science lesson.

She glanced up at him just in time to catch his expression. "What are you smiling about? Do I have grease on my cheek or something?"

"No—no grease. I was just wondering how you felt about snakes."

"Snakes? I hate the things! I wouldn't touch one with a ten-foot pole." Amy shivered. "Why?"

From beside Paul, Brice and Dayton produced stifled snickers. "What are you guys doing out of the van?" Paul asked, trying to maintain his "displeased parent" demeanor.

Without another word, they clambered back into the vehicle, mischievous merriment dancing in their eyes. Even though they would have to face their punishment, Paul knew they sensed they were back on their father's good side.

"What's the deal with the snake?" Amy asked suspiciously.

"Believe me, you don't want to know," Paul said, sweeping away the whole subject. He didn't exactly want Amy to suspect he was comparing her to his fiancée. "What do you think about the van?"

"Well, bad news and good news."

A low roll of thunder accompanied her words. Paul looked up to see a band of dark clouds threatening rain. "Oh great. All I need to round this day off is to get rained on. If ever there's been a black Monday, this is it for me."

"I'll give you a lift to wherever you need to go."

"So you can't fix the van?"

"No. That's what I was about to tell you. The bad news is that the timing chain broke and I can't fix it. It's too big of a job. The good news is that the mechanic can fix it for you," she said with assurance.

"How did you learn so much about engines?" Paul asked.

Amy smiled. "I was an only child, and since my father never had a boy, he poured all his knowledge into me."

"So you run your own bridal shop, and when business is slow, you cruise the streets to rescue non-mechanical men in distress. Is that it?" Without realizing it, Paul had begun to flirt. He and Amy seemed to have gone past the stage of speechlessness with this encounter. At least, she had seemed more comfortable in speaking with him than the last time they saw each other.

Until now.

Her face flushed, and she lowered her eyes.

"Er, Dad," Dayton called from the van's front seat. "I think it's about to rain."

As if Dayton's words invoked the clouds, fat drops of water splattered the van. In seconds, Paul shut the van's hood, locked the doors, and he and his boys climbed into Amy's shiny blue car. Just as they slammed the car doors, another roll of thunder rumbled across the skies, and the heavens released their fury.

"Where to?" Amy asked with a can-do attitude.

Paul liked that attitude. He liked her. He liked her too much. Way too much. And it was growing. This was not good. Not good at all. "I was headed home to leave my boys, then I was going back to work."

She checked her sporty watch. "Okay. I've got time for that. Stacy and I have a wedding party of eight coming for a fitting in an hour, but I'm free until then. If you want, go ahead and call the mechanic from home. I suggest you use Ken Weatherly; he's my cousin. He has a wrecker service as well, and if he's not busy and has the right part in stock, maybe he can get right on your van and have it fixed before five today."

"But that's just four hours from now."

"I know, but sometimes Ken can make it happen."

"That would be great."

"If he can't get the van fixed today, give me a call, and I can give you a lift back home."

"That's nice of you." Paul exposed her to his most charming smile. And he was tempted to leave the van at the mechanic's a week if he could catch a ride with Amy every afternoon.

She produced an indifferent shrug. "You're a customer. It's the least I can do," she said practically, and Paul felt thoroughly put in his place. He felt that Amy was reminding him he was an engaged man who met her because of his pending wedding. He was only a customer to her. That was it. And that was the way their relationship should stay. After all, his wedding would take place in a month.

Paul silently looked out the window but couldn't concentrate on the beauty of a small town in spring's full bloom. With a sterile voice, he gave Amy directions to his house, and she silently complied with his instructions. After the easy way they related with one another regarding the van, the mounting tension between them left Paul more than uncomfortable.

At last, she steered into his driveway, and he and the boys got out of the car. Amazingly, his sons had turned into perfect, respectful gentlemen in Amy's presence and expressed an honorable amount of heartfelt thanks for her help, replete with a good dose of "yes ma'am, thank you, and it's a pleasure to see you again." Who would ever guess Brice and Dayton had just released a king snake in Jill's desk?

"I'll wait here while you call the mechanic," she said, an edge of resentment to her voice.

What does she have to be resentful about? Paul wondered in exasperation. But he knew without an explanation that Amy's resentment resulted from his already being engaged, for in the depths of her hazel eyes was the look of a betrayed child, crying, "How could you?" The unsaid words were so strong between them that Paul had to bite back a retort. He wanted to say, "But I didn't even know you when I proposed to Jill! How was I supposed to see into the future?" But he didn't. Instead, he turned and followed his sons.

As Paul entered his home, devoid of feminine influence, a haunting thought began a slow torment. Had he ever really prayed about marrying Jill? Both of them were Christians. They attended the same church. Jill worked with the children. Paul sang in the choir. Their families had known each other their whole lives. When Paul moved to Rusk, he had been delighted and surprised to discover Jill in the same town. Readily, they had rekindled their childhood friendship. Never having married, Jill was ready for a husband and family. Paul needed a wife. And Paul's rambunctious boys desperately needed a mother. So when Paul suggested marriage, Jill readily agreed. Both seemed to think marriage was the logical choice. But was it God's choice for them? For the first time, Paul began to seriously doubt his decision, not only from a human perspective, but also from a divine perspective.

❧

Within fifteen minutes, Amy drove Paul onto the Rusk High School parking lot.

"Thanks so much. . .for everything," he said, turning an appreciative smile to her.

"Any time," she replied, wondering how much of his smile was in appreciation for what she had done and how much was in appreciation for her alone. There was no way she could ever deny the chemistry between her and Paul, a chemistry that defied their chances of ever having a normal friendship.

He started to get out, then stopped. "Um. . .would you agree to sharing dinner tonight with me and the boys?" he asked. "I put a large roast on this morning, and there's plenty."

"Oh, I couldn't—"

"Please. You're a new. . .friend, and I feel like I owe you for all your help today."

"But—"

"You'll be in good company," he teased. "My parents

will be there, too. I called them when I called the mechanic. I was going to take Brice and Dayton to the farm tonight, but since the van broke down, my parents will be coming to pick them up. The boys will stay on the farm until Thursday."

"Aren't they supposed to be in school?" Amy asked, at last venting her mounting curiosity about why Paul had been taking his sons home during school hours.

"Uh, yeah," he answered dryly. "But they got themselves suspended for three days."

"Does this have anything to do with your question about a snake?"

"Yes." He chuckled. "They put a snake in a teacher's desk."

"Oh," Amy answered, her lips holding the *O* shape.

"And not just any snake. It was one of those black and red and yellow king snakes. You know, the kind that looks almost like a coral snake except for the order of the bands of colors."

"What fun," Amy said with feigned enthusiasm. "I guess this all does wonders for your reputation as the high school principal."

"Oh yeah, just wonders." He rolled his eyes. "I've thought about skinning them both alive at least a dozen times. And it doesn't help at all that the teacher they chose to torment happens to be my fiancée." He rubbed his eyes as if he were weary of the whole ordeal.

"Don't they like her?"

"What do you think?" He pinched his upper lip and gazed across the rows of cars in the parking lot.

A companionable silence settled between them, and Amy sensed that her presence somehow encouraged Paul.

At last, he spoke. "So, will you join us for dinner?"

"What about Jill?" Amy challenged, suddenly resentful that he should ask her to dinner. *I can't pretend Jill doesn't exist, even if you can,* she thought spitefully.

"Jill's coming, too," he said, a troubled gleam in his eyes. "But there's plenty for everyone."

At once, Amy felt petty. "Oh, well then, I. . .I. . . guess I'll come."

"Good. Is six okay?"

"Yes, six is fine," she agreed, wondering if she had lost her mind.

Five

That evening at six o'clock, Amy stood outside the front door of Paul's Victorian home, debating whether to knock or turn around and run. Before she could make up her mind, Paul's older son opened the door. He greeted her with an admiring, lopsided grin, which reminded Amy of Paul.

"Hi," he said, his voice cracking.

"Hello."

The younger one arrived and pushed aside his older brother. "How are you," he said. "I'm Brice. I don't think we ever told you our names." He extended his hand in greeting.

"I'm Dayton," the older one said, rudely shoving aside Brice's hand and extending his.

"And I'm Paul," a deeper voice said from behind. "Why don't you guys just let Amy in?"

With a new supply of admiring smiles, the boys stepped away from the door in deference to their father. Paul no longer wore his business suit. Instead, he had changed into a sporty pair of golf shorts and a polo shirt. He looked relaxed, at home, and more masculine than Amy cared to admit. Her heart fluttered. She should never have let him talk her into coming over. Was she suddenly bent on tormenting herself? He was the unattainable, and she desperately wanted to attain him.

"You two get back to the kitchen," Paul ordered. "Brice, finish the salad, and Dayton, you finish setting the table."

Amy stepped into a living area with floor-to-ceiling windows that looked onto a scenic view of piney woods and rolling hills. The room, sparsely decorated in masculine tones, virtually cried out for a woman's touch, something Amy was sure Jill would supply.

"I'm sorry about the boys." Paul produced an admiring grin exactly like Dayton's. "If you want the truth, I think they have a crush on you."

"What?"

"Yes. You won a fan club when you correctly diagnosed the van's problem."

"So it was the timing chain?" Amy asked, desperate to change the subject. Given the appreciative glimmer in Paul's eyes, Amy wasn't sure Brice and Dayton were the only ones with a crush on her. Once again, she lambasted herself for agreeing to this dinner.

"That's right. And, believe it or not, your cousin worked me in and the van is now residing in the garage."

"Great."

"So my parents won't be here. I'm going to drive the boys to the farm after dinner." He directed her to an overstuffed sofa.

"I would have enjoyed meeting them," Amy said, trying to sound disappointed but feeling nothing short of panic. That meant she would be dining alone with Paul, his sons, and his fiancée. What a twist of cruel irony.

The telephone's ringing interrupted any reply from Paul. As he retrieved the cordless phone, Amy fidgeted with the strap of her leather purse. The smell of roast beef, which usually left Amy salivating, now made her nauseous. Somehow, she needed to get herself out of this fix. Amy was normally more cautious than this. She didn't usually tread where there might be potential danger. Paul Moore was the personification of potential danger. Trying to still her heart, now racing in desperation, Amy rubbed her clammy palms against her denim skirt.

Please, God, she begged, *get me out of this!*

Amy hadn't been able to pray since she flopped herself over the altar in the chapel. Even at church yesterday, she couldn't penetrate that steel wall that had sprung up between her and her Lord. But at this point, Amy was so desperate that she would have agreed to anything. Anything! If God would just get her out of this fix. Being a missionary to the penguins at the South Pole seemed a positive alternative compared to sharing dinner with Paul and his fiancée. Why had Paul ever invited her? Had he been temporarily insane?

By the time he got off the phone, Amy was ready to bolt from the room. Paul's words only heightened her resolve to leave.

"That was Jill," he said, a grim twist to his lips. "She just politely told me she didn't think she could stand an evening with my boys right now. She's still so exasperated with them she says she doesn't quite trust herself in their presence."

"So it's just us for dinner, then. Just me and. . .and you. . ." A hard swallow. "And. . .and Brice and Dayton?"

"Yes. It looks that way." His questioning gaze lengthened. "Is that okay with you?"

"No," she blurted honestly. "It isn't. I'm beginning to think I was crazy for ever agreeing to come in the first place. I've. . .I've got a TV dinner at home. I think I'd better go eat it." Amy wasn't even sure she was making sense. She could think of only one thing at the moment. *Escape! Escape! Escape!* To share an intimate, family-like dinner with this man and his two charming boys would only make her heart explode with "what might have been."

Without another word, Amy rushed for the front door.

"Amy, wait!" Paul said, gently gripping her wrist.

His touch sent her emotions careening into another sphere. "Don't. . .don't touch me," she said, trying to sound firm. Instead, her demand came out on a whimper.

He released her.

Amy stumbled toward the door and gripped the knob.

"Please, Amy, don't leave. Not. . .not now. Not like this."

His pleading tone stilled her. Biting her lips, she

stared at the doorknob, trying to will herself to leave anyway. But she couldn't. Amy was too weak. Or rather, Paul was her weakness.

She felt him move toward her, felt the light pressure of his hand on her shoulder, felt his own uncertainty.

"Why did you invite me over here?" she rasped.

"I. . .I don't know. I. . .guess for the same reason you stopped to help me today. You didn't have to do that, you know."

"Yes I did," she replied, her back still to him. "You needed me." Amy's admission surprised her. She hadn't taken time to examine her motives for stopping to help Paul. Perhaps because Rusk, Texas, was a small town. In small towns people helped each other. Amy probably would have stopped for any of her customers that she recognized. But her reason for stopping for Paul had gone much deeper than small-town friendliness. Somewhere in the deepest part of her psyche, Amy had recognized that Paul Moore needed her. The whole van episode was only symbolic of a much deeper truth.

After a long pause, Paul finally whispered, "I think you might be right." His grip on her shoulder tightened. "I do need you."

In desperation, Amy turned to face him. She shouldn't have. He was much closer than she had gauged. Mere inches. With a compulsive swallow, Amy tried to back away but only managed to press herself against the door. "This is crazy. We only just met."

"No, we didn't. We've known each other a long time. Or at least, that's the way it seems."

Amy felt as if she were trapped in a vacuum.

"Tell me you don't feel it, too." His gaze lowered to her mouth as he stroked her cheek.

"I feel it," she whispered huskily and closed her eyes to steel herself for this forbidden moment. He was going to kiss her. And with a deep longing only loneliness can birth, Amy wanted him to kiss her more than she had ever wanted anything. But she wanted more than just this one kiss. She wanted his kisses for life.

"Amy?"

She opened her eyes and impulsively leaned toward him. His hands cupped her face. Something inside her screamed *This isn't right. Paul is engaged. I should run. Run now! Before. . .* But another voice within, a more compelling voice, bade her enjoy this moment of forbidden paradise. His lips brushed hers in a gentle caress. Amy clutched the front of his shirt as her purse slid to the floor. While the kiss deepened, Amy felt as if a bolt of lightning struck her. Paul's gasp testified to his own emotions.

How long the embrace would have lasted, Amy was never to know, for a loud crash from the kitchen brought the moment to an abrupt end.

"Oh no," one of the boys groaned. "Uh. . .Dad. We broke the—woops!"

Still in Paul's embrace, Amy turned toward the voice. Brice and Dayton stood on the kitchen's threshold, wide-eyed and curious.

Like two teenagers on their first date, Amy and Paul couldn't disentangle themselves fast enough.

Amy's face felt as if it would ignite. There was no explanation that would in any way suffice for this situation. Brice and Dayton were too old not to fully understand the implications of their father's predicament. With shocked expressions, their gazes flitted from their father, to Amy, and back to Paul.

Shuddering like a sapling in a hurricane, Amy silently retrieved her purse and acted on the impulse she should have long ago obeyed. She fled. Like a doe pursued by wolves, Amy raced to her car, scrambled into the driver's seat, and careened away. The last she saw of Paul, he was standing on his porch, forlornly watching her departure.

❧

As Paul closed the front door and turned toward his living room, he stared mutely into the questioning eyes of his sons. They hadn't moved from their spot on the kitchen's threshold. The silence between them was like no other silence Paul had ever experienced. He was, in a word, speechless—dumbfounded at his own behavior. What kind of example was he setting for his sons? He was engaged to one woman and kissing another. At once, Paul was disgusted with himself. He had never been a womanizer. Even when he had been given ample opportunity to experience the opposite sex with his college friends, Paul had chosen not to play that mindless game. Now, he felt as if he had failed himself, Jill, his own sons. . .and especially God.

What had possessed him?

"Does this mean you'll marry Amy now?" Brice

asked hopefully.

Dayton elbowed his younger brother.

"I'm not sure what it means," Paul said in self-disgust. Trying to make the most of the situation, Paul decided a change of scenery and subject was the best, the only, alternative. "Let's just put the roast in the fridge and grab a burger on the way to the farm. You guys go get your duffel bags. You did already pack like I told you to?"

As if they were as glad as their father to escape the awkward situation, they nodded readily.

"Good. I'll take care of the roast. You guys get loaded into the van."

"But, Dad," Dayton said. "We dropped the salad on the floor. The bowl broke. It's a mess."

"It's okay. I'll clean it up. Just get into the van."

They blinked in obvious confusion. The rule around the Moore household was, "You make a mess; you clean it up." Paul had never lambasted his boys for being boys. Sometimes things were spilled, glasses broken, salads dropped. It was all a part of life in Paul's eyes. Nonetheless, Paul stood firm on cleaning up your own messes, and his sons weren't used to seeing their dad so willing to fix their blunder.

"Go on," Paul urged, an edge to his voice he didn't intend. "I'm ready to get out of here. The sooner the better."

In response, they rushed to their rooms.

Paul was desperate to do anything to expunge Amy Matthews from his mind. And right now, his home seemed flooded with her presence. Even though she wasn't physically present, Paul felt as if she had left her spirit behind her.

This was exactly what he had felt with Vivian. Even when she wasn't physically present in their home, Paul had sensed her influence. For one year after her death, he still felt as if she lived with him and the boys. The whole wretched ordeal had been nothing short of torment. He hadn't fully realized the powerful influence of a wife and mother until his own wife had been ripped from him.

Now, Amy had crashed into his life and infiltrated his senses. How had she managed what Jill had never even touched? Perhaps the whole thing had something to do with God's plan and very little to do with Paul's decisions.

Like a man in a fury, Paul viciously swept up the mound of lettuce and tomatoes mixed with glass. He would take his sons to the farm, then he must go to Jill's.

He had a confession to make. They needed to talk.

Six

As she stumbled into her living room, Amy released the first in a series of sobs. For years, she enjoyed the casual appearance of her home, decorated in southwest decor. But compared to the boy-worn look of Paul's house, Amy's living room suddenly seemed sterile, deprived of life.

Empty.

She collapsed on the striped sofa and allowed the grief to have its way with her. After a quarter hour of wallowing in the misery of a woman denied her heart's desire, another emotion gripped her in its talons. Anger. Anger with Paul Moore for subjecting her to more agony than one woman should be forced to endure. What kind of game was he playing, anyway?

Amy sat bolt upright and marched to her bedroom for the box of tissues always on her nightstand. "Well, I can play your game!" she fumed into the dresser mirror as if talking to Paul. "I'll cancel your whole account at Bride to Be and tell you to find somebody else to plan your wedding! I'm through with it, and I'm through with you." Her final words came out on another sob.

Weakly, she lowered herself to the bed, gathered her legs against her chest, and placed her forehead on her knees. "Why, God, why?" she bit out. "Why have You put Paul in my life? Why are You tormenting me like this?"

There were a few times in her thirty-five years when Amy had experienced an instantaneous moment of insight. The thoughts that immediately invaded her mind would qualify for one of those moments. God wasn't tormenting her. Amy was tormenting herself. God showed her long ago what she needed to do, and Amy was less than willing to follow through. A lack of peace had left her in this turmoil. If only she would relinquish her dream of marriage and motherhood to God, she would gain the precious peace.

But how? Amy had never given up such a deep part of herself before. How was she to dissect her dream from the core of her being? For the first time, she desperately wanted to rid herself of this element in her heart that was dealing her misery, but she simply didn't know how to go about the process.

Oh Father, Amy moaned in her spirit, *please take this dream from me. I don't in any way know how to remove it from my spirit. It's been a part of me for so long, I think I've confused it with who I really am. Please, please make me satisfied to be just Amy. Miss Amy Matthews. No husband. No children. No romance. Just me. Alone. Oh God, make me happy and content as a single woman who gains her strength from You. You're going to have to do it because, in myself, I'm miserable alone.*

Amy sensed that those words created weblike fractures in that steel wall between her and God. A rivulet of peace began to trickle through those fractures, gently lapping at her soul, bathing her emotions in the cool waters flowing from the Holy Spirit. In reaction to the relief penetrating her spirit, Amy began to cry anew. This time, the tears were joyous. And that wall of steel dissolved, allowing a rushing river of peace to immerse her heart in comfort.

❧

By 9:30, Paul had delivered his boys to the farm, chatted with his parents for awhile, and arrived at Jill's duplex apartment. Like an uncertain schoolboy, he hes-itated outside her door, trying to shape some organization out of his scrambled thoughts. He had been so distracted while visiting with his parents, they had eventually scrutinized him in speculation. Paul was certain his boys would receive nothing short of interrogation from their grandmother. Paul could never hide anything from her. She always knew when her eldest son was troubled.

With the crickets chirping and a cool spring breeze nibbling at the surrounding oaks and pines, Paul decided he had deliberated long enough. He needed to face Jill. He had a confession to make. And they had some serious decisions ahead of them. At last, he rang the doorbell.

As if she had been awaiting him, Jill immediately turned on her outside light and opened the door. The shadows couldn't hide her red, swollen eyes.

"Hello, Jill," Paul said in a hollow voice.

"Hello," she said simply. "Somehow, I knew you'd come."

"I just got back from taking the boys to my parents' farm."

She opened the door wider, and Paul stepped into the simply decorated room. One of Jill's favorite phrases was "simple yet elegant." It fit her. Just like the room fit her personality. The Chippendale sofa had the same graceful lines as her regal face. The understated mauves and grays spoke the same language as she. Jill was one of the most elegant women Paul had ever met. Even with her extra pounds, she carried herself like a princess. Then, there were her blond hair, blue eyes, and porcelain skin. Jill Spencer was a woman to be admired, both inside and outside.

"How are your parents?" she asked.

"Fine. They're fine. Dad's arthritis is acting up a bit. Come to think of it, after that long ride, mine is, too." Paul flexed the ankle he had injured in high school playing basketball.

"Would you like some ibuprofen tablets?"

"Yes. That would be nice. Thanks."

In minutes, Jill delivered the medicine.

"You're always so good about having everything I need right on the spot," Paul complimented, feeling miles away from the woman he had promised to marry.

She responded with a sad smile, and an awkward silence settled between them.

"Mind if I sit down?" Paul asked.

"No. I don't mind at all."

Paul claimed a spot on the sofa. He contemplated how long it would take his boys to mar this perfectly clean couch with some sort of unremovable stain. Jill's black cat, Midnight, vacated his spot in a wing chair and left the room. Midnight, the possessive sort, had always hated Paul. And Paul's boys disliked Jill. What a way to start a marriage!

"There's something. . .something I think we need to discuss," Jill said, sitting beside him on the sofa.

"Does it have anything to do with a snake?" Paul asked, his spirit tense.

"Well. . ."

He hated this kind of situation. He should tell Jill he had kissed Amy, and there was no way to soften the blow. But as he looked deeply into Jill's troubled, swollen eyes, Paul wondered if she might have her own news to deliver. She had obviously been crying. Hard. Paul's own dilemma so distracted him that he had given precious little attention to Jill.

"I. . .I guess." She swallowed hard. "I guess I've always known somewhere in my thick head that your boys didn't like me, but it didn't really dawn on me until today that they're serious about this—the way they feel. It's not a p–passing aversion they're going to get over when we get married!" She waved her arm as her eyes filled with unshed tears. "I keep wondering if, after I move in, I'm going to wake up one morning with a boa constrictor staring me in the eyes."

"Oh, Jill, I. . ." Paul wished he could tell Jill her concerns weren't valid and that he believed his boys would come around, but he knew that would be short of the truth. Paul recalled the candid conversation he and his sons shared that evening in the van. . . .

"Why exactly don't you like Jill?" he had asked, hoping perhaps to get to the bottom of their true feelings.

"I don't know." Dayton shrugged and looked him full in the eyes. "I don't guess she's so bad. I mean, I liked her okay until—"

"Until you decided to marry her," Brice added begrudgingly.

"So you don't dislike her as a person necessarily?" Paul asked.

"No. We just dislike her as a mom," Brice blurted.

Dayton produced another of his shrugs. "Yeah," he supplied as if Brice had said it all.

And that was the end of getting to the bottom of their true feelings.

With a sigh, Paul reached for a tissue sitting on the nearby lamp table. He handed it to Jill, who blotted her eyes. "I'm so sorry," Paul said, pulling her into his arms for a comforting embrace. He felt as if he were hugging his sister, and he hated to see her hurting. The snake episode was bad enough, but how did you go about telling a tearful fiancée you had kissed another woman?

"I think we should call off the wedding," Jill said against his shirt.

"What?" Even though Paul wondered if Jill might be having thoughts in this direction, hearing the words surprised him.

Immediately, she pulled away from him. "I. . .I hate to hurt you. I really do, Paul, but. . .but. . .there's something. . ." She looked at him helplessly.

"This isn't just about a snake, is it?"

Mutely, she shook her head. "I've been praying. And I've come to realize that we never did seek God about this—about our marriage. We just sorta fell into it. I mean, we get along just fine and. . .and we've known each other for forever and all, but. . ." She hesitated as if she feared her next admission would injure Paul beyond repair. "But. . .I. . . ," she gulped, "I don't want to hurt you, but I don't think I'm in love with you." She held her breath, her eyes pleading for him to understand.

With a disbelieving chuckle, Paul slumped into the couch and stared at the ceiling. What a turn of poetic justice. He was supposed to be the one to do the breaking up.

"It's not that I don't care for you, Paul," Jill rushed sympathetically. "It's just that. . .that. . ." She began to weep again. "I've really been praying about this the last few days, and God seems to be showing me that you just aren't the right man for me. It was really hard for me to accept this, too, because here I am, thirty-eight. Never been married. With no prospects in sight. And I'm turning down the opportunity to marry a wonderful, attractive Christian man. It seems like the craziest thing I've ever done. I couldn't quite believe that I really shouldn't marry you, and so I asked God to please give me some kind of sign if we weren't meant to get married. And here I am today with a. . .a king snake in my d–desk." Abruptly she stood up and grabbed a handful of tissue. "I've got to get a grip on myself." Jill hovered near a lamp stand, sniffling against the tissue, as if she expected Paul to lambaste her.

"It's okay. Really. You've had a horrible day by anybody's standards."

"You mean, you aren't furious?"

Paul hesitated and carefully chose his next words. He leaned forward, elbows on knees, and looked her square in the eyes. The time had come to be completely honest. "You're never going to believe it, but I came over here to tell you a similar story, except mine's way more scandalous than yours. I kissed another woman today."

Jill blinked in shock. "What?" she gasped, a hint of jealousy in her voice.

"Yes. I did. I didn't plan it. It just happened."

"Who?"

"Do you remember Amy Matthews."

"The woman at Bride to Be?"

He nodded.

Jill waited, and Paul sensed she expected some explanation. "We were. . .er. . .immediately attracted to each other, from the first time we met."

"Oh," she said a bit peevishly. "That explains why she practically gaped when we went into the shop the first time. But don't you think she was a bit obvious?"

"I think she was in shock. Like I was. If you want the truth, I was borderline gaping myself."

"I guess I was too busy wondering why she couldn't learn to be more discreet," she snapped.

Paul scrutinized Jill, a tad exasperated with her indignant reaction. She was breaking their engagement, why should she care who he found attractive? "I'm sorry I've upset you," Paul said tightly. "I was simply trying to be honest."

"Sometimes the truth hurts," Jill stated flatly. With a heavy sigh, she walked to a window and rested her forehead against the pane.

"You really aren't handling this well, are you?" Paul asked.

"What do you think? It's bad enough that I feel that I should break off the engagement without your being thrilled about it because of some other woman."

"I never said I was thrilled—"

"Tell me you aren't relieved then." She spun around, daring him to deny her claim.

Paul, holding her challenging gaze, didn't reply. He couldn't. Anything he said at this point would only make matters worse.

"So, are you in love with her?" Jill finally asked.

"No. Not yet, anyway. We barely know each other. But I will be perfectly honest and tell you that I think I could very easily fall in love with her." Paul determined to keep his voice even. "And I think God used this whole attraction with her plus the boys' dislike of you to show me that we were making a mistake. I've been having the same thoughts you had—that we never really sought God over whether or not we should get married. I guess I thought that since I was a mature man with two boys I should just make the best logical choice about a wife."

"It seemed like an intelligent decision." Jill's voice

held less of an edge.

"Yes. And a friendship marriage might be God's will for some people." He shrugged. "I don't know. I've been told that sometimes those marriages can grow into something beautiful. But I guess it just isn't God's will for us."

Feeling as if a huge burden had been lifted from him, Paul stood, walked across the room, and dared to take Jill's hand in his. "I'm sorry our engagement turned out like this. We're probably going to be the talk of the town for a while."

She produced a strained smile. "Do you want your ring back?"

"No, you keep it. Maybe you could have the diamond reset as a necklace or something."

"Okay. Thanks."

"Whoever you finally do marry, tell him I said he's getting a great catch."

"Do you really mean that?" she asked as her eyes pooled in unshed tears.

"Yes. I really mean it."

Seven

After Amy finished praying, she curled up on her bed, exhausted. Her spiritual journey, her emotional turmoil, and her busy day at work had drained her of all energy. Within minutes, she drifted into a deep, dreamless sleep.

A strange-sounding bell from what seemed like a great distance began to disturb her sleep. At last, she realized the ringing was her telephone. Groggily, she reached toward her nightstand, fumbled with the cordless phone, and eventually rasped a sleepy "Hello" into the receiver.

"Amy?" Paul's voice affected her like a bucket of cold water. She sat straight up.

"Yes?"

"I woke you up, didn't I?"

"Yes."

"Can we talk?"

"Yes." Her mind spinning in a whirlwind of emotions, she seemed unable to utter any word but "yes." Amy glanced at her digital clock to see 11:00 P.M. glaring at her. She had been asleep several hours.

"I'm in my van, outside your house, on my cell phone. Can I come in?"

"Uh. . ." She deliberated, trying to decide whether she wanted to see Paul Moore again. Ever. "What about Jill?" she blurted, not in any way interested in pretending Paul's engagement wasn't an issue.

"That's part of what I wanted to talk with you about. Tonight, Jill and I came to a mutual understanding that we were out of God's will in our engagement. And. . .I also wanted to apologize about earlier."

"Oh." She looked down at her crumpled oxford shirt and denim skirt. At least she hadn't changed into her nightclothes. "Can you give me five minutes?" Amy asked, already on her way to the bathroom to wash her face.

"Five minutes it is," Paul said, a smile in his tone.

The whole time Amy straightened her clothing, brushed her teeth, and tried to camouflage the evidence of her crying, she prayed. Hours ago, Amy had totally released her dream of marriage to God. Now, it seemed as if the whole situation were about to reverse. What did she do at this point? Deep within her soul was a peace she had never known. Would a relationship with Paul disturb that peace? At long last, she was content to be single. Now what was she supposed to do about this thing with Paul?

When the doorbell rang, Amy's confusion had mounted to hurricane proportions. As if she were in a daze, she opened the door to greet a man with dark circles under his eyes and uncertainty draped across his shoulders.

"I didn't really know whether you would hang up on

me or what," he said, stepping into the house.

She closed the door behind him. "Your call caught me off guard. I fell asleep shortly after I came home from your house."

"So, if you had been wide awake, you might have hung up on me? Is that what you're saying?"

"Uh. . ." Amy swallowed as her heart began to pound in reaction to his presence. "I. . .no. I don't make it a habit of hanging up on people."

"Oh." As if he were floundering for the right words, Paul looked around her home, decorated in hues of indigo and burgundy and sand. "You've done a nice job decorating this. It's attractive but not sterile."

"Thanks."

"I bet my boys could clutter it up in about two hours flat," he said with an unsure smile.

"Probably. But. . .," it was Amy's turn to flounder, ". . .they seem like really nice boys. That is, except maybe for the snake thing."

With a weary chuckle, Paul rubbed the back of his neck. "I can't believe they did that. But then. . .," a flicker of mischief twinkled in his eyes, ". . .my friend and I put a rat in a teacher's purse when we were in junior high. I guess I can't be too hard on them. They were probably born with these tendencies." He looked deeply into her eyes. "I guess you can consider yourself forewarned."

Amy's palms began to produce a film of cold sweat. What was the man implying?

"I guess I've beaten around the bush long enough,"

he finally said. "I need to address the reason I came over so late. I didn't feel like I would have a moment's peace until I took care of what I mentioned on the cell phone." His next words were spoken slowly, deliberately. "Like I said, I wanted to apologize to you in person. I shouldn't have kissed you. It wasn't right. I am—was an engaged man. And I don't know if it will make any difference to you or not, but I have never done anything like that in my life. Even when I was a teenager, I was always true to my girl. Quite frankly, I blew it tonight, and I haven't had a moment's peace since I did. I want you to know that after I took the boys to my parents, I went to confess what I did to Jill."

"You told her?"

"Of course. It was wrong. And I had to be completely honest with her."

"So she called off the engagement when she found out. . . ," Amy paused, not certain exactly how to frame the words.

"No. She called off the engagement before she found out what I had done. She had been seeking God about it and discovered what I had seen. Our marriage just wasn't God's will. I went to her house to tell her, but she beat me to the point."

"So you. . .you. . ." Amy swallowed. "You were going to break off the engagement, too?"

"Yes."

"Because of me?" The words came out a soft, husky whisper.

"No. Because it wasn't God's will. And I think God

used my boys' aversion to Jill and my attraction to you to show me that I shouldn't marry her."

"I see." Amy's confusion mounted as she deliberated whether to accept what she sensed Paul was ultimately leading to. Did she want a relationship with him? Hours ago, she had released—truly released—her dream of marriage to God. Now, she felt that she must guard that hard-won peace. Would a relationship with Paul threaten the peace?

"Given all that, I guess it's fairly obvious that I've got a third reason for being here." He stepped toward her. "I also wanted to ask you if you would agree to our beginning to see each other."

Amy stepped back. "I. . .I don't know," she rasped. "You. . .you see, I've got a story, too." With faltering words, Amy related her spiritual journey. She finished with, "If you had come to me last night with all this, I would have jumped at the chance. I don't guess there's any way I could ever hide the way you arrested my attention from the start. Don't ever think that I'm not attracted to you, because I am."

A heady triumph exuded from his every feature.

"But now. . . ," she shrugged helplessly, "I'm more interested in making sure a relationship with you is what God really wants for me than I am in having that relationship. And right at this moment, I'm so confused, I barely know my own name."

"I respect that," he said, evidence of that respect in his eyes. "And, believe it or not, I came to some of those same points after Vivian died. I had to finally release the whole thing to God and be perfectly content to raise my boys without my wife."

Even though Paul had never mentioned his wife to Amy, she had learned from her mother that Paul was a widower. "What caused Vivian's death?" she asked gently.

"Breast cancer." He stared past Amy as if she weren't there.

"Do you still miss her?"

"That's a tough question to answer," he supplied with a sad turn of the lips. "Like I said, I finally had to get to the point that I would accept her death and be at peace with God about raising my boys alone. So in that regard, I guess I don't miss her. But on another level, I do miss her, especially when Brice or Dayton has done something I know Vivian would have been proud of."

"Like the snake episode?"

He rolled his eyes. "Oh yeah, now that's something Vivian would have just been thrilled over," Paul said sarcastically.

They shared mutual laughter, and the tension between them eased. Amy spontaneously offered Paul a soda. When he settled in her living room as if he planned to stay a while, she wasn't certain whether or not the soda was such a good idea. The longer she was with Paul, the more she was reminded that he could very easily become her weakness. With great caution, she sat on the edge of the recliner. Somehow, their conversation strayed to likes and dislikes, favorite hobbies, and college backgrounds.

Without realizing it, Amy began to relax, to let down her guard, to really allow herself the luxury of enjoying Paul's presence. Nonetheless, a tiny doubt still plagued her mind. Amy still hadn't agreed to see Paul. Was this time of getting to know one another the wise choice? The more she learned of Paul Moore, the more she liked him. Eventually, she saw that she was going to have to seek God on a very deep level regarding their relationship.

At 1:00 A.M. Paul insisted on leaving, and, with a yawn, Amy agreed she needed to go back to bed.

"So," he said uncertainly, "where do we go from here?"

"Uh. . ." Amy was at a loss. At last, she decided to revert to humor. "I still haven't figured out what you see in me."

"You greatly underestimate yourself," he said with warmth.

She looked down, not sure how to handle this man's admiration. Her attempt at humor had failed.

"Perhaps you don't quite understand just how much I want us to start seeing one another." Slowly, Paul trailed his index finger down her cheek and traced the length of her jaw.

Amy swallowed and fought not to close her eyes and lean into his touch. She reacted to Paul Moore like a volcano, tormented by its inability to explode. "Have . . .have you prayed about this yourself?" she asked, desperately trying to cling to her senses.

"As a matter of fact, I have," he muttered. "I prayed

all the way to the farm, all the way back, and after I left Jill's, I went home and prayed. I already made one mistake in thinking I should marry Jill. I didn't want to make a mistake about seeing you. I know that to you I probably look like a Don Juan, but the truth is, Jill is the first woman I've dated since Vivian died five years ago." His earnest eyes reflected that his words were truth. "And since I'm telling all, here, I might as well tell you that I didn't have the guts to call you from home. I was afraid you wouldn't agree to my coming over. So I drove over here on purpose—"

"You manipulated me," she accused with feigned indignation.

"Yes. But I prayed like crazy the whole time I was doing it."

"And?"

"And. . ." With a daredevil glint in his eyes, he slipped his arms around her waist and tugged her toward him. "I feel more certain of this than I have of anything in a long, long time."

Mesmerized by the fire springing up between them, Amy knew in her spirit she should resist his kiss. It would be yet another step toward a relationship that she was no longer certain about. Would the peace she had so eagerly embraced be shattered were she to follow the dream of a husband and family, once so dear to her?

As if Paul sensed her hesitancy, he didn't attempt to kiss Amy, but simply held her. She relaxed against him, soaking up the essence of him. His strong arms. His heart's rapid beating. The spicy smell of his aftershave.

"I really need to go," he finally said, a quiver in his voice. "It's been a long, long time since I felt like this, and I. . .I. . .really need to go." As if he were exerting great effort, Paul removed Amy from his arms and produced a grin, stiff and restrained.

"Before you go, I want you to know that I'll think. . . think about our seeing each other." *That's probably all you'll think about,* her own mind taunted her. "But I basically need some time to pray about it."

"How long?"

"A week?"

"Okay. You've got yourself a deal. I won't call you for a week. But after that. . ." His ardent gaze roved her features, and Amy wondered if Paul were going to pull her into his arms again. Instead, he moved toward the door as if he were forcing himself to leave.

"I'll let you know. I promise I won't leave you hanging," she assured.

"I'll call you in a week then?"

"That's fine."

His gaze never leaving hers, Paul lifted her hand to his lips and placed a light kiss against her palm. Then he opened the door and hurried toward his van.

Amy, shuddering with reaction, collapsed onto her sofa. She stared at the ceiling, uncertain of what to do. When she relinquished her dream to her heavenly Father, she meant it. Amy chalked up the relationship with Paul as an impossibility and had been perfectly content to live her life single. Now, she felt as if her dream were being handed back to her by God Himself, all wrapped in silver, topped with a pretty red bow and a note that said, "Now that you've released your dream, I can give it back to you, and you can truly enjoy it because you won't depend on it for your happiness. You are now depending on Me."

The more she tried to pray, the more that same, recurring thought circled her mind. And she saw for the first time that until she released all her dreams to God, those dreams would never make her happy, would never give her peace. Only God could do that. Amy was learning to be content, whether married or not, wealthy or poor, successful or a failure. For contentment came from her Lord.

From Monday night through Friday Amy prayed about her relationship with Paul. Friday night, she joined her mother in a prayer vigil. The two sought God and shared well into the night. With a fathomless peace filling her soul, Amy got home in the wee hours of the morning and only slept when dawn's golden light began to peek over the horizon. Once again, she was awakened by the telephone. This time, the caller was Stacy.

"Is everything okay? You're late."

Amy groaned. "What time is it?"

"Nine-thirty. And there's a tall, dark, handsome somebody here to see you, holding a dozen red roses. He just verified that all his wedding plans were canceled and now insists on seeing you."

"Is it Paul Moore?" Amy asked.

"Yes, and you're keeping secrets from me, aren't you? Quite frankly, I'm surprised at you, Amy. Did you break up his engagement to Jill Spencer? At this rate, we're going to lose customers."

"It's a long, long story," Amy replied. All week she planned to tell Stacy about the situation with Paul, but the two had been so busy they barely had time to look at each other. Spring and summer were by far the busiest seasons for weddings.

"Tell him I'll be there in an hour."

"Will do. But I wouldn't keep him waiting too long. He seems pretty intense."

Within forty-five minutes, Amy drove into her usual parking place near the town square. As if he had been watching for her, Paul exited Bride to Be and met her in front of her car.

"Hi," he said admiringly.

"Hi." As she had the first time she met him, Amy felt more beautiful than she had ever felt in her life. How did Paul manage to make her feel so special?

"I. . .just came by to make sure Jill had canceled the wedding plans and to say good morning." He extended the roses to her.

"Thanks," she said, her voice husky. She suspected that checking on the cancellation was a convenient excuse. Nonetheless, Amy was flattered. She took the roses and buried her face in their softness—anything to distract her from his casual male appearance in pleated shorts and an oxford shirt.

"I was also wondering if you had been praying—"

He held up his hand as she tried to interrupt. "I'm not rushing you. I know it's been five days, not a week, but I just—yes, I guess I am rushing you, aren't I?" He smiled his apology.

"It's okay," Amy said. "Really. The truth is, I've had time to pray and think, and I came to some rather encouraging conclusions."

"Oh?"

"Yes. I think I had to release my dream to God before He would fulfill it for me. Otherwise, I was putting my dream in front of Him. And He wanted to be first."

"So. . ." He raised his brows in expectation.

"So. . .I think it would be okay for us to pursue a relationship. But—"

"But. . .," he said in disappointment.

"But, if for some reason it doesn't work out, I'll be okay."

"Oh, but it's going to work out."

"You seem extremely sure of yourself."

"Let's just say I'm experienced in the ways of love, and I know the beginnings of the real thing when I feel it."

"I do hope you're right."

"I am. I've always been known as 'Mr. Right'." His eyes twinkled with merriment. "But let's give it several months—maybe a year, just to get to know each other, and we'll take it from there. We don't need to rush into anything."

"I agree. And I certainly need to get to know your boys."

He rolled his eyes. "Believe me. You've already made two devoted conquests of them. I think the only person they'll resent is me. They're going to be jealous!"

Amy giggled in delight. And as they turned and walked arm in arm toward Bride to Be, she hoped that at long last she was the bride to be.

DEBRA WHITE SMITH

Debra White Smith lives in east Texas with her husbandand two small children. She is an editor, writer, and speaker who pens both books and magazine articles, and has approximately 20 book sales to her credit, both fiction and nonfiction. Debra also has about 200,000 books currently in print, and her works have appeared on the CBA best-seller list. Both she and her novels have been voted favorite by **Heartsong Presents** readers. Furthermore, Debra holds a B.A. and M.A. in English, and her Barbour novellas appear in *Only You, Season of Love,* and *Spring's Promise.* Her **Heartsong Presents** titles include *The Neighbor, Texas Honor,* and the coming series books to *Texas Honor—Texas Rose, Texas Lady,* and *Texas Angel.* A portion of her earnings from writing go to Christian Blind Mission, International.

You can write to Debra at P.O. Box 1482, Jacksonville, TX 75766, or visit her web site at www.getset.com/debrawhitesmith. She loves to hear from her readers!

A Letter to Our Readers

Dear Readers:

In order that we might better contribute to your reading enjoyment, we would appreciate your taking a few minutes to respond to the following questions. When completed, please return to the following: Managing Editor, Barbour Publishing, Inc., P.O. Box 719, Uhrichsville, OH 44683.

1. Did you enjoy reading *Spring's Promise*?
   ❑ Very much, I would like to see more books like this.
   ❑ Moderately—I would have enjoyed it more if ________

____

____

2. What influenced your decision to purchase this book?
   (Check those that apply)
   ❑ Cover ❑ Back cover copy ❑ Title ❑ Price
   ❑ Friends ❑ Publicity ❑ Other ____________

3. Which story was your favorite?
   ❑ *E-Love* ❑ *The Garden Plot* ❑ *Stormy Weather*
   ❑ *Bride to Be*

4. Please check your age range:
   ❑ Under 18 ❑ 18–24 ❑ 25–34
   ❑ 35–45 ❑ 46–55 ❑ Over 55 ________

5. How many hours per week do you read? ____________

Name ________________________________

Occupation ____________________________

Address ______________________________

City ________________ State __________ Zip ________